WILSON JOHN HAIRE was born in 1932 in Belfast, just off the Shankill Road, and entered the shipyard at the age of fourteen, joining a workforce of 36,000. At sixteen he began a five-year apprenticeship as a joiner; he soon became a trade union militant and was part of a committee that organised the first ever apprentices' strike for a living wage. At twenty-one he left Harland and Wolff and went to work in the Plaza Ballroom. In 1954 he left Belfast for England, where he worked on building sites. In the early 1960s he began to have stories published and joined the semi-professional Unity Theatre; in 1968 his one-act play *The Clockin' Hen* was performed. In 1971 *Within Two Shadows*, described as "the first play on the Ulster Crisis", won major drama awards. His other plays for the theatre include *Bloom of the Diamond Stone, Echoes from a Concrete Canyon* and *Lost Worlds*; and he has written television plays for the BBC: *The Dandelion Clock* and *Letter from a Soldier*. His work as a playwright has been produced at Dublin's Abbey Theatre, the Royal Court and the Royal National Theatres in London, the Lyric Theatre, Belfast, and in many other theatres throughout the world.

The Yard

Wilson John Haire

A Brandon Original Paperback

First published in 2002 by
Brandon
an imprint of Mount Eagle Publications
Dingle, Co. Kerry, Ireland

10 9 8 7 6 5 4 3 2 1

Copyright © Wilson John Haire 2002

The author has asserted his moral rights.

ISBN 0 86322 296 X

Mount Eagle Publications receives assistance from
the Arts Council/An Chomhairle Ealaíonn.

Cover design: Wendy Dunbar
Typesetting by Red Barn Publishing, Skeagh, Skibbereen
Printed by The Guernsey Press, Channel Islands

CONTENTS

FLEAS

This is Belfast in 1933. Carlisle Circus to be precise, not far from the city centre. It is around three in the morning. A pall of smoke from the hundred of thousands of coal fires is still trapped and held in by the ring of mountains to the west of the city and by the Castlereagh Hills in the east. South of the city, at the city boundary, the ground begins to rise into County Down by way of the Three-Mile Hill. North-east is Belfast Lough, running between Carmoney Hills on its west bank and the Castlereagh Hills on its east bank to the Irish Sea. The foul smoke therefore has little chance of escape, and in a few hours more smoke will be added by the newly built coal fires of the tiny houses. The spinning mills, the shipyard, the ropeworks and any other works that have barely survived the Great Depression now devastating the city will add their great furious smoke stacks.

But let us concentrate on one little house just off Carlisle Circus. In the bottom half lives Lipman the tailor with his workshop and tiny room to live in. Upstairs is one room that is habitable. The other room has been closed off due to its total dereliction.

Lipman hears a disturbance and looks out of the window. A baby further down the street is bawling its eyes out. A sudden gust of wind blows and mixes the unsweepable tram tickets that blow down from the tram stops with the dried tobacco of horseshite and slowly circulate in Carlisle Circus. The howling child, the gusting wind through the narrow streets is sufferable normality to Lipman. It is another sound that disturbs him – the heavy steel-shod footsteps of a member of the Royal Ulster Constabulary

A peeler known over the whole city as Pig McNeilly is striding out. He wears a night helmet, felted and corked. A begrudging dark-green uniform has turned to black under the gas lamps. The tunic is buttoned to the neck. Around his waist is a thick, wide, black, polished belt from which hangs an open-topped holster containing a .45 revolver on a black lanyard. Also on the belt is a black leather case containing a baton of green heartwood. A huge black-green cape tacks him into the wind.

Almost a caricature for a *Punch* cartoon of the nineteenth century, his face is red and as big as a large platter. His teeth could chew the hind legs off a donkey.

He shines his bull's-eye lamp up a dark entry.

"Now, you're pissin' up that entry again, Mary."

Mary quickly pulls up her knickers and her voice echoes in the entry: "You might give me time to pull m'drawers up, so you might. Shinin' your flashlight there on my business premises, so you are."

"Come away out of that now, you oul brass nail," says the Pig.

"Not a make or a wing to be made around the Circus any more," says she, wafting away the steam.

"It's near time to take your bird's nest somewhere else," thunders the Pig.

"Want a free rub?" she asks.

"Not tonight, Josephine," he answers. "Now get to hell's gates before the sergeant comes this way."

"Give a body a chance to comb her face and powder her hair," says she, and when the Pig tries to correct her she says it again and laughs. Then repeats it again, but the Pig doesn't laugh.

The cobblestones, bedded in sand, are a plentiful harvest this year. Like last year and the year before. Growing down these streets for half a century and ripe for the picking. But with the recent street riots of the unemployed they are being slowly concreted over.

The first horse and dray is on its way to the market to pick up vegetables. The great shire slips on the greasy square setts and skids the iron-hooped wheels across the tram lines. The tired carter is in corduroys with strapped-on leather leggings, calf length. His hessian apron flaps in the gusts of wind. He holds the reins as if sculpted.

"The Humane Society says a horse mustn't load up more than two tons. But load her up and don't let the horse see the dockets." He laughs loudly as he turns into Carlisle Circus.

As Pig McNeilly passes again, Lipman leaves the window and sits down at the sewing machine.

Upstairs, Annie can bear it no more. It is three in the morning, and the fleas are beginning to bite. She nudges Alex, gently at first with her forearm, then a rat-a-tat with her elbow when he fails to awaken. Finally she holds him down, at the same time saying, "Get up in the name of Christ! I'm being eaten to the bone."

She whispers this as if the fleas might hear. As he struggles to rise, she holds him even more firmly, whispering, "Do it slowly or you'll disturb them."

He slides out of bed, dizzy and in such an uncoordinated fashion that she has to guide him to the cretonne-covered orange box where he sits as if every joint in his body is broken. She then reaches under the bed and feels for the delft chamber pot, pulls down her baggy pink knickers, sits on it for a moment, farts, and gushes like a mountain stream in flood. The po rings like a bell from alto to bass, vibrating on the bare floorboards as if hit by a cloudburst.

"Shush," he whispers. "Lipman below will hear."

"To hell with Lipman," she replies. "I'm sure he's heard his oul ma on the po often enough."

He tuts. "That's not very nice language. It's rough to talk like that."

She is about to light the gas mantle but remembers that the meter needs a penny. She lights the stub of a candle that has been remoulded with the tallow that ran on to the cocoa tin lid earlier. She holds up the pale light and directs it at him.

He is peering into the chamber pot. "I hope you left me a bit of room." He sways slightly, holding the sagging crotch of his ragged lambswool combinations.

She looks into the po, notes the drowning flea with a smirk, and pulls her knickers up until the elastic digs a white weal around each thigh.

"He's a terrible man for work. Dreadful altogether is Lipman. Hear his sewin' machine still at it? He's no five-eighter."

"Is that a hint," he says, "for I'm not the only one who's out of work in this city."

He picks up the po angrily. The smell of ammonia reaches his nostrils and gives him a sudden erection. He turns his back to hide it. It is a good five seconds before his own urine flows. Still slightly dizzy after being so suddenly awakened, he almost drops the po. In catching it with his wrists he causes a mini tidal wave.

"God save us this day and this night, it'll drip through to *his* ceiling below," says she.

Taking a piece of cotton cut from an old bed sheet, which she had been saving for her period, she wipes the floor furiously.

"One of us better empty the po," she whispers loudly.

He shakes his head.

"You're willin' for me, a bride of less than a year, to go down to the yard, with a pot of piss in her hands, attired in her knickers and vest, and risk a face-to-face, with a man, in the middle of the night?"

"Ach, him, he's too religious to be a proper man."

She looks at him a moment before an amused smile spreads across her face. She tries hard not to laugh out loud. Every now and then she passes the palm of her hand across her face as if rearranging her features. But the amused smile remains there. She goes to the window and lets up the sun-blasted blind. The gas lamps from the streets throw a bluish white light into the room and light up a bunch of cherries on the wallpaper. The other bunches are obscured by the repairs of the now-yellowing newspaper. Her firm jaw with its perfect white skin flickers like a cinema screen as she holds up the candle. She undoes her black hair, which is pulled tightly behind her head and done up in a bun Spanish-style, and lets it fall with a silken whoosh audible only to her own ears. Then she looks daggers at him.

Transfixed, his heart beats breathless and his crotch jerks. He tries to smile through his desire, but his face has turned pale and frozen. One eye peeps out of her jungle, observing him. On quivering legs he advances on her, but with a cruel movement she sweeps the hair from her face and remakes the bun at the back of her head.

Wet, wrinkled below the waist, angry, he lifts the po with one hand, threatening her with his strength. The tendons in his forearm burn, the muscles ridge hard as he strains to keep the lemon liquid as calm as a pond while his other hand strays to support his sagging crotch.

"There, the door is open. Did I hear you say wider?" she giggles.

The candlelight sends his dark reflection down the stairs in one dimension. She holds the candle aloft as if she is the Statue of Liberty.

"Thinkin' of going to America?" she asks.

"Again!"

"Ay, again," she answers.

"Stand clear," he says, "out of my light."

"You'll not lose your way?" she taunts.

"Hurry, what are you tryin' to say? This po's breakin' my arm."

She waves a tiny hand towards his combs: "The map!"

Suddenly he is aware of the urine from the overflowing po as it turns cold on his combs. The candle flame flickers erratically in the draught coming up the stairs. Yes, indeed, he is looking at the map of North America. The Gulf of Mexico is quite clear now. He watches the scraggy neck of Central America form. He decides to move before the advent of Latin America.

"Wash down there. Do you hear me?" she says. "Don't come back up here smellin' of oul parboiled cabbage."

In his anger he straightens his arm and pushes the po in front of him to show his mastery of the trivial, but Annie has ceased to watch him. The door bangs.

"Ay," he says bitterly.

A sudden short howl of wind rocks the building. He carefully grips a tread of the stairway with his toes to test it for creaking and decides to use alternate ones in order not to alert Lipman. It is pitch dark. It is a darkness akin to that which comes from within the head when the eyes are closed tight and the heels of the hands are pressed into the eye sockets. Cast on a lonely island in the middle of the Milky Way with the occasional star bursting into a drifting wisp of spotlighted smoke.

There is a smell of gas, and his forehead touches the lead pipe that carries it to their room. It always has a tepid feel to it, even in winter. There is another sharp howl of wind, and a slate from the roof toboggans over its brothers and sisters with a rasping noise before shattering on the pavement. An icy draught comes up the chimney of the stairway almost icing his Americas.

He thinks of that black sheaf of hair in the snowy field lighted by a green eye. Then onwards down the stairs; one hand holds the po and one is still on his crotch to prevent the bishop wandering too far and catching its mitre on a thread.

The sewing machine is still rattling away. A fine line of light shows under Lipman's door. Alex exhales a shower of whistling spittle. The buckin' latch on the door to the yard won't budge. The sound of screeching rusty iron mingles with Alex's heavy breathing and the whispered whistling to cover up the noise. The sewing machine stops. He stands still, listening. Light begins to filter into the narrow hallway as the door to Lipman's room opens a cautious inch. His dark eye seems to send a ray through the widening crack. As the door opens wider, the single gas mantle throws a brilliant light on to the whitewashed walls of the passageway. This projector now shows a very fat man holding a very fat po.

He fights the latch again – this time as a trapped rat.

"My bloody finger – whoor's hell!"

There is a dull thud as he drives his foot through the rotten floorboards in pain and rage.

"I'm terrible sorry, Mr Lipman."

There is silence except for the hissing of the gas mantle. He says under his breath, "Is there somethin' you want, Mr Lipman? Maybe I don't owe you enough rent."

Lipman steps into the hallway, looking over his half-moon glasses, and lifts the latch without effort.

"I've always meant to take that latch off, straighten it, grease it and put it back with fresh screws. That's definite for tomorrow, Mr Lipman."

Lipman makes no effort to let him into the yard but stands there looking at the floor. He is wearing a black frock coat that shines at the seat and elbows like a bus driver's uniform. It is rusty where it creases and folds on his thin body. In the lapels are stuck a dozen needles of all sizes as if he has just done battle with the Lilliputians. Wisps of many-coloured threads are stuck all over his coat. His waistcoat is big enough to be an armless jacket. His grey-striped flannel shirt seems to grow out of the top of his waistcoat. One side of the long-tipped collar appears lopsided, as if it is getting more than its fair share of light. He stands there thinking, gently but unconsciously scraping the top layer off the flaking floorboard with his soft leather boot. He shakes his head as if denying something. His red hair and beard are as silky and integrated as the coat of an Irish setter. His beard suddenly ripples as he screws up his face. He lifts his glazed-straw skullcap an inch but drops it again in alarm. Effortlessly, absentmindedly, he sends the latch home again and disappears into his room, leaving Alex to the cosmic darkness.

"Hey there, oul hand!"

In a blinking, purple-black flash of gaslight, Lipman re-appears, lifts the latch, but sends it home again when Alex enters the yard.

Upstairs Annie is pondering on how to deal with the fleas. The brown-paper moon sticks its face through the ragged cloud and joins the bluish-white light of the street gas lamps. Each illuminates a corner of the room. The moon, so stark, steady and merciless, leaves nowhere to hide. The gas lamp, uncertain because of a hole in its mantle, sends out an uneven rhythm of light with its sporadic flare. She carefully takes the coat that acts as an additional blanket off the bed, breaks the candle from the cocoa tin lid and carefully pulls back the sheet. Microscopic spots of black digested blood show after the human feast.

"Thought as much, you dots of cannibals," she whispers.

She feels for the warmest part of the bottom sheet and slowly opens a crease. Four fleas are hiding there. She carefully hovers her left hand flat above them, opens her fingers slightly then snaps her fist into a trap. She feels the electric buzz from their hard shells as they give all their energy to escape. She tightens her fist and rubs her fingers together hoping to kill or even disable them. The first flea she moves from the hollow of her hand towards the tips of her fingers by feeling it and guiding it through the spasms of her flesh until she has gripped it between the pads of her index finger and thumb, and then on to the anvil of her left thumbnail. Bringing down the hammer of her right thumbnail, in a split second she dispatches it. There is a last desperate reverberation before the satisfactory crack. A splodge of blood colours her thumbnails, mixing with the flea pelts.

"Will wonders never cease! That wee body hardly bigger than an apostrophe can drink so much and have my blood flow in its body, like an equal."

The second flea wriggles free through the soft web between her finger and thumb. She pounds the bed as it springs away, sledging down enough blows to kill a cat. She deals with the third and fourth fleas.

"I'm not so mean as to skin a flea for its hide," she laughs to herself.

Blooded now, she begins the hunt for the escapee – setting up road blocks with interlocked fingers, raiding out-of-the-way crevices, descending into the cave-pockets of the coat, bombarding the canyons of the lapels, floodlighting the snow plains of the sheets with the put-put-putting candle. There is no sign of the insect. In escaping it is taking a lot of experience with it.

"God's curse on you for even being invented!"

She kneels down and carefully pulls the blotched-skin cardboard suitcase from under the bed and welds the candle to the floor. Under there is a murky world of worn floorboards with the knots of the timber appearing as lumps. A thin mist of grey fluff begins to slowly rise, propelled by her breath. The springs of the bed have a living layer of crystallised rust that sheds when touched, only to reveal another equally yielding layer. As she fretfully picks away, one of the springs decides its springing days are over and invites the mattress to bulge in that area. She quickly rolls back the flock mattress and finds that the underside has an exact copy of the wire mesh in sepia. The springs, after a moment, relieved of their burden, twang like a great harp. The grey mist whirls and runs from the gathering wind. For a moment she could swear she saw a tiny insect springing away in the eye of the storm.

"You'll be back, and I'll be waitin'!"

Alex can't get the cistern to flush. He pulls the handle, but the great weight in the iron box above his head only shudders. Here he sits on the cracked wooden seat, hoping that it will fill up again soon. But the water in the pipes is a mere trickle, and at times there is a faint gurgle a long way off. The door of the lavatory is tongued and grooved and painted the usual black. It has been cut to fit the middle of the opening, leaving a twelve-inch gap top and bottom. He begins to shiver and feels the wet Americas return to the ice age. His two bare feet become cold meat. The moon is now above the little walled-in yard, and as it cannot see through the upper gap, it sends its fluorescent light spilling under the door. The rough concrete floor, covered with a thin coating of frost, shines as if embedded with a thousand diamond chippings. The normally dirty-white of the peeling whitewash now radiates, renewed.

His feet stick to the floor. He lifts each foot in turn and scrapes away the salty texture. He exhales as if trying to get a fire started and watches the steam – a greenish colour now in the moon's neon – escape by the top gap. He attempts to flush the lavatory again. The water has even stopped its old man's cough. The droplets of water on the rusty iron are slowly turning into buttons of ice. He pulls down his combs, defecates, and feels the momentary warmth of the turds on his bare bottom before they die of cold in the inch of water. He reaches for the newspaper squares of paper on the string and pulls off a couple. One he uses to push back his piles. He feels the squares and guesses correctly that the thick ones are that of a weekly county paper sent to Annie by her better-off sister. The whole cistern has gone to sleep. He feels around for the Jeyes Fluid bottle and grabs its ribbed glass. It is empty. He has no water to put in it and shake. Anyway, that has been done so many times before it now only smells of stagnant water.

The heavy brass tap in the yard, covered in icicles, looks like the scaly foot of a crocodile. The cold is slowly ascending to his hips while his piles are descending quickly. Any more of that and they'll soon be down to his knees, he thinks. He knows from long experience that unless he can be perfectly relaxed he cannot push them back up without the ring muscle of the anus nipping them. Then they would become swollen and a section of them would refuse to return.

"M'guts are comin' out!"

All the Zambuk in the world would not relieve them. A greasy snail-trail would appear on his combs and come through his blue-serge trousers or, worse, darken the seat of his grey flannels that he keeps for best.

He tries to relax but the cold is vibrating his jaw. The ring muscle tightens. He can't push back the piles. But every struggle has its last ditch. He gets down on his hunkers, makes his right foot stand on its toes, sits on that heel and puts his body weight behind it, but being very careful not to flatten the piles. They will not move at first, but finally they begin to slide.

"They're home, tucked up safely in bed. What a friggin' relief!"

A tram in the distance approaches at speed. Its electric motor gives off a high-pitched hum. Its steel wheels rock in the lines.

It's not stopping, probably making for Glengormley at the end of the line to start picking up early-morning passengers. Its hullabaloo floods each narrow street as it rocks past. It bursts into Carlisle Circus with a grinding of sand, of metal savaging metal. As it passes Lipman's house, it causes a fine, almost invisible mortar to spill from between the bricks. Alex coughs. Its trolley flares as it hits a joint on the overhead wire and heliographs a garbled message across the blue slates of the little houses.

"In the name of Christ!"

The water in the lavatory bowl rises in a fit, and there is a sudden draught under him. Wet-arsed, he jumps up. The water then subsides just as quickly, drawing in a rush of air. Now the bowl has no water at all. He stands, waiting for the noise of the tram to stop. An electric clamour hits the sky a few more times before the flashings grow weaker. But just as it seems to have gone, it revives briskly with a loud sudden sound of metal dropping from a great height, followed by a very faint sound, followed by a tinkling bell, followed by nothing, as if cut off by a great knife.

The moon gets tired of showering its silver at him, and he is able to see a little of the sky. This little oblong at the top of the door, though tinged at the edges with the city lights and obscured at times by the drifting smoke of thousands of dying household coal fires, still contains one or two sooty stars. Now and then these worlds take off at speed when an extra-thick band of smoke drifts within sight of the oblong. The pungent smell of the smoke is normal, even reassuring. It means a warm fire on a winter's night. Sometimes the sulphurous acidity comes mixed with the aroma of a good soup.

He is thinking of stewing meat, onions, floury potatoes, parsnips, carrots, barley, lentils, peas, turnip, leeks, parsley and the great knee bone, still in its socket, down in the depths of a two-gallon oval pot, slowly softening and giving off its marrow – and all sitting on a rosy fire. He sighs: "Will there ever be another Friday pay night?"

Another band of smoke passes the oblong. It smells of sweat-saturated rubber and canvas plimsolls, singed raw potato peelings, mixed with the cold black cinders of newspapers and the stinging sprinkling of coal-slack to give it the name of a fire.

"Where is that chronic smell comin' from?"

He decides to think no more about it. It is coming from the chimney of his own room. But he is afraid now of never-ending poverty. The fear is breaking through his fantasies. He looks in the direction of heaven but looks away quickly.

"That's only for the oul dolls."

In a microsecond a red spark is born and dead. It could have been a meteorite or a stray piece of flaming soot. And then there is another. And another. Flaming soot. Nothing much ever comes to us out of that great universe out there.

"Well, surely to God she's stopped crackin' fleas by this time."

One more attempt to flush the toilet, followed by a string of dirty oaths.

He struggles with the latch again until Lipman reappears and performs another miracle.

"Tomorrow, Mr Lipman; it'll be like a Swiss watch, tomorrow."

Lipman doesn't look at Alex, but it is obvious he is still trying to say something. His lips move clockwise and then anti-clockwise. His cheeks grow into a fat frog about to deliver a

thousand jellied eyes. Alex almost asks Lipman if he could wash
the po in his kitchen, but Lipman looks so profound he doesn't
want to bother him about trivia. Startled, as if he has spoken
Tibetan, Lipman looks at him. The spring in his brow has his
face glistening. He moves a hand to dismiss himself, goes to his
room and closes the door.

With the tailor gone, the pencil-line light at the bottom of his
door begins to fade as he slowly starves the mantle, and a faint
red crayon draws itself in its place briefly as the mantle cools to
a chalky white.

Climbing the stairs in the total darkness of outer space, Alex
ponders his own little universe as it whirls within his head,
throwing off pinpricks of light – or is it the gap below his own
door? Climbing further his eyes level with it. Dot, dot, dot,
dash, dot, dot, dash. The gap is giving off an erratic light as if
from a Morse lamp.

Annie glares at him as he enters and tells him to close the door
quickly.

He says, "You might give me time to get through it first."

"That bloody draught would founder a body," she answers.

The look on her face, deeply etched by the shadows, turns it
to granite. She has started a miserable fire. It's made up of whole
pages of newspapers folded lengthwise to an inch broad, then
plaited tightly together. In the midst of this lies a pair of old
plimsolls.

"My second best footwear! What have you done?" he
complains.

"Your mutton-dummies were crawlin'," says she. "It's time to
put them out of their misery." She lets out a wild laugh.

The plimsolls writhe in the yellow-blue flame, so worn that the cardboard insole has scarcely an edge to cling to any more. The running, bubbling rubber catches fire and throws out an incendiary light that floods the room for a second to an intense brilliance. A series of these flare-ups, in close sequence, causes a flickering that stars the couple in a penny-peepshow. Shadows flit, die and are born as if fifty people occupy the room. The blemished brown oval of the wardrobe mirror flashes Annie's face in a scowl and then changes to a transparent one chuckling on the window-pane. Alex's own lanky frame shoots across the room in profile – in an advancing position, in retreating fashion, pleading, whipped-cur-grovelling, quarter stance, on his knees showing his teeth.

"I'm supposing you had a titter of wit and washed the vessel."

"No," he mumbles incoherently, "tap iced up, couldn't sneak into Lipman's scullery."

"You didn't try slipping into his scullery again! But that's a mortal sin in his calendar."

"Ay," he says bitterly, meaning, I heard you and I don't like what you're saying.

"And don't eye the water in the bath. That's for the washin'. Certainly you were down there long enough to rinse every po from here to the River Po."

How relieved he is when she gives that little chuckle. But the fire still goes very black and dead looking. Six layers of char-coaled paper peel away in a black-death confetti and quickly whirl up the chimney. The rest of the half-charred paper bursts into instant flame and shines on the sizzling raw potato peelings as they wrinkle and give off steam. She digs into the coal slack that has baked hard and exposes its red underbelly. But it is the red of a rotting dead animal. She quickly controls its putrid flame by spreading another layer of coal dust over it and setting it crackling as if it were a mixture of gunpowder. When she is satisfied that it is giving off a steady temperature, she backs away slowly as if she has at last managed to put a teething child to sleep.

At the zinc bath, she begins to scrub every inch of the bed sheets with a hard yellow soap and while doing so remembers what five shillings once bought: Newcastle Nuts. Those little squares of shiny black coal that burn quietly and cause soft steady shadows to caress the room. They catch fire easily and give off a white pure smoke for a time. Thereafter, their consumption is invisible. For a long time, such a fire is almost white in its intensity. At the outer edge of the fire, half-cooked coals give off little geysers of gas. Each jet lights with a soft plop and roars its tiny life away. All burnt away now, the white ash leaves the shape of the coal behind it, forming the ghost of a fire in the coming dawn.

But the coal he once stole from a railway siding is a different beast. Stone-like, hit it with a hammer and it breaks without warning into sharp spearheads. And having failed to kill, it lies there in the grate as an alien, spitting and crackling ill-temperedly, aiming at the eyes and the soft spots of the neck. Then comes the down-draught that will fill the room with thick greasy sulphurous fumes. The door and window have to be opened until it decides on naturalisation. It glows there as pumice stone from a raging volcano. And in the morning its stone hearts are as cold as the Arctic rocks.

She passes each inch of the sheet between her thumbs, rubbing the material between her fingers, rubbing the material

against itself, then douses each square inch one by one, pushing
each one under the cold water, pulling it out quickly, repeating
the process several times, as if changing and unchanging her
mind about a drowning.

Finally she seizes the sheet and twists it to the thickness of a
cobra. She lets the dryer end climb her arm to the elbow while
concentrating on crushing the vital organs of the struggling creature, finally laying the pacified monster on the bare deal table.
For a moment it lies still until some nerve reaction begins to
unwind the twisted, tormented creature. Quickly helping the
movement, she spreads its flattened skin over the battered cage
of the fireguard. Nothing happens for a while; then very slowly,
it begins to cure in a faint cloud of faltering steam. She reaches
for the second sheet.

"It's ah. . . it's ah. . ." He wants to say it's almost four in the
morning, but it may sound like the beginning of an argument.

"Never you mind what time it is," she says, reading his mind.
"I'm not lyin' down where fleas have been." She spits out the
words, and he watches the falling spray glisten in the light of an
eruption during the death fit of the weaker plimsoll.

"Do you have anywhere to go later this mornin'? Something
terrible urgent to attend to?"

He says, bitterly as usual, "Ay," then enlarges on this after
thinking a moment. "You think I can just ignore the slump and
get myself a job as a joiner, or at anything. But even if 'anything'
was there for the gettin', far too many men are lookin' for anything. And another thing, the very last ship being built at the
shipyard went up in smoke. I saw the flames above the rooftops
as I was making my way there to look for a job on her. I turned
and came back. Would there have been any sense in burnin' shoe

leather as well to ask a stupid question like 'Do you have a job for me?' Have you ever thought of my dignity though I'm signing on the buroo. I had to pawn the violin, for you thought I was too happy without work. And dare I try to write a bit of a poem! That was resigning myself to my fate in your eyes. Paintin' . . ."

She gives a cynical laugh. He answers with a cynical laugh.

"A sailin' ship on a run to Botany Bay via cardboard and household paint from the three dee and six dee stores."

She interrupts him to say, "It would fit you better to give the mantelpiece a lick of paint. You're not to spend any more money on buildin' castles in the air."

"Ay," he says bitterly yet again. "Is my soul to be unemployed as well?"

She turns to the steaming sheets and slaps them roughly into a new position so as a new portion can dry. Picking up a newspaper, she spreads out the double page and is about to cover the mouth of the fireplace when she tries to read it.

"Found me *another* job?" he asks, still cynical.

She doesn't answer but again spreads the paper to act as a bellows. Nothing happens for a few seconds; then a whisper begins, followed by a slight tremor running across the print. The paper is almost sucked out of her hand, and the fire shines its light until she can read every word clearly: "Labourer wanted for rag warehouse. Protestant only. Apply to Box No. 66."

"That job would suit you right down to the ground," she says.

He doesn't know how to answer. He doesn't want any conflict with his Catholic wife over what this statelet is doing to her kind. They are no Romeo and Juliet healing the divisions. If anything, their mixed marriage has widened the divisions. His family looks on him as a traitor. Her family thinks she has married beneath her. At least if he had had money they could have talked business. And in talking business, who knows? He could have been talked into converting. But he is just a shipyard worker. And he claims to be an atheist. There's no converting an atheist Protestant. So they gave her up as lost.

The advert turns brown and collapses inwards, and the little blue flames make a dash for the headlines: "HERR HITLER APPOINTED CHANCELLOR."

The paper quickly bursts into flames and the carbon races up the chimney like a flock of birds.

The transparent flames dance in the grate without giving off much heat. Annie lifts the pram-axle poker and nudges the sick fire carefully in case she kills it. Taking another piece of paper, she rolls it into a ball and pushes it into the ashes under the grate. It catches fire slowly, but its white flame cannot penetrate the congealed mass of the plimsolls. She carefully drives the poker into the coal-slack and twists it. Thousands of minute sparks appear as if out of a fountain and pour up the chimney. A piece of blazing soot falls and lies in the grate for a long time, brighter than the fire itself, before expiring like the lights of the city at dawn.

"Those combs are a disgrace. Take them off and throw them in the bath this very minute."

He stands looking at her. She picks up the coat from the bed and throws it at him. He turns his back and takes off the combs.

"You're wearing no underpants, you dirty hound!"

"They came to pieces in my hands yesterday," he protests.

She flings the combinations into the bath and immediately batters them with the block of yellow soap.

"That coat shouldn't be on the bed," he says. "I brought it back all the way from America. Pure wool. Silk lining."

He turns around wearing it fully buttoned to the neck, with the collar turned up, the belt tight.

"Pawn it," she say. "We need the money."

"Squeeze it all day and it will never wrinkle."

"Fifteen shillings in the pawnshop," she says softly in a seductive voice.

He begins to gently parade up and down in the small room, whirling occasionally, making the coat into a carousel.

"What a coat for those New York winters!"

"Even twenty-five shillings?"

He watches her Neptunian taming of the sea creature. The drowned combs resume their shape again and begin to breath. Triumphant, her queenship secure over water, she turns to the terminal fire and tenderly coaxes it away from death's door. But it still needs nourishment. She points silently at the orange box. He hesitates before taking off the cretonne cover.

"Now don't batter it on the floor or Lipman'll think we're taking his floorboards up for the fire."

Sitting on the bed, he takes the box on his lap, as if he were about to castrate a young pig for fattening, and lets fly with the badly burred hatchet, smashing its ribs in. The wooden shrapnel flies around the room. She races after the shards as keen as a terrier and feeds them to the chronically ill fire as anxiously as chicken soup to a dying man. He tries to split the grain of one of the two heavy ends.

"The grain's runnin' around the knots and makin' my life desperate altogether. But you won't get the better of me, you fuckin', dyin'-lookin' bastard of a whoor!"

Shocked by his language but more interested in feeding the fire, she gives him a long hard stare instead. But he isn't looking at her.

He seizes the timber and makes every vein in his head, throat and arms throbbing rivers as he endeavours to pull it apart. The timber suddenly gives, and he is on his back spitting out splinters. Flinging himself upright on the bed again, he takes the other end of the orange box. He lambastes the wood as it lies stretched across the palm of his hand until it splits in zig-zag earthquake fashion.

The box is now completely in smithereens, and he looks around the room wild-eyed, the hair on his head sleeked back with sweat, his eyes drowning. Fearful that he might go on to demolish the room, she gently lays her hand on the hatchet and silently shakes her head.

Except for the occasional rocket, the timber burns evenly, sending out slow drifting sparks. The sheets begin to turn white and crisp, giving off a slight scorched smell. She continually offers up their patched material to the fire, checking the material, from time to time, against her cheek for dampness. The combs slowly shrink back to their original size and become light and free as if they have a life of their own.

"The water, you've got to empty the bath. I'll give you a hand downstairs."

But he is fast asleep, still buttoned to the neck in his overcoat. She searches the bed for splinters, taking some from his hair and feeding them to the fire. Then she begins to tidy the room before sitting on the bed and looking into the fire. She opens her legs to warm herself and watches the wood sweat out its moisture. One piece explodes with a faint thump before bursting into flames. To save her thighs from the measle-pattern created by the toasting fire, she stretches her knicker legs to cover them.

One by one the dancing flames bow out. The stage is empty. The cold ash leaves nothing but the aroma of wood in the room. With Alex looking settled for the rest of the night, she decides against dressing the bed with the born-again sheets. She gets under the blanket and makes a place for herself by pushing him over with her arse. He flings out an arm across her breasts. She lifts the arm as if it belongs to the dead and folds it back upon him. Then finding her indent in the old worn-out mattress, she too falls asleep.

In the breaking dawn, the knight of light and darkness bicycles into the Circus and thrusts his lance at the jugular of the gas lamp to shut it off. Pig McNeilly, sheltering in a shop doorway from the rain, looks at his watch and discovers his shift is over. He clatters away down the pavement. The sewing machine starts up again.

THE SHILLING

It was about midnight when the women set out with a boy of about six to act as a scout. The fields glistened with frost under a stark-white moon as big as a bin lid. Ragged pieces of cloud attached itself to its face from time to time but were soon blown away. Down the hill and across the road was the waterworks. The moon shining on it made it a huge sheet of glass, and the anti-boat wire stretching across it made it a three-pane window. Facing the waterworks was the 1930s motor inn called the Ivanhoe. Its sloping roof and extended eaves and green tiles made it look like a Chinese temple under the moonlight.

The windows of the small farmhouse on the edge of the fields were blacked out. The farmer had been to market that morning at four, his wife had hand-churned butter all day, and his two young sons had to be in bed early for school, so the whole house was sleeping. The boy was sent forward to check the farmhouse. He was friends with the dog – a huge Rhodesian ridgeback, chained to its kennel in the farmyard. He petted it and played carefully with it to keep it quiet.

The women, bent over, crept forward until they reached the curly kale drills, went on their knees and began cutting kale out of the ground with an assortment of kitchen knives. They filled their bags and retreated backwards, still doubled up, until they were back in Fairview Gardens.

Fairview Gardens, better known as F.U. Gardens, was nothing more than a track with an unmade surface of protruding rocks. On either side were twelve corrugated-iron roofed wooden shacks divided roughly inside into bedrooms, kitchen and living room. They had no electricity, though the power lines ran past the waterworks up the Saintfield Road. A single outside water tap, to serve all the shacks, was in an corrugated-iron alcove just off the track. Down the hill the waterworks took on a mauve sheen as the ragged clouds annoyed the moon's face again. A petrol-operated pump in a field near the Ivanhoe filled the tank in the tin alcove each day, but some days it broke down. Paddy Mallin, owner of the Ivanhoe, also owned Fairview Gardens. He was a man in his eighties who had five young children by a new, younger wife, his first wife having died ten years earlier at the age of seventy-two.

The inhabitants of Fairview Gardens were mostly economic refugees from Belfast. Among them was an Englishwoman from Coventry with a Belfast husband and a southern Protestant from County Cavan with a Belfast wife. There was also a gypsy couple with a young son. They wore colourful clothes the type of which no one had ever seen before. Their son was dressed as a girl in a blue frock and had long hair. They had strange accents. No one knew where they came from. This family kept to themselves, and their boy didn't attend the nearby Clontonacally School, nor did he attend any school. The gypsy wife did attempt to sell handworked lace around the shacks when they first arrived, but no one had the money. The inhabitants puzzled as to their origins for a while. They didn't think of asking which country they might have come from because their vista didn't extend much further than Fairview Gardens, McCormack's shop at the foot of Manse Hill and the local school. Belfast was, for most of them, a no-go area. They had, in the main, fled from the debt collectors or tick-men. True, one had a job shovelling coke in the Belfast gasworks and another had sporadic work in the Belfast shipyard, but mostly they lived on the dole which kept them at almost starvation level. They were Catholic and Protestant. Some were in mixed marriages. One Protestant woman and her Catholic man weren't even wed. The only sectarianism came from the County Cavan Protestant who, it seemed, thought he had to continually prove himself – being from the south – to his Protestant neighbours, though they weren't interested. It took all their energy just to survive as human beings without being burdened with tags.

Though it was winter, the round iron stoves, with just enough room for a kettle or a pan, had been allowed to go cold after the evening meal – such as it was – to save coal or coke. The stove-pipes coming through the tin roof were covered in a film of ice already. The tin oil lamps had also ceased to give out their yellow light to save paraffin. Even the stubs of candles had to be saved.

Out at the back of each shack, in the tiny garden, was a sentry-type box that contained the bucket for the dry lavatory. The garden grew nothing but high nettles, and somewhere in the nettles was an ash-covered hole to empty the bucket into.

It was five months before the outbreak of the Second World War, and a drunk or mad old man in one of the shacks was singing, "It's a long way to Tipperary . . . It's a long way to go . . ." and volunteering for the next war.

Next morning there were "curlies" for breakfast for everyone in Fairview Gardens; boiled in water and sprinkled with vinegar, the kale, fresh from the fields, was a treat. Waring, the coke-heaver, set off at half past five to walk the six miles to the Belfast gasworks on the lower Ormeau Road. He would walk home again, though exhausted by his day's work. With four young children, he couldn't afford the bus fares. Harper took out his gate of a bicycle and pedalled off at half past six to look for work in the shipyard as a joiner.

The Alderdyce parents – who seemed to owe the most money – took off, with their two children, at the same time down Manse Hill, across the Saintfield Road and into a by-road called the Cut and made vaguely towards Drumbo to avoid the tick-men. They were said to owe the half of Belfast. They wouldn't return until dark. The food they had with them this morning comprised of the heels of loaves, called catskin, and a tin can of cold tea. They didn't look at the ground going down Fairview Gardens, for nothing was ever found there. There were better prospects going down Manse Hill as the schoolchildren and teachers passed that way. One lucky day one of their children found a shilling wrapped carefully in paper as if carried by a child on its way to McCormack's shop. The mother bought a pan loaf and a tin of syrup at the shop for their wanderings.

The children of the shacks next appeared at half past nine to make their way to Clontonacally School. The three Harvey children, who were Catholics and attended the same school, didn't set out until a quarter to ten as they were excused Protestant prayers.

Maguire, the Cavan man, next appeared in a pair of recently acquired white trousers and rattling two halfpennies in his pocket to make it appear he had money. He paraded up and down the rocky, potholed track. Some of the inhabitants peeped out at him from behind their flour-bag curtains but made sure not to be seen in order not to gratify him. His thin, ginger-haired wife – whose shape and posture were said to be those of a greyhound shiteing – called him into breakfast. But she said it in such a way as to give the impression he was having a boiled egg with bread and butter, when everyone knew she was in the fields last night cutting the curlies like a beaver. Somebody laughed as he was about to go indoors. He turned quickly but couldn't identify which shack it came from. He noticed a cat wandering into his nettle-infested garden. A ring of blue appeared around his mouth like a lightning strike, his face con-torted, his hair electrified, and with a mad rush he seized the cat and beat its brains out against the side of his shack. He then threw the dead cat into the middle of Fairview Gardens, imi-tated the laughter he had heard, and went indoors to eat his curlies.

A batch of children came home from school and discovered the cat, which was now frozen, with the fur stiffened with frost, and tried to revive it. Even a stick forced past its clenched teeth and down its throat didn't bring it back to life. They ended up throwing it at one another until the Waring children rescued it and ran crying indoors.

The shacks were alive with excitement at the prospect of a fight between Maguire and Waring. They boiled their potatoes, carrots and parsnips, stolen from a previous raid on the fields, and shook the maggots off the bacon – if they had any – and pre-pared to fry it in the rancid lard. Through all this they peeped through the windows or opened the door a crack to watch for the coming of Waring, though he wasn't due for at least a half-hour. Maguire sensed the excitement at his expense for his wife was beginning to howl, in between telling him he had murdered the Waring cat.

Waring was a quiet man who rarely came out of his shack once he got home. He just rested up for the next day's work and listened to the wireless, which was one of the few existing in Fairview Gardens. If he found a newspaper on the way home, he read that though it might be a week old. He would turn off the wireless to save the battery and accumulator. A battery could last about three months, and the accumulator was usually charged at Jameson's garage every two weeks if he were careful. Any old paper could last him all evening as he read every word of it, including the adverts. The cat, which he called Skinnemelink after the foreman of the coke-heavers, would climb upon his coke-dust-saturated, dungareed knees, sniff a while and then revolve a few times to make its bed before settling down and purring. His children were delighted with the cat, for it meant their father was in a good mood. The heavy leather belt, with the huge brass buckle, around his waist remained buckled.

Sometimes in summer, on a Saturday afternoon after work, he might shave and wash and – if his newly washed dungarees were dry enough from the heat of the stove – go down to McCormack's Corner and just watch what was passing along the Saintfield Road. Sometimes it was a horse pulling a red-oxide coloured cart with two high wheels, an Austin Seven, a motor-cycle with sidecar, a single-decker bus going to Drumaness or a double-decker going to Ballynahinch, a pretty girl, a nice plump woman, a steam tractor pulling a mobile watchman's hut to

Lowe's quarry, an Ormo Bakery bread van, a door-to-door vegetable van, a spring cart loaded with tinkers (the pony's head high in the air chaffing at the bit as it raced towards Belfast), a low, flat hay-shifter with small wheels pulled by a slow plodding horse, a group of racing cyclists coming from the direction of Belfast, a tandem bicycle ridden by an elderly couple, and once a Crossley tender of policemen with rifles probably flying towards Downpatrick. The country people nodded extravagantly at him as they passed, including the country bus drivers. Being a Belfastman, Waring rarely nodded back. But he did acknowledge them with a slight tilt of the head which looked as if he were agreeing with them. Winter didn't see too much traffic except for the odd bus. As the nights drew in, all that could be heard was the wind humming along the telephone wires, and if it snowed not even that as the snow froze on the wires.

It was greyish dark now, and the only light shining on to the track came from the yellow flickering oil lamps of the shacks. A luminous patch on the clouds indicated the trapped full moon. Away in the distance, the incandescent horizon indicated Belfast. Two miles from Fairview Gardens, in the direction of the city, a few lighted windows of Purdysburn Lunatic Asylum could just about be glimpsed through the cedar trees.

The inhabitants still peeped, and a few hearts beat fast when Waring appeared at the bottom of Fairview Gardens, as if they were to be his punch-ball. Waring was a muscular square slab of a man. His children met him down at McCormack's Corner, and as they told him the news, he began to outpace them despite his exhaustion. He didn't roar or curse as he made for Maguire's door.

He gave a heavy rat-a-tat knock on the door with his knuckles. The door didn't open, so he began a sustained knocking so heavy that the flimsy door began to loosen at the hinges. There was a sudden scream inside from Mrs Maguire and a whimpering from the children as if from a basket of puppies. The door opened to darkness inside, for they had not lighted the lamp, in order to peep out more secretively. Out of the gloom came Maguire with a coal hammer and clinging to him his screeching wife and two children now crying hysterically. Maguire swung the hammer in a wide arc and almost hit his wife on the head. He roughly detached himself from her and sent his children flying with a swing of his hips. He now faced Waring on the rocky track. They were both black silhouettes, and the hammer, being held high, was totally blacked out.

Maguire was advised to put the hammer down and fight like a man by an onlooker, for they were all standing outside their doors by now. Scraggy mongrels, provoked by the excited humans, barked madly or growled and snapped at one another. Mrs Featherstone called out for somebody to fetch the police from the barracks down the road and was told, "You're not in your own country now!"

The silhouettes stood facing one another while Waring told Maguire quietly to put down the hammer or it would be all the worse for him. The crowd began to chant for him to put the hammer down. Maguire stood there, the hammer still upraised, paralysed by the chants of the crowd. He knew he couldn't attempt to hit Waring now, but he also didn't want to put the hammer down. Suddenly, Waring made a mad-bull rush and Maguire was flattened.

The hammer was twisted from his hand and flung through

the window of his shack. Maguire, thinking it was all over, even asked for a hand-up from Waring as a way of showing he had given in. The crowd booed for they wanted to see more. But Waring wasn't finished. Somebody brought out the only tilley lamp in Fairview Gardens and held it at an angle in order to throw an oval of light on to the rocky track. Waring had other ideas, and it wasn't going to be Gentleman Jim versus John L. Sullivan. He grasped the still-flattened figure by the ankles and began swinging, slowly at first, then faster until he had swept him off the ground, then faster until he was waist-high and going around him as precisely as a flywheel. He moved closer and closer to Maguire's shack, as balanced as a perpetual-motion spinning top, before letting him go. Maguire hit the side with a tremendous bang of bones on wood. The rag doll lay there moaning. There was complete silence for a few moments until his wife and children, now quiet and fearing the worst, rushed to him.

Maguire had a broken arm, and a large lump was beginning to rise on his forehead. Blood flowed from a broken nose. Mrs Maguire, relieved at her husband being still alive, began to berate Waring in a tongue that was not foreign to the inhabitants. Mrs Waring, heavy-arsed with pillar legs, rushed at Mrs Maguire and tore a clump of ginger hair from her head, skin and all. The crowd now egged on the two women. The man with the tilley lamp angled the lamp again to make a bright oval on the rocky track, but both women went indoors. The inhabitants stood around waiting in hope when they heard Maguire raving inside his shack, threatening what he would do with Waring. They waited until the lamp was lighted inside, watched as Mrs Maguire put a square of pasteboard over the hole in the window to keep out the winter cold, and then they, too, went inside reluctantly.

Later that evening, Mrs Maguire slipped down Manse Hill to McCormack's Corner and crossed the Saintfield Road to the telephone box. She called an ambulance through the emergency number, but the control centre was outraged at her cheek – "He has a broken arm!" She only had six pennies in her purse, but she used four of them to call a doctor in Saintfield. The doctor, who was in bed after a hard day attending people around the countryside, sleepily, grumpily told her to phone for an ambulance. She said she did and they weren't coming. He then suggested she bring her husband to his surgery in Saintfield. She said she didn't have the bus fare. He suggested she borrow it. She said nobody had that much money in Fairview Gardens; besides her husband was bleeding badly. He asked where the bleeding was coming from, and she said his nose. He told her in a cool, cynical voice that nobody died yet from that kind of injury.

"And what about his ear," she asked.

"What about his ear?"

"Bleedin'," she said.

"Outside or inside," he asked without much interest.

"I think inside," she answered.

"You don't sound too sure," he said. "And how did he get his injuries?"

She almost said fightin' as she was now a bit proud of her husband even daring to face the brick wall of Waring, but saying fightin' could mean him putting the phone down. She said he was kicked by a cow and lied by saying he was a cattle drover. The doctor mentioned the possibility of him catching lockjaw and said he would come out under some Rural Act or other;

other than that she should call an ambulance or bring him to his surgery in Saintfield.

The doctor arrived at two in the morning in his old Morris car. His breath smelt of whiskey, and the whiskey had not helped. He was in a foul temper. He found Maguire trying to make a splint from a walking stick and shouting every now and again as the shattered bones rubbed against one another. His children watched him with tears in their eyes. The doctor chased the children back into their bedroom and examined Maguire's ears and found no blood. He blew a whiskey exhalation towards Mrs Maguire as a way of calling her a liar. He didn't bother about Maguire's nose as that was a common enough event amongst the down-and-out. He opened his bag and told Mrs Maguire to hold the oil lamp properly for he wasn't a bat of the night. He took out some splints and said it was ten shillings for the first visit and five shillings for the loan of the splints, which had to be returned clean as he had brought them.

The rent was five shillings a week for the shacks, so Mrs Maguire calculated that he was asking her for three weeks' rent when she could scarcely pay one week and owed two months' already. She said there was only two pence in the whole house. The doctor again asked her to borrow it from a neighbour. She laughed and he made for the door. She apologised and asked him if he could take her husband to a hospital in his car as he now couldn't walk for he had also twisted his knee. Maguire stood up to demonstrate a twisted knee and then fell heavily on to the leatherette couch with a sharp shout.

The doctor said the nearest hospital was Purdysburn and that was a lunatic asylum. Mrs Maguire reminded him that part of it was a fever hospital. The doctor took Maguire's temperature and pronounced him normal. He had an idea: if Maguire were fit enough for the lunatic asylum, they would also fix his bones free of charge and right away at that. He could sign him in though he would have to walk the two miles, for he wasn't going to gallivant all over the country in the middle of the night. He could check him in the morning as he had to go there to sign a certificate to get another one of his patients admitted. He told Maguire again he could sign him in, but he wasn't certain when he would get out again. He looked at Maguire who was now gnashing his teeth and saying strange things to himself. The sweat poured from his face as his wounds burned.

The doctor decided he wouldn't use his brand new splints but instead suggested that Mrs Maguire look around for some sticks of wood somewhere. She remembered she had some wooden palings in the back garden for the fire which she had pulled off a fence around the garden of a retired policeman about a week ago. The doctor examined them. They were the right length. He reset Maguire's arm amid a lot of shouting and groaning. He told Maguire to stay still and asked for something to tie around the palings, a bed sheet cut into strips would do. They didn't have a bedsheet, neither spare nor on the bed, so she cut up her flannel nightdress. Before the doctor left, he advised Maguire to go to the Royal Victoria Hospital in Belfast in the morning as the work he had done was only temporary. What the arm needed was a cast of plaster of Paris. They might even X-ray it, but that cost money. He said it was free there for emergencies as long as you put something in the Poor Box.

Mrs Maguire asked him if he would like a cup of tea but knowing he would refuse. She had no fresh tea but yesterday's old tea leaves. He looked around the barely furnished room with the walls distempered a dirty apple green, looked at the smoking tin oil lamp and its sooted-up yellow funnel and said, "No thanks. I won't bother tonight." He mumbled something about being owed a ten-bob note and left.

Maguire wore the palings for six weeks amidst a lot of banter from neighbours, who said he should have them round his head instead.

It was summer and someone sang, "Doing the Lambeth Walk".

A wireless played, "With a shillelagh under my arm and a twinkle in my eye, I'm off to Tipperary in the morning."

An oul doll shouted to a group of children, "All of yez stand at the corner and luk out fer any strange men on bikes with bouler hats and guid raincoats."

They were spotted often enough. All doors were locked and silence reigned except for the thunderous knockings on doors.

A coalman once sat on Mrs Wright's doorstep all night and still didn't get his money in the morning. She had three children who were known to the other inhabitants as the "starved rats". Stale bread fried in rancid dripping was mostly what they got. The hair of the older girl gleamed with blue ointment to kill the lice. The boy had his head shaved against a similiar condition. Once the coalman was gone, Mrs Wright came out into the middle of Fairview Gardens with a glass of Tony wine in her hand, shouting, "I owe the world and they'll never see it! Fairview Gardens? It's F.U. Gardens!"

A pony came up the track pulling a cart with a large milk can on it. "Skimmed milk! Skimmed milk!" shouted the man.

This was followed shortly afterwards by a pony pulling a

spring-cart loaded with boxes of Ardglass herrings: "Sixpence for six! Sixpence for six." It was the food of the poor, but not the very poor.

In the course of the day, there would follow the ragman with his horse and spring-cart. And afterwards – to catch the children who had arrived back from school – the horse-drawn carousel with its tiny hobby-horses and small Austin Seven cars swinging from chains would stop at the bottom of Fairview Gardens – for the track wasn't wide enough – and an old motor horn would sound as the man pressed on its bulbous rubber. Any child who had a halfpenny for the horses or a penny for the Austin Sevens would climb aboard, and the man would turn the handle to set everything in motion. Then the chains carrying the rides would begin to revolve and the horses and cars would rise, higher and higher, and the music would begin from the music box – usually something from *The Barber of Seville*. But there were very few halfpennies or pennies around there in Fairview Gardens.

One night the Wright family got a telegram with the simple message: "Mr Herbert Wright . . . Stop . . . Lost at sea".

Their father, a ship's stoker, was dead. When Mrs Wright contacted the shipping company, they said he had fallen overboard off the East Indies while drunk. No alcohol was allowed on board ship. No compensation. He couldn't drink because of having ulcers. Mrs Wright couldn't prove this to their satisfaction.

The Wright family wailed that night into the small hours. No one went near them. They had nothing to give but useless rhetoric. No one even sympathised the next day – it was too much like spitting into an open wound. The day after that the children were laughing and playing again.

*

One night Maguire turns up the volume control of the wireless as it plays "God Save the King". He wants to annoy the Harper family who live opposite because Harper, a Protestant, has a Catholic family. Harper tunes in to Athlone and gets the national anthem of the Irish Free State. He turns up "A Soldier's Song". He thinks he's pacifying his wife, but she's scared in case Maguire comes over looking for a fight. The two Protestants battle it out each night until the batteries fade and the accumulators discharge.

Two old people move into the shack beside the Harper family. The old wife airs the blankets on the line. Printed on them are the words "Union Workhouse". The old man gets on his messenger boy's bicycle every morning and hunts the country roads for branches and twigs to light their fire. He goes to McCormack's shop to buy a packet of Epsom salts every week for his constipation.

The bailiffs arrive one day suddenly. They have hidden their bicycles and bowler hats under a hedge and cut across the fields to Fairview Gardens. They are stoned by the children and threatened with death by the adults. They disappear with bloody cuts but come back with four armed policemen. Maguire's wireless set is seized. Harper's wireless is also seized, but he pretends he has just got a job in the shipyard. He gives the bailiff their last two shillings towards his debts with a promise to pay the same amount each week. He gets his wireless set back.

When Maguire starts whistling "God Save the King" at night, Harper is able to drown him out with "A Soldier's Song". Mrs Harper is still afraid of Maguire starting a fight and goes all out to become friends with the Protestant Waring family. Maguire, noting this, still whistles but not so loudly. Harper drowns him out, but not so loudly any more. Maguire stops whistling. Harper stops tuning in to Athlone.

McCormack's shop sells everything. Hanging in the shop is a whole side of bacon. Joe, the owner, flips the maggots off with a cloth when no one is looking. Beside the bacon is a large round tank of paraffin oil. He is in his dotage and repeats a customer's order over and over again in order not to forget it: "An 'envelop', two Woodbine, a pint of paraffin, a barmbrack, box of matches, a stick of cinnamon."

The superior light of a tilley lamp throws out its white light over the enigmatic rows of mahogany drawers in the shop. Mrs Wright enters, followed by her three starved rats. She asks them to wait outside. When they won't, she threatens to cut their "thoats" with a rusty "raisor" blade.

Her starved rats peep through the window as she buys a bottle of Tony wine. They wail. She produces a razor blade. It is rusty. Joe takes the opportunity to swipe off a few more maggots.

Joe McCormack has four elderly sisters, unmarried and living in the house, plus a younger brother of about fifty. The sisters occasionally peep through the curtains that divide the shop from the rest of the house. They all have pale and wan faces that quickly disappear if someone looks at them. No customer has ever seen their complete bodies. They never leave the house. The younger brother looks after their small farm adjoining the house. He keeps a bull in the apple orchard. The bull has permanent diarrhoea from eating the fallen apples. Some boys from Fairview Gardens once went there to rob the orchard. They had discovered the bull couldn't charge because the apple trees are growing too close together. Young brother McCormack heard the bull bellowing in frustration and ran out and fired his shotgun in the air.

Later he threw off his coarse-cut black suit, turning green with age, and dressed in a smart sports jacket and flannels. He was seen getting the bus to Belfast, one morning, and returning late at night with a stout lady his own age. She never serves in the shop and takes to peeping through the curtain like the four sisters.

The four sisters die one after another within a few weeks. The shop, attended by Joe, stays open during all the funerals.

Their coffins are carried through the shop despite the customers.

One day Joe is whipping a young stallion with a knotted rope when it crushes him to death with its forelegs. The younger brother inherits everything, but he still won't have the stout lady serve in the shop. She peeps through the curtain and her ruddy face is turning pale. She is never seen outside the house.

Her new husband whacks the maggots off the bacon like his late brother and repeats every order over and over again as if he were in his dotage. He isn't in his dotage.

Mrs Wright takes a bottle of Tony wine over to the Maguires' shack, and they sit down and drink it. Mrs Maguire sends one of her children down to McCormack's for another bottle. The wine is at the bottom of the list for quality, but it is strong and has an immediate effect on the undernourished. The door flies open and Mrs Wright, still in her tattered mourning black, comes racing out screaming, followed by Maguire, who has his risen cock in his hand, followed by Mrs Maguire with the fire-poker. All three race up and down the track and on to the Manse Hill. Up and down Manse Hill as far as McCormack's Corner at one end and the Clontonacally School at the other end. The inhabitants watch Maguire trying to catch Mrs Wright to rape her and Mrs Maguire trying to catch her husband to kill him. As exhaustion sets in they all three collapse into a ditch, breathing heavily and eyeing one another in a paranoid fashion. Maguire starts towards Mrs Wright, who gives a spent scream, and Mrs Maguire starts towards her husband who closes his eyes and falls asleep. Their children watch them from a distance, afraid to go near them because of their condition. Darkness falls and they eventually stagger back up the track one by one with a hundred yards between them.

Maguire joins the army reserve for the few shillings it pays each week. He wears the khaki uniform, with jacket buttoned to the neck, and peaked cap and puttees which wind spirally from his ankles to his knees. He parades Fairview Gardens. Someone laughs. He can't identify the shack it's coming from. He spots a cat but leaves it alone; instead, he kicks a feral dog and sends it howling down the rocky track.

It is September 1939 and war breaks out in Europe. To his shock, Maguire is called up. At the army medical he points to his deformed arm, the bones of which have knitted crookedly. He is passed A2 and almost faints. That night his family wails as if he were dead. The neighbours don't go near their shack. They are afraid they might wish him well for his journey across the water to Aldershot.

Somebody sings, "Yes, we have no bananas, we have no bananas today . . ."

One day during the school holidays, Jimmy is sent down to McCormack's to buy a loaf of bread. The shilling is wrapped neatly in a piece of paper torn from a back issue of *Titbits*. He is to ask McCormack to wrap up the change, and he is to bring it straight back. But instead of going directly down Manse Hill, he stops halfway to taunt a bull in the field. It has red fierce eyes. There is also a herd of cows in the field. The bull's penis is almost dragging on the ground. He shouts at it, makes funny faces at it, waves his arms. The bull watches him for a while with its ill-tempered eyes before charging the hedge. It doesn't break through because it falls into a ditch at the other side of the hedge.

The boy is terrified and shouts, "Mammy! Mammy!" and begins to run back home but realises he has lost the shilling in his panic. He forgets the bull and searches the spot where he taunted it. He can't find it anywhere. He retraces his steps almost back to Fairview Gardens, but at the same time knowing he had it in his hand when he was taunting the bull. He goes back to that spot and combs the long grass again but still can't find it. Sick with fear he walks back up Manse Hill, past Fairview Gardens, past Clontonacally School and turns into a lane leading to the Carson farm. He likes to play with Sidney at school. They are both in Senior Infants.

Mrs Carson welcomes him into the farmhouse kitchen and sits him at the table where the family are having their meal. The old grandmother sits by the large open fire. She is dressed in a long black dress that was fashionable at the beginning of the century and has a grey hand-knitted shawl around her shoulders. She directs a large ear trumpet towards the table from time to time before turning it to the horn of the large music box. She turns the handle and it plays, "When you and I were young, Maggie . . ."

In the middle of the bare-scrubbed table is a pyramid of potatoes in their jackets, a huge bowl of stewing meat mixed with carrots, twin loaves of home-baked bread, a large jug of sweet milk, a larger jug of buttermilk, enamelled mugs for the sweet milk, tin mugs for the buttermilk, about two pounds of farm-produced butter on a wooden, ridged butter pat, two-pound jars of home-made gooseberry jam, blackberry jam and strawberry jam – the fruits of which are full. Mrs Carson carries in a platter of stewed pork ribs and onions and puts it on the table. Da Carson says a quick prayer while stabbing a potato with his fork. He stabs again and again until he has seven on his large plate. Sidney is laughed at by his father for only stabbing two. Jimmy is shouted at by Mrs Carson for not joining in. The potatoes are eaten with the skins. Jimmy is shouted at again for being too cautious with the butter. Mrs Carson throws a huge dollop of it on his plate. Da Carson takes about a pound of stewing meat on his knife and devours it, patting his stomach and laughing at Jimmy for not stuffing enough down his throat. Sidney manages five large potatoes and about half a pound of meat before he starts on the ribs. He pulls up his jersey to show his bulging belly and laughs until he almost falls off the chair. Granny swivels her ear trumpet around to listen to him and smiles before cackling. She turns a lever on the music box to change the disk and turns the handle: "I walk beside you. . ."

Jimmy feels something under his feet. He peeps below the table and sees a twelve-month-old baby girl in a hessian nappy pulling a piece of potato from a hen who has wandered in from the farmyard. He points out the child to Mrs Carson, who says, "She's an independent one. . . that wee we'an."

Mrs Carson, wearing a hessian-bag apron, doesn't sit at the table but fusses around trying to get Granny to eat. Granny will just have a potato and a mug full of buttermilk. Da Carson reaches over the table and cuts a whack of bread, butters it liberally and spreads on a pile of gooseberry jam. This time he shouts at Jimmy to do the same.

"Eat up, put some arse on you."

Mrs Carson shouts at him for using *that* word again. Granny swivels her ear trumpet and asks for a repeat from her son, Da Carson.

He says, "It's goin' to be dark again tonight, Mammy."

Jimmy laughs at the sight of such a big man addressing his mother as "Mammy". Da Carson says, "If you're able to laugh, you haven't ate enough."

Seemingly out of nowhere comes a boy of about fourteen. He is desperately thin, bent double, his face an amber colour. His jacket hangs on him as if on a peg on the wall. His pitifully thin arms hang in the sleeves of his jacket like twigs. His thin wrists and long bony fingers are also amber. His family look at him in amazement, as if he has never entered the kitchen before. He sits down at the table, coughing as feebly as a kitten, and reaches for the platter of ribs. He begins devouring them as if he has never seen food before. Da Carson cries. Mrs Carson cries. Granny cries. Sidney grins with embarrassment. Jimmy just stares at Sidney's older brother, afraid. The boy gets up and disappears again to an outer room somewhere. Mrs Carson examines the platter and counts the remaining ribs.

"Cecil's just eaten about a pound of ribs," she says in amazement.

The ear trumpet swivels.

"He's ate about near two pounds of ribs – my poor wee Cecil . . . did you hear me, Mammy?"

The old lady doesn't answer, and he asks her again, almost shouting into her trumpet. But she won't answer.

Mrs Carson throws a large bleach bottle into the fire and covers it with coal. Jimmy watches, his eyes blinking, in case it explodes, but it only melts down to another shape and then finally to a lump of smooth glass.

Sidney takes Jimmy to the shed where the boxes of seed potatoes are stacked to look for rats' tails sticking out of the boxes. He puts his finger to his lips, and they both move silently on tiptoe. The rats hear them, of course, but they think they are hidden well enough and aren't conscious that their tails are peeping out of the boxes. Sidney finds one and yanks the squealing rat out of the box and, whirling it quickly around his head, flings it into a corner where it desperately tries to climb the stone walls. Jimmy finds a tail but is afraid to touch it. Sidney grabs it, but the rat is alerted by Jimmy's hestitation. It nips Sidney and runs up his jersey to his head and jumps off to flee. Sidney sucks his bleeding finger and squeals with laughter. After discovering four more rats' tails, Jimmy manages to yank one rat out, but before he can whirl it around his head, the rat jumps on to his shoulder and sits there a moment. He hears himself cry out, "Mammy! Mammy!"

Sidney knocks it off his shoulder and stamps on it, breaking its neck. He then kicks the convulsing creature through the door into the farmyard where it is attacked by a gander.

They next enter the barn and turn the handle of the turnip slicer, feeding it huge purple turnips. Sidney eats a few slices, pulls up his jersey and pats his bulging belly. A wren's nest is stuck on a wall within reaching distance. Sidney puts a finger to his mouth and they tiptoe past it. The bird doesn't stir from its nest.

They next enter the hayloft and bury one another in the hay.

Then it's on to the pigsties. Da Carson is boiling potatoes and various discarded vegetables in a huge coke-fired copper for the pigs. Now and then he reaches in, takes out a piece of potato and eats it. A sow is feeding her litter in a pen. Sidney reaches over the fence and takes out a squealing piglet. He gets a piece of hessian and a piece of hayrope and dresses it up like a doll. Da Carson roars with laughter and keeps on stirring the copper and eating the potatoes.

Jimmy forgets about the lost shilling for a while, but when he remembers he longs to stay with Sidney and the Carson family, though he doesn't say this to them. He wants to stay for ever. He doesn't want to go back to Fairview Gardens. He knows what will happen when he gets home. Finally, he just has to leave, much to Sidney's disappointment, and to Mrs Carson's disappointment for she wants a companion for her son. He says byebye to Granny, who hears him without her trumpet, says bye-bye to Da Carson, and wanders slowly down the lane followed by Sidney, who keeps asking him not to go. He reaches the long iron gate, between the two pillars with a stone lion perched on each, and Jimmy swings it open on its screeching hinges. Sidney kicks the gate in frustration as he goes.

He comes to the duck pond and watched the ducks wag their tails as they dip their heads below the surface in search of tadpoles, walks on to Clontonacally School, travels on slowly until he comes to the entrance of Fairview Gardens. His two sisters are there looking for him. They say nothing but run up to their shack.

He walks even slower up the rocky track. A stray donkey is being chased by a group of children. They are trying to climb on its back. Normally he would join them, but he has a more pressing engagement. He knocks at the door, but it is already open.

His mother strikes first with a still-green stick cut from a hedge. His father, hiding behind the door, strikes out indiscrimately with a heavy leather belt, striking him everywhere and anywhere, not seeming to care that the buckle on the strap is also digging into him. Jimmy's screams don't stop them. He isn't given time to breathe or cry. They belabour him until he thinks he will die. Finally they stop to ask him where the loaf is, where the change is, why was he so long. When he says he lost the shilling, they begin all over again, striking him, pushing him away as he tries to cling to either parent. Nobody from the shacks intervenes as they understand that children must be taught a lesson on occasion. Exhausted, red in the face, sweating, his nose continually running, drooling spittle, hurting from weals caused by the belt, bleeding from the buckle, hurting in the bones from the stick, he is so injured physically and mentally that his emotions evaporate. He can't hate them or love them, feel sorry for himself, feel sorry for them, be frightened, be brave; not able to cry any more, or laugh, even hysterically, he can't wish himself dead, or wish his parents dead. The boy is dead and alive. He can't feel either sensation. He is taken by the ear and led out of the door. He doesn't know which parent holds his ear. He is so numbed now, the world has disappeared under his feet; he sees himself walking down Fairview Gardens and on to Manse Hill. He must have pointed out the spot where he lost the shilling for they are searching the road and combing the long grass as he had done a hundred times before. Then he thinks he sees them beginning to search the whole of Manse Hill, right down to McCormack's Corner. Maybe they even go into McCormack's shop and ask McCormack the Younger if he had picked up a shilling wrapped in a piece of paper torn from a back number of *Titbits*. And maybe he just repeats, like his late brother, over and over again, "A shillin' wrapped in paper. A shillin' wrapped in paper. A shillin' wrapped in paper..."

On the way up the hill, one of them finds the piece of paper – the piece torn from a back number of *Titbits*. Just the paper. He might have received a few slaps across the ears and a punch in the back, but he doesn't feel anything. Maybe he hasn't been thrashed after all.

When they get back indoors and one of them is snipping the blackened tip of the wick of the oil lamp, filling it with paraffin from the pint can, turning up the wick slightly, cleaning the glass funnel, putting it carefully in its holder, letting the glass heat up first before turning up the wick a bit more, cleaning the tin reflector for it to cast its light on the dirty-cream distempered walls... after all that, he wonders why time has flown so fast. They seem to be going on and on about the lost shilling, repeating themselves over and over again – how they have searched Manse Hill, combed the grass again and again, asked McCormack, how they mistrust him now, how they mistrust everybody in Fairview Gardens, how they mistrust the whole world, how somebody must now be laughing up their sleeve at the Harper family when they found the shilling, the only shilling they had left. They might be looking at the boy with hate-filled glances as they speak, even still throwing out the odd slap or punch, but it has all already happened, and each slap or punch becomes history immediately. He doesn't even anticipate the next blow as it comes toward him – it is already spent, a thing of the past.

He is in the single bed, sleeping beside his younger sister while his older sister sleeps at the bottom of the bed. His father

drowns his kitten because it keeps squeaking for its mother all
night. Somebody tells him that vaguely through a mist. He isn't
sure if it is a dream he is having or had. Then one of his sisters
appears and says the mammy cat has come to the door and taken
its baby away because she heard it squeaking all night. Daddy
said that.

He senses his sisters getting out of bed the next morning,
hears their welcome-to-the-sun voices and the patter of their feet
over the worn linoleum. He can't get out of bed but just lies
there looking up at the ceiling blackened by innumerable oil
lamps. He senses being dragged out of the bed and just lying on
the floor unable to move. Then he is lifted into the bed again by
someone. He fades away a few times. Someone is desperately
trying to spoon-feed him. It might be egg. If it is egg then he is
sick. The shadows grow longer, the yellow glow of the oil lamp
falls on his face a few times. Two people are arguing about him,
over him, blaming him, blaming each other, quarrelling, shouting, whispering, holding a flickering stub of candle near his face,
washing his face with a cold wet facecloth, then spoon-feeding
him again, nursing him, holding him like a baby, crying over
him, arguing, whispering, shouting, lighting the oil lamp, snuff-
ing the wick, holding the flickering candle to his face, lifting him
into a tin bath, gently washing him, dressing him, undressing
him, putting him to bed with his sisters, putting him to bed by
himself, his mother taking him to bed and holding him against
her warm body; the tin bath rattles, the warm water pours from
a jug, then a mighty light switches on. He is in a chair beside the
round iron stove, the chimney pipe is roaring as his mother puts
more and more wood in. He looks around and sees his father.
He looks embarrassed and then averts his eyes from him. His

sisters jump up and down in delight when he focuses on them. He asks for his kitten, but there is silence.

He bursts into tears, feels sorry for the kitten, feels sorry for himself – his emotions come flooding back.

Sidney calls for him but he is too weak to go outside and play. Sidney says God sent the angels down for his big brother after he ate a pound of pork ribs. Where the sun shines through a hole in the clouds – that's the way they took him to Heaven.

A few days later he goes outside to play but he doesn't feel like playing with the other children. He goes into the back garden and walks through the stinging nettles. They sting harder because they are in seed. He rubs a dalkin leaf on some of the blisters, but there are far too many. He finds about six Tony wine bottles that must have been thrown there by Mrs Wright from next door. He puts them together and begins breaking them up with the coal-hammer. A piece of glass shrapnel hits him in the thumb and cuts a gaping wound to the bone. He goes indoors without a word. His mother bathes it and dresses it with a piece of one of his sisters' old cotton dresses while at the same time saying it should be stitched. His father doesn't want to take him to the doctor because he is still black and blue all over his body from the beating.

Sometime in healing, the bandage is overgrown by the flesh. It isn't released until the thumb is agonisingly bathed for hours. Mrs McNally at school refuses to believe it is taking so long to heal, grabs his hand and guides it on the slate. He suffers agonies but says nothing.

The thumb eventually heals, and he shows the vivid scar continually to his mother for sympathy. She says if he is ever lost she can tell the police he has a scar on his right thumb.

Maguire becomes a military policeman and gets a soft posting in India.

Waring collapses and dies outside the gasworks while on his way home. The whole of the lower Ormeau Road always smells of escaped gas. It is raining heavily, and the coke dust on the pavements is now a black sludge. Skinnemelink, his foreman, runs to the pub across the road and comes back with a drop of whiskey at the bottom of a dirty cup. He holds Waring's hand while at the same time trying to feed him the whiskey. He tries for ten minutes, but Waring died a long time ago. Then they call an ambulance.

The Waring family wail. No one in Fairview Gardens goes near them. They still have nothing practical to offer.

They're testing the new air-raid sirens in Belfast. Everyone in Fairview Gardens can hear the distant banshee. They see the smoke in the distance rising above the Ormeau Road as rubber tyres are burnt in oil drums to create a smokescreen. Barrage balloons rise above the military camp near Cedar Valley.

Jimmy watches a German reconnaissance plane streak across the sky to Belfast in broad daylight. He still looks at the ground hoping to find the shilling. . . or any shilling.

THE CRAB-APPLE TREE

Sam Adair, a man in his late eighties – known behind his back as Oul Dried Balls – was having his usual stroll down Laurel Hill. Laurel Hill was a well-worn narrow lane hemmed in by high hedges of hawthorn with the odd clump of woodbine. In times past, the steep lane was called the Lane or the Humpy Lane by the older inhabitants in the area. But Bobby, his son – known behind his back as Dolly Mixture – had given it the definitive name of Laurel Hill. Laurel bushes were fighting the hawthorn for living space now. Sam remembered his father planting the laurels in the vicinity of the old thatched cottage where he had been born. It was said they drew away the damp. He walked on, inspecting the laurels, picking off the odd brown, dried-up leaf, counting the bushes, having a good look at the trees, until he came to the cottage.

He looked at the ground for a while. This was his most recent habit since that family had moved in. It was about all the hostility he could muster up in his old dried-up body these days. He would eventually raise his head and look at the cottage face on, but in the meantime he studied the ground. Once the floor of the lane had been soft and green with soil and short grass. The hoof marks of cattle could no longer register on the barren ground. And the sunken tracks of horse-drawn carts had long

disappeared. It was all rock now, worn rock, with the more hardened granite beginning to come up like daggers. Cattle today cut
their hooves on it if they were driven too fast. The lane fell away
rapidly, humping its way down to the Drumbo Road.

There was a lot of rock around here. That's why there was a
quarry in the vicinity, and if it didn't stop developing it would
one day come right up to the cottage door. He didn't feel the
lane would ever be green again. The ground was too shrunken
now. And there was that family, five children – seven of a family, including the parents – here to wear it down even more,
cause more daggers to stick up. He had begged his son not to let
it out. But no, Bobby lost no opportunity when a few more
shillings a week could be gained. Bobby had cleared out the animal feedstuff, spent a couple of days shifting the sacks further up
the lane to an outhouse near their new house, which he had had
built about ten years ago. A flight of poles carried the cables for
the electricity. It had been put in two years ago by his son,
around about the time when the old man had started his decline.
Bobby had wanted another run of cable to the cottage so as he
didn't have to use the storm lamp when he entered the old dark
and damp cottage in winter to fetch meal for the animals. Sam
had stopped this by implying that he wanted the cottage left as
a memorial to Bobby's grandfather. There was just something
too expensive about it all. At night he could hear the buzzing of
the electricity as it jumped over the insulators at the side of the
house. They were paying for that. Even when you switched off
all the lights inside the house, this buzzing still continued.

He finally lifted his head to look at the cottage. The thatch
was ageing; it was losing its flexibility, breaking here and there,
like the hair of a mad woman, but there would never be repairs

made while that family remained. The heavy stone walls could do with a limewash, but it wouldn't be done in his day. And the door needed a lick of paint. To hell with them. He was sure they were watching him from the tiny windows. He slowly cast his eyes along the length of the cottage. Such a building had already stood for well over a hundred years, and it could stand for another hundred if only the stone quarry would stop their blasting and pneumatic drilling. One day you could step through that half-door and fall into a hole two hundred feet deep.

He caught a sight of the crab-apple tree growing in the side garden of the cottage. His father had planted that. It no longer gave its small sour apples that he once enjoyed as a boy. It was old, almost dried up, old like him. But it was a friend. He looked a while and his look turned to a stare. There was something odd about the tree; something was missing. He counted the branches again. One was missing. The one as thick as a man's arm. He was certain of that. He counted them every morning as surely as he was aware of his own limbs, including his heavy hawthorn stick. He leant on the large gnarled top from which many branches had sprouted at one time. In leaning he almost fell. The top was as smooth as glass with the use it had had from his father and maybe *his* father.

It was summer, a beautiful morning, and the dragonflies flew a foot above his head, coupling. He didn't feel the heat of the sun or the cold of the winter any more, or the wet of the rain. The weather meant nothing to him now. The passing of the seasons even less. He wore his heavy black overcoat, greening with age, rusty at the creases, the whole year round, and in the last year he hadn't bothered taking it off at all, even when going to bed. He looked at the crab-apple tree again. They spoke about the good weather often enough up at the farm, but he could hardly remember the joy it had brought to him once when he was young. He was tired of it all – the same seasons, the same weather. The same tired old talk about the benefits when it rained cats and dogs or how the heavy winds that almost tore the crops out of the ground brought something good like clearing the trees of their rotten branches and stimulating the sap. But it was summer and there had been no winds, yet a branch was missing from the crab-apple tree. His eyes were no longer good enough to see properly up into the tree, though it was maybe only about ten feet tall. He looked over the loose stone wall, on the ground, beneath the tree, but couldn't see any evidence of a branch having fallen. But he would get to the bottom of this mystery. He walked away slower than usual to give anyone watching from the cottage the impression that he was pondering the mystery of the missing branch. He made sure that they would know that his wisdom was now turned on fully to the subject. He knew every damned blade of grass in this area around the farm, and he was sure that all forms of life were aware of him.

Eina Connor, a hefty girl of sixteen – known behind her back as Bull Connor – was weeding the carrot beds in a field adjoining the lane. She was hunkered down doing a sort of slow Cossack dance along the rows. Hunkering down prevented her holding her water for any length of time. The weather being warm, she felt the need to dress for it, or undress for it. She let go a long and fierce gush as if she had sprung a leak. Some of it changed direction, wetting her inner thigh. She stood up to shake her leg. It was a very large leg, covered with purplish blotches got from toasting herself in front of the fire when she would pull up her dress and open her legs to welcome in the heat. The result was what is called measled legs. Summer and winter she did the same in the evenings in front of a large open fire that was kept going, for there was little human warmth around for her kind. Shaking off the urine, she grabbed a handful of her dress to finish drying herself. She turned around just as Sam passed, exposing him to a great tuft of pubic hair. But as he was an old man, she didn't bother turning away. Also, being a great muscular hulk of a girl with a coarse red face with bluey-black hair as tough as a mare's mane, there was no point in worrying about what men thought about her, never mind this old doter. She therefore, quite deliberately, took the end of her dress and wiped her crotch dry again before turning her back and hunkering down again.

He watched her for a while as she progressed down the rows of young carrots. Things grew better when she was around, he thought, but didn't give his usual dry mean chuckle which signalled that he was joking. He didn't usually take much notice of Bella's daughter. She and her mother were practically beggars who called soda bread pastry. She did her work all right, dawn to dusk, and had her food in the shed, while her mother, a battered-looking pullet of a woman, roamed the countryside all day picking up twigs for the fire. Eina scarcely got any money for her toil in the fields, but she did have as much potatoes and vegetables as she could carry each week, along with a quart can of buttermilk and a jug of sweet milk. People in the area could never see her getting a man of her own. She was a "get" – a bastard – and gets begot gets. It ran in the blood, and no one could do anything about it, even if anyone cared.

He thought of returning and asking if she had seen the branch of the crab-apple tree. Maybe her mother had seen it, but

he decided it might make her slack if he started a conversation
with her, even if it was a one-way gruff conversation answered
fearfully with monosyllables. But he did go back to the cottage
and take another look at the crab-apple tree. He looked again on
the ground for sawdust in case it had been sawn down. He
found nothing.

As he entered the farmyard, the speckled grey rooster, red-
dening in the comb, flew at him with wings outstretched, beak
poised like a dart. It didn't recognise him again. He had been
hale and hearty up to a year ago, with ruddy complexion and at
least two stone heavier. One morning he had awakened feeling
old and tired. This feeling usually wore off within a couple of
hours. But this day that feeling had lasted until midday, and
before the week was out it was nightfall before he felt better.
Then one morning he had awakened and known he would never
feel right again. The joyless dawn had come, and sunset could
mean death. He gave up working in the fields, announced it at
the breakfast table one morning at four thirty and went back to
bed, stayed there for a week, wondering how an old man was to
occupy his time, unable to remember what his own father had
done. He decided he had to get out of bed if he was not to lose
the use of his limbs. After a few weeks he set up a routine, visiting the borders of the farm, counting the animals, inspecting the
machinery, counting the laurel bushes, having a good look at the
trees, lingering outside the old thatched cottage. Now that his
son had rented out the cottage, his last bit of peace of mind had
been taken away. And the crab-apple tree had lost a limb.

He lifted his stick, and for a moment was tempted to break a
wing of the rooster. What for? The bird didn't recognise him any
more. It too was old.

"Have ye gone off yer head again?" he said. "Ay, and me that remembers ye from a wee chick?"

The bird stopped beating its wings against his legs, cocked its head and looked at him with its one eye clouding momentarily before moving off to the dung heap and letting off a crowing that could no longer reach the high notes.

Only when he entered the kitchen did he realise that it was baking day. Beatrice, his wife, and his daughter-in-law Mina were belabouring the mounds of dough on the large scrubbed pine table. It was only then that he was able to smell the potato bread in the oven of the American range. A few years ago he could have smelt it halfway down the lane, and he would have gone quickly to the house. Hot potato bread with the butter running on it was his favourite. But now it didn't set the saliva welling. Eating was becoming too much like hard work now. The women were silently annoyed at his lack of interest and didn't greet him or look at him. He stood silently before going to look at the range to see if they were using coke or wood. Coke, just as he thought. It took a day to bring a load of it up from the coal quays by horse and cart from Belfast harbour.

Beatrice banged down the flour sieve on the table as a signal that he should leave the kitchen. When he took no notice of that, it was Mina's turn to send a cloud of flour in his direction, saying, "Ach, sure m'head's gone this day and night. I must have been dreamin'. Sorry."

The old man looked at them. In the old days they would have heard his tongue ushering out great oaths until they fled the room. Now he could only stare at the brown tile floor, pretending he was thinking up some retaliation, and lift his head slowly to look at them. But his slow movements only set them to working harder as a way of emphasising his tortoise-like movement.

He moved into the farmyard, and the old rooster set about him again. This time he beat it off with his stick, leaving a couple of flight feathers to float in a stagnant pool of diluted pig shite.

Beatrice – known behind her back as Jamjaw because of the eczema covering one side of her face – came into the farmyard holding a bread knife. A gaggle of geese stepped stiffly towards her, expecting grain. She studied them a moment and chose the second in line. Their leader was a fine bird, fat with gleaming feathers, but its second-in-command was approaching that condition. There would be less fat, maybe two oven-tins less, on the second one. The leader was, anyway, becoming a pet. He once honked an hour before a great storm ripped the roofs off the byre and milking parlour. What they could have done in the face of the great storm was anyone's guess, but they had been warned.

She hid the bread knife behind her back as the geese gathered around her and suddenly plunged for what she thought was the second goose, but it was in fact the fourth goose. It had its head half-severed from its neck. Holding the bird by the stem, she let it spend the rest of its life beating its wings against her legs, revolving as it did so, its purple blood spouting. The slaps from its wings were painful at times, but it wouldn't last. She noticed her mistake and felt sorry for her victim for a few seconds. Blaming it on the wiliness of the second goose, she attempted to kick it, but her foot would only rise a few inches. Instead she tried to beat the bird with the dead one. The leader took his gaggle back a few feet. She took some grain from her apron pocket and threw it at them. The leader got most of it.

Mina – known behind her back as a Good Thing: available for sexual encounters – came into the yard. Once old Sam would have shouted at her and asked where she was going. It still mattered to him where she was going, but his shout had also withered. His neck out of order now, he twisted his whole body in watching her progress towards the hay loft. She was a beautiful young woman with blond hair, but a subtle blond that could pass for very light brown hair in the shadows. Her skin was snow, and to look into her sky-blue eyes was fatal. She wore a frock that seemed handtailored. Everything she wore enhanced her slightly plump figure. Even the wellington boots emphasised her shapely calves. Around her waist was a hessian-bag apron. That apron took nothing from her but gave her the look of a woman ready for anything.

Old Sam suddenly connected hay lofts with girls, and for a moment something stirred in his groin, but he suppressed this self-torture by wondering if she was about to betray his son. He hadn't got round to looking in the loft yet. A dog whimpered and some puppies whined. Gathering his strength, he made for the loft door and looked into the gloom. She was tying a bib around the tiny neck of a puppy. Taking a baby's bottle, she began feeding the young canine.

"Has she no milk?" he said after a few minutes.

She didn't answer or look up as she held the young cocker spaniel in her arms in the manner of holding a baby. When it had sucked its fill, she tapped its tiny back to bring up the wind. He watched this scene until his old dried eyes grew painful, as if someone had thrown sand in them. She dried the pup's mouth and put it back with its mother. He blocked the doorway to the loft, and as she was leaving he couldn't get out of her way quickly enough. He sensed her hot breasts as she squeezed through. But she was passing an inanimate object as far as she was concerned. He raised his stick in a threatening manner, but she was already back into the house.

His son, so far, had no heir to Laurel Farm, though five years had passed. This woman, being twenty years younger than his son, would get the farm on his death. Some waster would marry her and drink it all away. What he had now was a grand-pup, a substitute for the real thing. She had given up all hope of having a baby. . . this small-town girl from Saintfield. Bobby had met her at a dance and brought her home as part of a cover-up when people began to wonder why he seemed to be bringing home so many young men. It was also thought odd of him to claim that he'd been to school with their fathers. . . especially when they had broad Belfast accents and this was Carryduff. They usually slept with him in the same bed. But that wasn't unusual in this age of innocence. Sam had himself shared a bed with other farmers when they got too drunk to go home after a cattle fair in Ballynahinch.

Bobby, when a schoolboy, liked to comb girl's hair. That worried Sam. He bought him a fine hunter to divert him. The animal was a mare, so Bobby set to combing its mane endlessly. Sam put the mare down one night by sticking a walking stick into its ear to scramble its brain. He did it with the stick he was holding in his hand. The local vet pronounced its death as due to an ear infection. Bobby cried bestial tears for weeks.

He was still annoyed about the renting out of the cottage to that ragamuffin family. The father was called Cocktail to his face, and he gloried in the name. He was a motor mechanic in Lowe's garage. Lowe was the quarry owner who was now extending the quarry towards the cottage. Cocktail was always slightly tipsy. In those days a motor mechanic was thought to be a better mechanic for the drink. And Cocktail was good. With the Second World War in progress, spare parts were hard to find. He would search the scrapyards in Belfast and always come up with something to keep the 1930s fleet of lorries going. Bobby had a three-wheeler van which looked like something built over the forward end of a motor-cycle. Cocktail gave it life eternal. When Cocktail made his frequent visits to the Ivanhoe, he sometimes bumped into Bobby; and Bobby would help him home on those occasions when Cocktail got stocious.

Cocktail, a sexual neutral in his cups, always gave Bobby a bloody good hug and a drunken kiss on the cheek. Cocktail, then regretting being drunk as an oul doll and licking up to the landlord, went indoors, woke his wife and five children and beat the shite out of them to show them who was master. His five boys from ten to fourteen were as battered-looking as the children of a tinker. Their white fearful faces were taut, with a constant snarl on them. Each had the arse of their trousers badly patched with large stitches, and sometimes the patches just flapped. The wife – known behind her back as Lady Muck of Laurel Hill – was rumoured to be from a well-off family from County Fermanagh because of a fox fur she wore both winter and summer. She also wore a hat with a veil which gave her an enigmatic look. It was also rumoured she was a Roman Catholic, and though she was sometimes taunted with derogatory names such as teague, mickey and fenian by the children coming out of Clontonacally School, it never seemed to fizz on her. Cocktail was beyond religion. He took no part in local Twelfth of July parades, though he mixed with the Orangemen when they celebrated at the Ivanhoe.

Old Sam decided he must do something about Mina and his
substitute heir. He entered the loft and stamped on the five
pups as they nuzzled around his feet. The bitch cocker spaniel
looked on, panting in the summer heat, as if this were an
everyday occurrence. This took a great effort, and he almost
toppled over when he slid in one of their pools of blood. One
still squealed with a broken back, so he helped it along with a
blow from his stick. The bitch then began sniffing the tiny
bodies, pawing at them, running to him and looking up into
his eyes. He dismissed her with a whack and left the loft. He
was sweating and his face had turned amber. He made it to the
kitchen, ordered buttermilk and sat down as the air filled with
clouds of fine flour. Finally he made his way to his room and
lay down, reckoning this was his last day on earth, before
falling asleep.

Mina's screams woke him, and she burst through the door
with Eina and Beatrice. He told Eina to go back to her shed. It
was built of rough concrete blocks, unplastered, with a concrete
floor and a corrugated iron roof. An old open fireplace was the
only compromise. She preferred the farmhouse and wished to
stay there as long as possible. Beatrice tapped her on the arm,
meaning for her to stay around a while longer. Still saying nothing, Beatrice looked hard at her husband. Her eczema glowed
like a cockscomb in combat.

Mina kept wondering who would do a thing like this, and
Sam said the cocker spaniel bitch must have turned on her own
as his own was turning on him. He was a fair man to animals,
he said, but nature knew better. He would have had Bobby
drown the pups anyway. They were reminded that he owned the
farm. He said he could starve them all out if he had a mind to.

Anything turning on its own blood had to go. The bitch had to go. Bobby would see to it.

Mina screamed and Beatrice led her from the musty-smelling room with its heavy Victorian furniture and its horse harnesses, which Sam was always promising to have repaired.

Old Sam, the next morning, had his usual walk. Eina was pissing as usual. It was cold and the steam drifted across the cabbage rows. Bella had an old pram full of twigs and was breaking a currant malt loaf and handing it to her daughter. Sam waved his stick to indicate that Bella wasn't wanted on his land.

Bella grinned a gummy grin. Eina wiped her crotch and fell to weeding. Bella made off, dragging the pram with its buckled wheels into the potato field; and though he tried to shout after her, he could make no sound.

Bella and her daughter lived under a hedge covered with a worn-out square of tarpaulin whenever Eina was out of work. Now, after she had roamed the countryside, Bella would sneak to Eina's shed at night to sleep and would slip out again about four in the morning before milking time.

Mina arrived with an enamelled can of milky tea and two thick jam sandwiches for Eina. Sam had ordered this so as Eina would have to stay in the field rather than go back to her shed for her midday break. Mina was talking earnestly with Eina, and they both threw glances in his direction from time to time. Eina, hunkered down, took great bites from the sandwiches as if tearing at the grass, mixing them with great gulps of tea. Then they began to laugh, and he knew they were talking about men. However, it wasn't a loving laugh about some sexual matters, but a laugh of hatred against domination. There was bitterness and anger against that sex for the moment. Then Mina, ever hopeful and maybe remembering or hoping for love, laughed softly. Eina glowed in this new conversation and began combing her hair with her fingers and taking little delicate bites of her sandwich and gently sipping at the can of tea.

Sam waved his stick at them as if performing semaphore, telling Eina to get on with her work, telling Mina to go back to the kitchen. But they were lost in some great romance to do with Clark Gable.

He walked slowly to the cottage again to inspect the crab-apple tree. They were peeping out at him in turns from the tiny windows. The five boys hadn't gone to school this morning. He was certain they would end up in an industrial school. He hoped they would. The oldest boy finally came boldly out and said something like, "A half a crown and you can look at my arse, mister."

Sam didn't understand. An arse to him was something you kicked.

The boy got bolder and came closer to him.

"Your Sissy Bobby wants to give me a half a crown for pulling my trousers down."

Sam raised his stick and tried to brain the boy.

The boy jumped back jeering, "I'd rather put my sausage in her jam roll. Your Mina I'm talking about. Do ye hear?"

Sam understood that and waved his stick. The boy suddenly frightened, as battered boys do, and escaped back into the cottage white as a sheet. Sam banged on the door with his stick.

Cocktail came out: "Away, ye fuckin' whoor's bastard of a cunt!"

Cocktail was nastily drunk and advanced on the old man, jerking his head back and forth like a bantam cock. His face was a scarlet-blue and his hair stood on end. Being a small man, he had got on to the tips of his toes. His fists were flailing like damaged aeroplane propellers, and the froth was coming out of his mouth as if out of an exhaust pipe. The old man cowered, hiding his head under his upraised stick.

Cocktail dropped his fists and began spitting at him, going deep down in his throat to bring up the phlegm, sucking in the snatters from his nose to use as added ammunition, shouting, "You whoor's whoor of a whoor! May you die shoutin'! I'll kick your balls into your mouth! Your cunt of a son sits down to make his water! He'll get a God Almighty kick in the plums! I'll cut his charlie off and give it to the cat!"

He then calmed slightly, shaking all over and white in the face. "We shit people like your cuntin' son on the road to Mons. Goin' over the top we blew their brains out – shot them in the arse."

Cocktail wound down like a clockwork toy. Mumbled about being shell-shocked, tried to shake the old man's hand and then stood with bowed head looking at the ground. Then, as if an unseen hand had rewound him, he was at it again.

"You're comin' round here every day to look at the tree like Lord Shite of Clabber Hill. Well, I cut the branch off the tree for the fire. You couldn't see where the branch had been cut."

He stopped to grab a handful of soil.

"I rubbed it over the saw marks. Ha, I camouflaged it. Ground the sawdust into the ground. Learnt that in the army. Ha, ye fuckin' oul blurt yah. Ha!"

He ran at the old man, trying to rub the soil into his face, but his sons came out crying and grabbed their father and took him indoors. Cocktail's wife came out wearing her fox fur and hat with veil and said in a strange accent, pronouncing the "ing", "Have you been upsetting my husband?"

She then closed the door. The last thing Sam saw of them was seven faces fighting to take it in turns to look out of the tiny windows at him. The spittle had dried on his face, and he didn't bother trying to wipe it off. He just didn't have the energy left. One great green snatter clung to the lapel of his rusty-black coat. It ran snail-like down his coat as he began walking.

In some ways he didn't feel too bad. Five years ago he would have gone back to the farmhouse to get the shotgun and threaten them . . . maybe firing one barrel in the air. But now, confirmed as an old man, he could no longer think of revenge at the moment. But they couldn't stay in the cottage after what he had learnt about the crab-apple tree. They had abused him, but he didn't worry too much about that. As an old man he had survived. It was the tree he was worried about. He stopped to study it. Eventually he saw the great wound darkened with soil. His father's tree!

He walked on up the lane and looked over the hedge at the hobbled red bullock. It was a devil. No hedge or fence could hold it since Bobby had castrated it as a young bull. It had escaped countless times. One day he told Bobby to get a long chain, nail it to a heavy log of wood and put the chain round its neck so as the log dangled level with its knees. It worked. The animal had to walk slowly or it would trip. Its fence and hedge busting days were over. Now he decided to have it slaughtered, but in an unusual way. It would be made to pay for all the trouble it had caused. Its death would also pay back Cocktail and his family for what he had done to the crab-apple tree. Animal squealing started somewhere up ahead.

When he got back to the farmyard, Bobby was sitting on a chair with a hessian sack on his knees. Near by were a number of young pigs with their legs tied, waiting to be castrated. One piglet was on its back, on his knee, while he cut into the testicle bag with a razor blade. When he had finished with the pig, he slopped some water from a bucket, now bloody, into the wound before sewing it up with cotton thread. The old man could scarcely make himself heard above the squealing, but he did bend over the pig and carry on a staccato conversation. Bobby nodded eagerly and smiled, his face white and drawn.

Cocktail entered the yard the next day with a bucket and was attacked by the rooster. Bobby was still continuing his work so as the young piglets would grow fat. He would also stop the young boars from breeding, in preference to his expensive blue boar. Cocktail went to lift the cover to the deep well when Bobby shouted above the squealing, "There's no water here for you any more!"

Cocktail again hooked the rope to the bucket to draw water, but Bobby put the bleeding pig under his arm and marched towards the well. "I said no water here any more."

Cocktail, visibly shaken by the squealing injured pig, melted down to a small boy and began calling him Mr Adair.

Beatrice entered the yard to enquire what was going on. Bobby said "no water" again and waved the injured animal towards Cocktail. Beatrice suggested a compromise: he could draw it out of the milk cooler. Cocktail began arguing about his rights. The rooster suddenly attacked Beatrice. Bobby crunched on it with his heavy boot and had it a matted mixture of blood and feathers with his ferocious stamping. Cocktail, now more frightened, ran for the milking parlour to fill his bucket. The water would be warmish and near stagnant, but he would bide his time and think up what to do next. Sam looked down at what was once a proud rooster. He put his hand to his eyes. He was crying, but there were no tears.

Bobby sat down again with his piglets and began slicing and laughing when Cocktail passed with the bucket of water. He tried to spit into the bucket and followed up with a piece of bloody testicle. He missed, and the leading goose gobbled it up before it hit the ground.

Mina turned the wireless up loud to listen to *Workers' Playtime*. She sang along to "Run Rabbit Run". She went off-key a few times as she tried to stifle her sobs.

Later that evening Cocktail found an old well under a hedge across the Drumbo Road in a lane called the Duck Walk. He bucketed until it was empty, then cleared out the stones which had fallen in or had been thrown in by boys. The water was ice cold, and he wondered why he had never thought of this before.

He fearfully told his wife everything about the episode in the farmyard, and her blood froze. The boys were frightened, and he calmed them by saying he would never lay his hand on them again, but later he smacked the eldest boy across the ear when he burnt the toast at the wood fire. They were having toast and home-grown lettuce and tomatoes for tea. Later they all gathered around the large open fireplace with its cranes for heavy pots and watched the wood lice come out of the rotten wood. Cocktail and the boys took it in turn to trap the wood lice with burning twigs and force them to commit suicide by running into the heart of the fire. They laughed while the mother belaboured them for their cruelty. Later they all listened to *ITMA* on the wireless (*It's That Man Again*) with Tommy Handley being asked by Mrs Mop, "Can I do you now, sir?"

And much later, as a special late-night treat, the boys were allowed to listen to the thin voice of Lord Haw-Haw: "Gammanee calling. . . Gammanee calling. . . This is the *Reichsrunfunk* – the English language service – broadcasting to the downtrodden masses of the British Isles. . . Did you enjoy the Easter eggs we sent you in April, Mr Churchill? You poor white-haired boy. . . we never. . . never. . . never forget our friends. . . We have many more gifts for your birthday, Mr Churchill. . . We here in the Third Reich sincerely hope that you are not too drunk to listen to our greetings. . . I have just been handed a special communiqué. . . to the people of Portadown under the English yoke: Why is your town clock five minutes slow?. . . It appears that your masters are neglecting you. . . Depend on us. . . We are your friends. . . The day is coming when we will liberate you. . ."

The radio stuttered and went dead. Cocktail cursed and swore. The accumulator needed charging or the battery had failed.

They dipped the wicks of the oil lamps, blew on them and went to bed by candlelight. It had been a good evening.

A few days later the family went down ill with vomiting and stomach pains. Cocktail made a list of the food they had eaten, but it had all been fresh. He thought of the water suddenly and went to the well across Drumbo Road. He fished in the water until he found a pebble of bluestone used in sheep dipping and a dead swollen frog.

He took the bluestone pebble and frog to the farm and accused Sam and Bobby of attempted murder. When he threatened them with the peelers, Bobby said it must have been Eina.

Eina had once stolen a horse's harness and been incarcerated in a convent for two years. There she scrubbed floors and was punched on the back by the nuns if they thought she was slacking.

A priest, in mufti, came out to interview her as she was out on licence. Later the police took her back to the convent.

Cocktail still blamed Bobby. He was interviewed at the local police barracks. When he named Bobby and Sam as possible suspects, he was threatened with a "fuckin' good kickin'".

Cocktail stopped drinking and lost his job. One day his boys were beaten at the school gates by a teenage gang whom they had never seen before. It was said they came from Saintfield where old Sam's family had originally come from in the last century.

Cocktail got a job driving sailors around for the Royal Navy. The sailors sometimes sang:

"One two three four five
A sailor took a dive
He skinned his cock against a rock
One two three four five."

They still lived in the cottage, but old Sam and Bobby wanted them out even more than before. Especially Bobby. That arse for a half-crown leaked by Cocktail's son was driving him mad. With all the soldiers and sailors pouring into Northern Ireland, he found more of his kind easier to meet in a pub in Cornmarket, in the city, but Cocktail and his family knew about him now. His father and mother might get wise to him with all this new cosmopolitan atmosphere coming in because of the war. Mina, as a woman lying beside him in bed at night, was not a happy woman. She just thought he didn't love her. Despite her beauty, she felt diminished and ugly. Beatrice made no comment, but she thought a lot.

American troops began landing at Belfast Docks. One convoy took forty-eight hours to pass along the main road to Ballynahinch. It was a continual deep roar of the engines of jeeps, peeps, beeps, heavy haulage trucks bearing machinery and truckloads of tired soldiers holding carbines between their knees. The roads were covered with chewing-gum packets. A local bus driver tried to edge his bus into this convoy and was told, by an officer through a loudhailer, to reverse back into a secondary road, but he refused to do so as these were his roads. He had driven on them for thirty years. A jeep drew alongside the bus, and the officer shot him dead.

Old Sam seemed to have forgotten about the red hobbled bullock, but Bobby reminded him. He also reminded him about the sawn-off branch of the crab-apple tree. Cocktail and his family were still at the cottage and refusing to leave despite eviction notices. The deflecting nature of this war was beginning to override local issues, local justice. Old Sam became alive again for a few days when the rage built up in him again after Bobby's taunts that he was afraid to do something about the crab-apple tree. Old Sam then ordered the red bullock to be brought to the farmyard. The women were to stay indoors and draw the curtains.

The animal was mild-mannered, though a persistent escapee in the past. It nuzzled old Sam's hand as he took off the chained log from around its neck. It almost won him over. For a moment he stroked its head. Bobby put an end to that. His first blow with the pickaxe knocked its eye out. The old man almost went into a state of shock, but when he remembered the crab-apple tree he recovered. The second blow dug deep into its neck, and a fountain of black blood drenched the ground. A third blow tore into its left side with such force that Bobby had trouble pulling the pickaxe out. The beast stood patiently, without a sound, rolling its one eye in terror. Then came the fourth, fifth and sixth blows to its body. The animal bent its forelegs as if praying. Its ears twitched to the sound of the pickaxe. Despite the seventh blow, the animal carefully moved its hind legs until it was lying down as if to chew the cud. But its cud-pockets had been rented, and the slippery pile of vegetation was slowly sliding on to the ground.

Bobby was sweating. He went to the well and drew a bucket of water and poured it over his head. Spitting on his hands, he delivered a mighty blow to the spine of the animal. The animal, again carefully, laid its head on the ground and didn't move. It still looked alive, with its one eye trying to see who was behind it. Bobby continued to hack into the beast until old Sam said it had had enough. There was a great sea of blood all around, and floating on it were bits of flesh and hide. Bobby sharpened a knife on a long, rounded carborundum stone used for sharpening scythes and cut off its red coat. He held it up to the sun and looked through twenty holes.

Satisfied, he carried it down Laurel Hill and spread it out to dry on the hedge opposite the cottage. Then he walked back to the farmyard and hacked the animal into pieces with an axe. Now, it looking like something in a butcher's shop, Beatrice came out to carry the animal pieces inside. Beatrice looked for Mina, to get her to help, but couldn't find her. A suitcase was missing with some of her clothes; also missing was about a hundred pounds from the old tea caddy on the mantelpiece.

Bella wheeled her battered pram into the farmyard and was given a leg to carry away.

Cocktail, without the booze, was a timid man. He went outside to the hedge, looked at the hide and counted the holes.

He knew it was the red bullock. His family gazed out, in turns, through the tiny windows. He thought of the peelers, thought of a kicking, went inside and signed the last-delivered eviction notice.

Later that day he found another cottage a long way off on the Moss Road. Using the Royal Navy windowed van, he loaded up his meagre collection of furniture, pots and pans, clothing and motor mechanic's tools and spare engine parts, and left with his family.

Beatrice told her son that Mina had disappeared. He flew into a rage and wrecked their bedroom with the bloodied pickaxe.

Later he transferred all the animal feedstuff back into the cottage and padlocked the door.

Old Sam seemed revitalised by the animal sacrifice. The bloom of health was back on his cheek. His voice returned and he was able to shout at Beatrice. He ate about a pound of the slaughtered bullock at one sitting on that wonderful day of renewal.

The next morning he was found dead in bed by Beatrice. The years, plus a few, had returned to his body. He lay there looking small and shrunken. His face didn't look relaxed as most new-dead look. His mouth was wide open as if he had tried to swallow himself. The undertakers had to sew the eyelids over his bulging, terror-stricken eyes.

There was a storm that night, and the crab-apple tree snapped like a rotten twig, falling through the thatch of the cottage.

Bobby was in town in the centre of Cornmarket talking to a
GI when the soldier suddenly punched him, splitting his lip.

Mina, linked between two Yanks, was passing through Cornmarket on her way to a dance at the American Red Cross building in Chichester Street. Belfast being in many ways a big village
meant that people who knew one another couldn't help bump-
ing into each another. He spotted her and followed them. Outside the Anderson and McAuley store, he threatened to knock
her dead between the two soldiers. He began shouting that she
was his wife. The Yanks politely said he could have his wife back.
Mina denied she was his wife and said he was just a drunk who
kept pestering her. He ran at her and kicked her in the stomach.
One of the soldiers hit him with a half-filled bottle of Black
Bush whiskey. He hit the ground unconscious.

Two young men in powder-blue zoot suits, from the nearby
Markets area, approached the prone figure to rob him. He
came to and tried to get to his feet, but one took a sharpened
bicycle chain from behind the lapels of his suit and slashed
Bobby across the face. They got about three hundred pounds
in white fivers. A police patrol found him and took him to a
cell. He insisted they phone his local police barracks. The
sergeant there was a witness to his good character. They did
and they let him go.

The next night he was arrested in Cornmarket for opportun-
ing for lewd purposes – "looking into the face of a man". A
detective read out a statement, in court, saying how he had been
under surveillance in Cornmarket for a month. He got two years
in prison. Beatrice died while he was in prison.

When he got back to the farm, he found Eina back living in
the shed. The storm that blew over the crab-apple tree had also

blown off the roof of the shed. She was in bed snoring while the rain fell on her. He closed the door of the shed silently.

The animals had been sold in an auction. The farmhouse roof was leaking. Doors in the outhouses were hanging from one rusting hinge. He took up his father's hawthorn stick and wandered slowly down Laurel Hill. The crab-apple tree was rotted to yellowish pulp with woodlice crawling over it. Opposite on the hedge was the rotting ragged remains of a red hide. Near by, a blackbird had built part of its nest from it. The thatch on the cottage had caved in. The animal feedstuff inside was mouldering, with the bags rotted away. He heard the squeaking of rats. A klaxon sounded from the quarry. The rock-grinding machinery stopped. There was silence, then an explosion and a sound of tumbling rocks. White powder drifted into the air and settled on the laurel bushes. The klaxon sounded the all-clear. The rock grinders started up again. He looked through the hedge and saw that the quarry had advanced about a hundred yards towards the cottage. In a few years the hawthorn hedge would be consumed, and the laurel bushes. Then the cottage.

He walked slowly back up Laurel Hill. The rocks were sharper daggers now. The fields had gone wild.

Eina was toasting herself at the fire. She stood up fearfully as he entered the roofless shed. Then he saw Bella quivering in a corner. She made to flee, but he put his arm out to stop her. He bade her sit down at the fire on an old broken stool. He drew up an old bucket, upturned it, and also sat at the fire. There was silence as they watched the crackling twigs. They watched him nervously out of the side of their eyes. He didn't know what to say but heard himself asking Bella for the hand of her daughter. He even got down on his knees. Bella cheeped like the ancient

pullet she was. Eina pulled him to his feet with a mighty movement and, while dusting down his clothes, said, "Yes," her eyes
rolling either in wonderment or terror.

Later that day it was announced that the Second World War
had ended.

CLONTONACALLY

My sister Martha wrote and told me that Stanley Lovell was dead. Some time before that she had written me a letter saying she had bumped into Stanley in town and he seemed anguished. One of the things he said was that she should convey his apologies to me for the way he treated me at school. I was startled at this news because I also had things on my conscience from those school-days during the Second World War. I also wanted to apologise, but not to Stanley – I call him Stanley now, but in those days I called him Lovell. I wanted to apologise to Charles Temple.

It was 1966, and Stanley had died young at the age of thirty-four. We were the same age. Martha claimed she didn't know how he had died or what he had died of. Yet she had read of his death in the death columns of the *Belfast Telegraph*. The first thing that a lot of people do in Northern Ireland is to turn to the death columns. You might have moved from the area you once lived in and lost contact with the deceased. Most knew some-body who had died. You can also get a fairly good picture of what people had done since you last had contact with them. The parents of the deceased and any brothers or sisters still living at home head the column in one composite unit. This is followed by uncles, aunts, cousins, grandparents – dead or alive – and married brothers and sisters and their spouses. You get a good overall picture of that family – were they or any of their relatives in the Orange Order, for their lodge will also put in a notice of condolence. Likewise if he were a member of the Freemasons, if he were a committed member of a church, did any of the family become Catholics or marry into a Catholic family, were any now living in England, Wales, Scotland, America, Canada or Australia? Their place of work might also have their condolences published. You would then have a good idea what they had been doing for a living. Did they die in hospital and, if so, was it the result of an accident, a disease? If a disease, was it cancer or a kidney problem, meningitis, a tumour on the brain? The death notice might not be so specific, but usually there was a clue appertaining to a terminal illness: "peace after suffering" was a favourite; or "the Lord called her before her time" for an accidental death.

Martha must have found out something about Stanley Lovell and his family when she read the death columns. I wrote and asked for this information. She wrote back but didn't mention Stanley Lovell. I suppose she still had it in for him, for he had also treated my two sisters badly. Of course, he didn't apologise to Martha formally. Maybe he may have thought even talking to her in Frederick Street was apology enough.

Some time ago, Maggie, my other sister, had worked briefly with him in the office of a large bakery. She could also have still had it in for him but she didn't, for in childhood reminiscences, when I visited her and her husband, she only mentioned his name in order to say she had worked with him for a number of weeks in the accountancy department. Anyway, I wasn't very interested in hearing about him at that time, so I didn't try to enlarge on the conversation. But in looking back now, his whole manner towards Maggie must have been an apology. He was a closed book to her now. Usually if any wrongs had been done to her in the past, she remembered them only with regret while Martha remembered them with anger.

My anger against him subsided immediately I heard of his apology. I'm glad he didn't apologise to me directly, for I wouldn't have known what to say. I might have felt like his victim again – standing there, unable to look him in the eye, not knowing where to put my hands, standing lopsided or standing with knees slightly bent in order to make myself seem smaller though we were about the same height at school. The apology coming through my embittered sister gave me time to savour it in the artistic environs of my American girlfriend's flat in London. Up to that time, when I thought back to my schooldays, the memories usually depressed me for I felt I hadn't really developed. . . though I was by now well travelled and well read, loved the theatre and the plays of Chekhov, Molière, Ibsen and Beckett. I also eagerly went to the concert hall – Chopin, Bach and Beethoven being my favourites. We visited art galleries, played bridge and poker occasionally with friends. I was head of my department in the British Standards Institute. Yet here I was throwing myself into a past where nothing of this new-found knowledge seemed to help me.

I didn't write back to Martha for a long time. I thought she was trying to drag me down to her own embittered level. She still lived with our parents though she was now thirty-one. She dressed past events up as tragedies in her life and lived and relived them until they became distorted and unreliable in her memory.

On my visits to my parents, she would go over my injustices towards her and Maggie. I would sit there, not saying anything in order not to provoke the situation or cause an argument that might become a shouting match. No, I just sat there and took it all. I was afraid of going down to her level again and never coming out of it. But, overall, I suppose I must have learnt something in life because I had a good reaction to Stanley's apology.

A few months after learning of his death, I paid a visit to my parents with the specific purpose of showing off Helen, my girlfriend, to them. I had already been divorced by the woman they sort of half-heartedly approved of, but I certainly wasn't bringing this woman back for their approval. I was worried about what she would think of my sister Martha. I didn't want Martha's behaviour to reflect on me, so I warned Helen that my sister was maybe sick and to please try and understand her. As it happened, there were no problems. Helen was so intrigued with getting inside an Irish family. She had a vague Irish forebear, but then she also had Dutch and German somewhere. Her mother leaned more towards that Scottish part of her, and she also claimed some English as far back as the *Mayflower* pilgrims.

Anyway, though we weren't married, my mother insisted we stay with them and gave us a bedroom. In a cautious conversation with Martha, I tried to bring up the subject of our old school. She didn't know anything about it any more as the family had moved out of that area years ago to Carrickfergus, which is about seventeen miles from Clontonacally. I suddenly had this urge to see our old school, walk in – not so much to show off as to credit the teachers with giving me the thirst for knowledge which I was sure it had given me. Martha said our headmaster Mr Torney had died in Downpatrick Lunatic Asylum. I was shocked at this sudden news, but I didn't remonstrate with her over her not telling me this in one of her letters. But I did correct the lunatic asylum bit, changing it to psychiatric hospital, though he had beaten the hell out of me. He was not a man to converse personally with any pupil, but he did with me on one occasion – and it was the only occasion during my whole school life – when he said he couldn't understand a boy like me getting up to so much destructive mischief. I was two classes ahead in arithmetic. No one could beat me. I remembered that compliment more than the beatings with the tae, and I never had any bitterness for him then or now. Most parents told their offspring – when they carried back such tales of woe – that they must have done something to provoke him. I know I did complain once and got a further beating from my mother for not behaving at school, plus yet another one from my father when he came home from work. Mr Torney was revered, in their eyes, as an educator, and I suppose he did show results by the number of pupils who were able to go on to further education.

There was no point in inquiring after Miss Flack or Mrs McNally, or Miss Dobbins or Miss Torney, the headmaster's sister. Martha only remembered them with contempt. She felt they were still alive, though, because their names hadn't appeared in the death columns. . . so far.

I decided to pay a visit to the school. Helen asked to be excused as we had toured so much of Northern Ireland already. She was tired and wanted to rest. I must say I had seen more of my homeland with her than I had ever seen when I lived there.

Rather than go by our hired car, I thought it better to travel by bus and walk some. That way I would see more. I took the bus to Belfast, then went to Ormeau Avenue and caught another bus heading south to Saintfield. Going along the Ormeau Road, I saw the Apollo Cinema, which I had once known as a boy,

boarded up and derelict. Crossing the bridge over the River
Lagan from the County Antrim side of Belfast into the County
Down side, I noticed the Curzon Cinema was still open; then it
was the suburbs, past Newtownbreda with the military hospital
on the left, up the Three-Mile Hill and then to the total red
brick of the Purdysburn Hospital complex, with its psychiatric
and contagious diseases buildings, to Cedar Valley. Suddenly the
bus took an elevated new road which I didn't know had been
built. Carryduff police barracks now lay in what seemed a valley
to my left. Then the bus went past what had been a military
camp with its endless rows of now-rotting Nissen huts – first
occupied by English soldiers, then by the US Army, during the
Second World War, its cricket pitch ploughed up with their
heavy trucks, then by refugees from Gibraltar when the Rock
had been cleared for war – past the waterworks with Paddy
Mallin's pub, the Ivanhoe, opposite.

I got off at the derelict shop of McCormack's and looked up
Manse Hill. But it wasn't called Manse Hill any more, though it
was still the narrow, steep incline I remembered from twenty
years before. I went up the hill, and near the top I looked for
Fairview Gardens to my left with its wooden, corrugated-iron
roofed shacks – they had once housed non-commissioned ranks
and their families during the First World War – but they had all
disappeared, and in their place were a number of modern brick
houses with neat gardens. Further up the Manse was still there,
surrounded by its cedar trees and with a new generation of crows
cawing in their branches. The cedars slowly nodded in the wind.
I looked over the Manse hedge expecting to see the Reverend
Crossley and his dog Patch, but I was beginning to expect too
much by now. Beside the Manse was Clontonacally Public

Elementary School, the name carved on a stone plaque set into the red brickwork.

The gates of the school were rusted and chained and the padlocks so corroded that I was sure the keys must have been lost long ago. It was a school conceived of humanitarian architecture, bang in the middle of green fields, its steam radiators once a wonderment in a once remote rural area, closed down for ever. I remembered that Mr Torney, with his balding head and his remaining hair ragged as a hen in moult, was also no more.

I climbed the gates and looked through the windows of the four classrooms. The oak stationery cupboards with their glassed doors were still intact. The hardwood floors still shone through the layers of dust. The large iron radiators I leaned against in winter looked as if they could be turned on again any time. The cookery room for girls still had the heavy scrubbed pine tables, though the tables were eventually used as desks when the school went up to a roll-call of eighty-two. In the other classrooms, even the desks, with their sunken inkwells, were still there.

I went to the back of the school, to its playground. Its once calm sea of black tarmacadam now had waves that were being powered by the blind albino dandelion spore. The drinking fountain produced nothing but the mortar from the bricks. A sudden wind sent the cedars nodding again, and from the undulating roof the hatchet of a blue note was flung down, as if aiming for me. It shattered at my feet; maybe it was a warning. It was as if some other power had taken over this crumbling school.

I moved on down to the plots where we were once taught horticulture. They were as wild and overgrown as if a Van Gogh had rearranged them – the marigolds grew in a manic fashion, the immodest eye of the forget-me-not seemed to have a cast, the parsley beds raced through the rusting wire, the strawberries grew so big it was difficult to trust them – one was the size of a small apple. The brambles snaked and zipped through the now-wire grass.

Mr Torney planned to grow a small orchard here. He gathered us around one spring for us to watch the first planting of an apple sapling. It was like a ceremony a head of state might perform in the opening of a memorial garden to the war dead of many nations. He dug into the rich brown earth, told a boy to hold the spade, and carefully interred the tree's roots, took the spade from the boy, filled in around the roots and patted the earth gently down. He gave the boy the spade to hold again, stepped back and admired it. It was Dig-for-Victory week. I suppose we should have applauded, but it wasn't the custom then. You remained silent and never spoke to the headmaster until you were spoken to.

He divided us into groups – some to get on with digging the potato drills, others to weed, and still others to turn over some rough, uncultivated ground. We fell to with enthusiasm, testing our young muscles, competing with one another. I was in the detail with Stanley Lovell and three other boys. We were racing one another in tearing up the ground. There was one small patch left, and Stanley was playing king-of-the-castle by standing on it and warding off the other boys. I sank the spade deep in the ground under his feet and levered the earth to create a mini-earthquake. He fell backwards off the patch and into a blackcurrant bush, got up and came at me with his fists, but stopped as Mr Torney turned round. We set to breaking up the hard compressed lumps of earth and removing any rocks or big stones.

A chip of flint hit me on the back of the neck. I turned round, but Stanley seemed busier than ever. When he turned his back, I threw a chip of flint at him and hit him on the back of his left ear as he straightened up; then I looked busy in levering out a particularly stubborn rock. His sallow skin glowed and his eyes turned black as he looked towards me. He was about to pick up something when Mr Torney came over to watch us work.

"Who's getting the soil on to the grass verge?" he asked; but knowing he would get no answer to that, he went on, "Don't be untidy, dirty horticulturists. Treat the soil with respect. Without it we have no future on this earth."

He walked to the next group to admonish them for handling the seed potatoes roughly: "Breaking the sprouts off is like breaking the arms off a new-born child."

I thought that was the end of my war with Stanley. I didn't want to continue the conflict as I knew it would lead to a fight after school. I was in a hurry that day as my mother would be waiting at the bottom of Manse Hill to put me on the bus to Belfast. I had to go to McKelvey the butcher on the Ormeau Road to pick up an oxtail for making soup. Suddenly, a sod of earth hit me on the back. Stanley, as usual, was busy, but I noticed that the other boys had moved away from him in anticipation of my return fire.

I bent down and picked up a fat juicy sod, healthy and writhing with purple earthworms, and hit him on the side of the face. He flew at me, knocking me to the ground. We wrestled, for the rules didn't allow for punching unless you were both confronting one another, on your feet, face to face. We rolled over and over for a number of yards, trying to pin one another to the ground. The boys continued to work, looking at us from under their brows. They didn't throw down their implements and gather around. No unlawful assembly was allowed. We continued wrestling, trying to push one another's face into the soil. That was allowed. A fight like this only stopped when someone gave up struggling. A pulling of the hair or a twisting of the arm of a prone figure was considered cowardice. Equally, while on your feet, if the arms were dropped as if standing to attention, then a blow on the surrendered person was also thought of as cowardice. Breaking the rules meant banishment from the football team for the rest of your days at Clontonacally School. You then had no one to play with – as most of the boys were keen footballers – except a small group of boys and girls who had also been cast out for breaking various rules.

Neither I nor Stanley was ever able to get the upper hand. By some miracle, Mr Torney must have had his back to us. We fought silently without a shout or a word spoken, oblivious to the headmaster and to the world.

I remember the sound of the snapping to this day. We had rolled on to the newly planted sapling. We had taken its young life. Its spine was doubled up, its leaves were looking down at its feet. Mr Torney turned round at the sound of the pistol shot and walked slowly towards us in his wellington boots, maybe not wanting to see what had happened. He examined the sapling in silence while we still lay transfixed on the ground. Stanley even momentarily put his head on my chest like a small child needing comfort. The headmaster continued examining the apple sapling, lifting its poor head to straighten it up, watching it fall again to look at its feet. When it fell a third time, he quietly told us to make our way to the classroom where he would deal with us at the end of the horticultural lesson. The boys kept working and peeping at us cautiously, for to start staring brought the headmaster's index finger pointing at the offender.

At the end of each practical lesson, we usually went back to the classroom and took dictation into our exercise books while Mr Torney spoke on drainage, seeds, times to plant, the care of bulbs and a dozen other things to do with growing. He spoke at a measured pace but continually, and you had to get it all down. He did sometimes stop to spell out a Latin name, but you had to have it down correctly when he read through your work. The dipping of pens into inkwells and the scratchings on paper must have made us sound like a colony of wasps chewing wood to make a paper hive. Handwriting, during this lesson, was not criticised by him as long as he could read it. Blots were also overlooked as long as the marine-blue didn't obscure a word. But every word he spoke had to be recorded by us. The smell of freshly disturbed ink wafted over the class.

Sometimes a nib would get bent, from too much pressure and desperation, and refuse to pick up the ink. Then there was a wild lifting of the desk top to look for another nib, but usually it had also been rejected some time ago and was now rusting and corroded. That meant having to put your hand up. You didn't say anything until Mr Torney said curtly, "Yes, boy, what is it you want?"

"Please, sir, can I have a new nib?"

He then tutted slightly and went to the stationery cupboard, unlocked it, took out a packet, took out a nib, motioned for you to come forward, waited for you to open your hand and threw it on to the palm. All this time he would keep right on with his dictation. You would go back to your desk and with inky fingers attempt to push the nib into the holder, but the metal was usually corroded. Push too hard and you drove the point of the nib into your hand. Then loading the nib with ink had to be done a number of times until the new nib had a fine, almost invisible film of ink. Then you had to wait for the nib to bend slightly in order to break it in to the angle of your hand and fingers.

By this time the headmaster was maybe two pages ahead. You whispered to your classmate sitting beside you on the two-pupil desk, asking what Mr Torney had said, but he would be too busy keeping up. That meant trying to look to see what he had already written, and, of course, he would have maybe turned over the page. Not getting it all down meant staying behind after school and copying it from the best pupil's exercise book. You didn't dare mention the fact that the non-functioning nib and the breaking-in of the new nib had made you fall behind.

While the horticultural lessons were going on, the girls were being taught knitting, embroidery and sewing. Sometimes a boy caught for some trivial offence in the plots would be sent up by Mr Torney to join the girls in their sewing class. He would be given a square of material and taught a hemstitch by Miss Dobbins. I was sent up there once, and I was so embarrassed I sat there paralysed looking at the square for a whole hour, despite being rapped over the knuckles with the cane by Miss Dobbins. But this was nothing compared to the tae.

The tae had a wooden handle with a long strip of heavy leather attached that ended in a forked tongue. It was applied once to a hand for more minor matters and three to each hand for more serious breaches of the rules. The tae, according to Mr Torney, originated in Scotland. It was designed to wrap around the hand, thus slashing the palm of the hand and the back of the hand at the same time. For extra punishment, the blow was delivered as near to the wrist as possible. The softer skin of the inner side of the wrist then came out in a very painful red raised welt. Not holding your hand steady, deliberately or nervously, could mean a sudden whack around the bare knees. The knee whack was also applied if you dared to smile. Some of the farmers' sons had hardened hands through working the farm after school. The wisest of them gave a pretended wince to escape the whack to the legs. The devil-may-care ended up with tiny tears running down their little red platter faces, their future great teeth leaking spittle, green snatters beginning to snail out of their noses.

I was up with Stanley Lovell sitting in the classroom. The sound of a spade hitting a stone could be heard from the plots, but other than that there was silence except maybe for a blackbird alarming somewhere in a bush or a thrush singing on the window ledge outside. The watermark of the sun danced on the ceiling. Stanley sat there looking more foreign than ever with his sallow skin and jet-black hair and brown, almost black eyes. My mother once called him a "yellow-faced rat" when he punched Martha on the way home from school.

A very fat old bookkeeper who worked part-time in the stone quarry office once caught Stanley imitating his walk of a pig waddling.

His retort to Stanley was, "Your arse in parsley!"

Ever since then, when we were on our way home from school and he was coming from his job in the quarry, we'd whisper to one another, "Here comes Arse-in-Parsley."

Arse-in-Parsley was known locally as a very knowledgeable man who read a lot. He could advise on law suits or how to treat a horse which had foolishly swallowed a thistle. He had it in for

Stanley, for he had eventually found out who had given him the nickname that had stuck. He never gave Stanley a nickname, but I'm sure he was capable of thinking up plenty because he was a rural man. One day a bunch of us were walking home, and seeing him waddle towards us wearing his usual flapping, faded, fawn raincoat over his black suit with waistcoat and soft, battered, grey hat, we asked him the usual question: "What time is it, Mr Shaw?"

We wanted to see him take his gold watch out of his waistcoat pocket again. But because of the nickname Stanley had given him, he wouldn't but used to answer instead, "It's wartime", or "It might be peacetime tomorrow."

One day he stopped to give us a lecture on Stanley and his ilk. He began by talking about the Huguenots who came here over two hundred years ago. He said that Stanley, by the colour of him and by his name, must have come from the French Walloon area inside what is now Belgium. He asked us if Stanley had a knife in his pocket. I said most of the boys had penknives. He walked on. We didn't understand what he was talking about. If he meant a big knife, then only Spaniards carried them, or people with dark skins, but darker than Stanley's.

I watched Stanley cautiously in the classroom that day, but the fight was knocked out of him. The large clock on the wall, framed in polished mahogany, ticked loudly, and he kept watching its minute hand jerk forward suddenly as if as an afterthought.

The heavy brass Yale door-closer shuddered once when a sudden breeze from the open window rocked the door. He nearly jumped out of his skin. I was in no better a condition. I felt sick and blamed it on the chalk dust twinkling in a shaft of sunlight.

Stanley looked at me for a full minute in a questioning sort of way, and I think I must have tuned in to his brain wave. We stood up without a word, ran out of the classroom and down Manse Hill like hares, almost falling head-over-shite because of our long legs. Stanley then turned left at McCormack's Corner and took to the Saintfield Road. He stopped to look back at me for a moment because I wasn't following him. I signed to him and dived into a thick hedgerow to hide. I had to meet my mother who was putting me on the bus to Belfast.

There was still a half-hour to go, so I sat there with a bird's nest above my head and listened to the squeakings of the fledglings and the constant wild chirping of the thrush as she flew above the hedge with a green caterpillar wriggling in her beak. I had to crawl further into the hedge in order not give my position away.

Eventually, about fifty of the eighty-two pupils of the school came tearing down Manse Hill – the long legs of Class Four first, followed by Class Three, Class Two, Class One, Senior Infants and Junior Infants. Those who had money went into McCormack's shop and came out sucking black-and-white-striped bull's-eyes, kalie suckers, sticks of cinnamon, dolly mixtures, shoelace liquorice, candy apples, yellow man, dulse – anything that a halfpenny and a penny would buy. A farthing was just about acceptable, though it only bought a small square taken from a grid of toffee.

Then came the teachers: the young Miss Flack, marching in military style with two long plaits of hair, each one lying on a bulging breast, followed by the stern Miss Dobbins, a woman of about thirty dressed totally in black and wearing a small born-again hat that looked something like half a pudding bowl on her head. Walking with Miss Dobbins was Mrs McNally, a prematurely grey woman in her mid-thirties. Then came Miss Torney, a woman in her mid-forties, wearing a navy blue dress and a grey cardigan. She walked nervously but as dainty as a fairy and didn't seem to make much progress down the hill. Finally, after five minutes, came Mr Torney, a tall, slim, well-built man in his early forties, wearing a brown sports jacket with grey flannels and a grey sleeveless pullover, and with a grey soft hat on his head. He carried his usual small leather attaché case. The headmaster seemed to peer across the road into the hedge at me.

Mother was standing at the bus stop only about ten yards away from where I was hiding in the hedge. I tried to move up through the hedge in her direction but met with a vicious patch of hawthorn. I whistled in her direction, but Sissy McCann, the boy of pink cheeks, fair hair and girlish lisp, heard me first. He was tying a red ribbon into the hair of one of the three girls who were with him and calling her a film star. I saw his blue calf's eyes peering into the hedge, and I managed to fart because that's one of the things that appalled him. I also shook my fist and he jumped back. I came out of the hedge with leaves in my hair and sticking to my jersey. He was about to jeer about something, maybe to do with my sudden ignominious flight from the school, but stopped when my mother took me by the ear and began beating the leaves out of me.

I said I was in the hedge looking for my ball, but she said I didn't have a ball. I was handed the shopping bag and the one and sixpence wrapped carefully in paper, plus my fare for a return ticket. She told me about six times that it was an oxtail I was going to Belfast to buy and not to go gallivanting around the shops looking for the *Dandy* or *Beano* as the change had to be brought straight home or my father would hear of it. Even with money it was hard to find the comics owing to paper rationing. Sissy McCann was smirking as he eavesdropped, so when the bus came and he went to the upper deck with his Hollywood starlets, I sat behind him and continually dug my knee into the back of his seat as he combed a girl's hair.

Next day, as I didn't want to go to school, I feigned sickness by saying I was too ill to eat my porridge. I hoped I looked pale. My mother felt my brow, but she didn't think I had a temperature. My sisters giggled, whispered to one another and took it in turns to stare at me. They had heard the news and, therefore, so had mother.

On the three-mile walk to school, I lagged behind them until they were almost out of sight. The thought of mitching entered my head. I would hide in an isolated hay shed I knew of. Running away from home was almost unheard of in those days, and the odd ones who did were soon picked up by the police. Everyone seemed to know everyone, even in the city, and strangers at a loose end were noticed quickly. My sisters jeered at my cowardice, so I ran like the wind, caught up with them, gave both their hair a good tug and ran on to McCormack's Corner, up Manse Hill and entered the school entrance hall with my face on fire and panting like a dog during a hot summer.

The other pupils were entering and hanging their things in the cloakroom. I went into the playground and had a drink from the fountain. Stanley was kicking a tennis ball viciously against a wall. He didn't look at me. Going back into the school corridor, I thought of what Stanley and I faced shortly. Any other boys would have been friends by now. It wasn't so much that I thought of myself as an angel and that he was the devil. It was that he seemed never to know when to stop fighting with me. I wanted to be friends with him, but he always seemed to have it in for me and my two sisters. He did have fights with other boys, but he never touched their sisters. I wasn't afraid of fighting him; it was just that I was getting tired of having to defend myself against him. We were about equal in strength, but I had the most hurting punch. This didn't stop him. A good punch on the nose would infuriate him so much I once thought he was fit for Purdysburn Lunatic Asylum. I generally took a couple of blows from him and let him win to get it over with. As I've said, we were more or less equal and neither one of us really won. Most fights, in reality, usually ended in draws.

Mr Torney, after prayers, had all eighty-two pupils gathered in the cookery room, which was big enough to take us all. The whole school knew Stanley and I were in for it, and they stared at us in sympathy. Posters were on the wall showing various types of bombs or anti-personnel weapons that shouldn't be lifted or even touched. The phosphorus bomb, the German hand grenade or potato masher, bombs designed as toys, the safety razor that blew up in your face when you twisted the handle, and so on. He then began to ask questions.

"Why does an aerial bomb have fins?"

No one answered, so I put up my hand and waited for him to give me permission to speak.

"Yes?"

"To make them fall straight, sir."

"Good answer. And so as the detonator cap hits the explosive charge. Good.

"We have been warned that German planes are approaching our school. You are in the playground. What do you do?"

No one answered. I again put up my hand.

"Yes?" he said, exhaling at the rest of the school.

"Run and flatten yourself against the walls, slide along them to the air-raid shelter."

"Good!"

We were then commanded to stand and file out of the school – infants first, the older last – hug the walls and enter the air-raid shelter. The shelter was dank and smelled of drying concrete mixed with the paraffin fumes of the hurricane lamps carried by the teachers. The noise of eighty-two children chatting and squealing brought a loud command from Mr Torney. We quietened down, and the only sound was of whispering. Mr Torney issued another command, and the only sound was the breathing of eighty-two pairs of lungs. We were packed in like sardines, and the smell of sweat became unbearable. I could smell the rancid lard breath of Skin O'Neill, the anti-nit blue ointment on the hair of Mary Weir and the waxed-lavender smell of Mrs McNally as if from funeral flowers. Miss Flack compensated with her subtle perfume. At last Mr Torney gave the command to file back to the classrooms.

On the way back, Vincent McConnell, who was almost fourteen and due to leave soon, castigated me for my answer to Bat's second question to the school. (Bat was for Baldy Alex Torney.)

Vincent said the first part of my answer was correct – flatten yourself against the wall – but the second part when we entered the air-raid shelter was wrong. He said a direct hit on the shelter would kill us all. It was far better to disperse over the fields and lie in ditches in groups of three or four, and even with bombs and machine-gunning the most of us would survive.

Although I knew he was right and that some day he would be

a great army general, I felt deflated – as if I had become the headmaster's pet against my will. He restored me by saying I was correct about the fins of the bomb.

We filed into our classrooms. I was now sure that I had escaped by giving the right answers. Especially the answer to the second question which was what Mr Torney wanted to hear. I might even have saved Stanley.

About an hour later while we were doing arithmetic under the direction of Miss Flack, the door opened and the headmaster entered. He called out quietly, "Lovell." And then my surname.

He meant business when he called us by our surnames. It was usually "Stanley Lovell", etc., but never "Stanley" on its own. He showed us to the juniors' classroom which had been evacuated for his purpose. He didn't have an office any more. This classroom had been his office, but the intake of pupils was increasing. Stanley was invited in first while I stood in the red-and-white-patterned terrazzo corridor listening to the next classroom sing:

"Oft in the stilly night

Where slumber chains have bound me. . ."

The tae fell – skin on skin – the skin of the sacrificed beast upon the sacrificing human. Each tanning blow measured with sufficient time to let the hand of the victim feel the full effect of the stinging, wounding it enough to make the successive blows ply their agony to better effect. (Quick blows would have numbed the hands.) Six blows in all, three on each hand. Stanley came out, his face darkened, his eyes black searchlights, his lips curled to reveal his teeth like that of a horse who has been drawn up suddenly by the bit. He didn't look at me, but I was almost certain he was blaming me for his woes.

I knocked and entered and was told by the headmaster to go out into the corridor again and wait. I waited five minutes, and he came out and asked why I hadn't knocked again. I remained silent. He closed the door and I knocked again. He said to come in. He began to button up the middle button of his open jacket in a quick furious manner so as the tae wouldn't catch on it. He lifted the tae again in the same furious manner, caught my hand impatiently to set it at the right angle and, with his face distorted and breathing heavily, brought the instrument down as hard as if felling a pig with a sledgehammer. The tae sang and snaked around my hand and whiplashed to cut across the inside of my wrist. He grabbed my other hand to set the angle and again tried to kill the pig. I knew the angle of the hand required by now and set it in order to get it over with, but he delayed even more than he did with Stanley. I felt the weals rise hot and stinging, and like the proverbial flea on the flea's back, I felt a weal upon a weal. Having suffered this punishment before, I knew I was allowed to leave the room without his permission, but I stood there pretending to waiting for the word.

"What are you standing there for? Do you want more?" he asked, undoing the button of his jacket.

I felt that six was the maximum number allowed in the school, and once someone was punished to the maximum, it didn't usually occur again for a few months. I therefore felt free to do what I wanted. As a further punishment for my insolence, which he was quick to detect, he ordered me go up to the tank room and pump up the water.

I climbed the stone steps to the room and entered the roof space. The room was full of small boxes containing sawdust in which daffodil bulbs were beginning to sprout. I urinated into several of them before grasping the pump handle. Hand-pumping was a monotonous task. A huge tank had to be filled with water from a well somewhere beneath the school. The tank supplied the water to the taps for drinking and washing, and also supplied the coke-fired boilerhouse for the radiators. It had to be filled at least once a week. Usually the caretaker did this job and spent the better part of a morning pumping. This was the middle of the week and the tank was half full.

It took five minutes pumping before the first water appeared from maybe sixty feet deep down in the well. The headmaster appeared suddenly to check on me. He then began to look at his bulbs. I had distributed my urine equally amongst the many little boxes by luck rather than design. He looked up at the naked blue of the slates and touched them for any sign of a leak and then left, turning on the steps to look at me a couple of times. My hands and wrists were painful, so I covered them by pulling my jersey sleeves down over them.

I then pumped furiously for five minutes until my arms ached and then rested for a few. I began again at an even more aggressive rate. The water was pouring into the tank as thick as a man's arm. I had built up so much suction it continued gushing while I rested. Not content with this flow, I pumped even harder, pushing the handle back and forth, listening to the great zinc tank change its tone from an echoing one to a booming one, then to a quieter one as it filled. Suddenly the cast-iron handle snapped off at the pivot. The man's arm of water was flexing its muscles. It began to overflow down the sides of the tank and on to the floor. Soon after, the little boxes of sawdust began to sail down the stone steps and into the corridor. I desperately tried to stop the water flowing into the tank but couldn't find the shut-off valve. Fear took a hold of me. I was a puppet with cut strings. I felt myself growing pale. My heart thumped. I wanted to flee, but in the end I decided I would just walk casually back to my classroom though my knees could scarcely support me.

Miss Flack was handing out the exercise books for the grammar lesson. My short trousers were soaking, as were my long knee socks, and my shoes were filled with water. I squelched as I walked. Miss Flack looked out of the window momentarily to see if it was raining.

There was a commotion in the corridor – the sound of voices and buckets. The water peeped under the door of my classroom, retreated and then came back in one sheet. Miss Flack ordered the classroom to evacuate into the playground. We did our air-raid drill. As she was doing so, the headmaster's voice rasped out my surname. I stood in the flooded corridor as Mr Torney looked down at me, shook his head, but said nothing and splashed away. He would get me another time. The caretaker, a dried-up old man wearing a flat cap and a dirty silk scarf tied around his wizened throat, looked at me with hatred as he mopped up the water.

Sports to me then meant nothing but an extension of war. I knew Stanley wanted me out of the football team for other reasons than he was saying now: I was "handballing too much". Though he was a hero for a time, as I was, after the thrashing with the tae, I was more of a hero for flooding the school. While I was dribbling the tennis ball towards the two turnips that acted as goalposts, he tackled me viciously, kicking me on the shinbone. Instead of shouting, "Foul!" I punched him on the nose. He shouted, "Foul!" The two teams stopped play immediately, and Stanley, who acted as trainer, captain and referee, ordered me off . . . for ever. I kicked the ball as hard as I could over a hedge and left.

I joined the small group of renegades playing rounders near the girls' lavatory. Two other boys were there: Sissy McCann and Charles Temple, a gentle boy who never fought physically or verbally and always got first prize for his drawings. He had been pushed out of the football team for refusing to fight. Sissy McCann had also got the heave-ho for kicking in ten own goals. There were three girls. Patsy, a red-haired girl with a fierce temper, was a skipping-rope expert who could walk into the long spinning rope being twirled by two girls no matter how fast it was going and hop out again unscathed. Other girls attempting it would either trip and fall or end up with the rope around their necks. At a slower pace six girls could skip in its spinning ovals. Patsy skipping with her own rope could spin it so fast that her footwork and the rope became a blur. She was as thin as a rake with twig-like arms. The two girls who always seemed to have to turn the long rope for the communal skipping one day, out of envy, pulled the rope taut and caused Patsy to fall heavily on to the tarmacadam. She didn't cry, and though the two girls said, "Sorry", Patsy pulled a clump of hair out of each of their heads, held the hair up as if after a scalping, and put it in the small knee-pocket of her cotton dress. The two girls screeched so much that Miss Flack came out to investigate. But no one would tell her what had happened. After that Patsy founded the renegade group with Sissy McCann and Charles Temple. Relations with the other pupils, boys and girls, still continued, but no one ever played with the renegades.

Of the other two girls, one, Ella, a jokester, had put a dead mouse in the coat pocket of another girl. The girl went into the cloakroom to get twopence out of her coat pocket and took out the mouse. She screamed and her face turned so blue that she had to be brought all the way to the cottage hospital in Saintfield on the back of an army truck that happened to be passing the school. Mr Torney set up an investigation but came to a dead end very quickly. Everyone knew about Ella and her tricks but said nothing and blackballed her. Then there was Maureen, who was ousted when, on having a pen loaded with ink stuck into her back by a boy sitting behind, told Miss Flack. Informing was a deadly sin. Maureen tried to ingratiate herself with the school, but no one accepted her excuse that she only shouted out the boy's name in pain. She even petitioned the Junior Infants and Senior Infants, who didn't know what she was talking about.

I joined the renegades, and though no welcoming speeches were made, I was accepted by being asked to recover the ball which Patsy deliberately threw over the wire into the Reverend Crossley's garden.

Vincent McConnell took no part in any of the games at school. Everything we played was puny to him. He sat most of the time with his pals – two aides-de-camp – near the boiler house, scratching out plans of strategies and tactics in the dust. Anyone coming near him was ignored until he went away.

Something was about to happen soon, for Vincent began surveying the terrain outside the school, looking into ditches, looking up at the trees, pacing the width of the by-roads and noting the number of horse-drawn hay-shifters coming along the roads: were they loaded with a haystack, what fields did they come from, how long would it take them to clear a field of their haystacks?

One morning his aides-de-camp spread the news that war was about to break out at lunchtime. That same morning, during our five-minute break for using the lavatories and water fountain, an RAF Spitfire flew so low over the school that most either threw themselves to the ground or hugged the walls. A few hysterics made for the air-raid shelter. Vincent and his army staff didn't flinch but stood saluting the visible pilot as if the fighter plane were part of his plans. Some of the school even thought he had planned the plane's buzzing of the school, so entranced were they by his leadership.

The gender divisions were quickly eradicated as he gathered the Third and Fourth Classes at a secret location in a nearby turnip field. Our renegade group was incorporated in his scheme, despite the protests by Stanley. We were divided into Germans versus English. Stanley was made commander of the German forces while Vincent headed the English. Patsy was made provost marshall, with a group of girls as her staff for guarding any prisoners. The boiler house was to be a prison. All prisoners, German or English, were to be brought there. There was to be no changing sides should the going get tough. In the middle of this highly secret meeting in the turnip field, a boy who was in Second Class was suddenly pulled out of a hedge by one of Vincent's aides-de-camp and told he was being held prisoner for the duration of the lunch hour or the war – whichever ended first. Military police were appointed to take any prisoners back to the prison. They were to be neutral. I was appointed one. The target was the Castle, which was a ridge of high rocks near a water-filled quarry. Vincent and his army would defend it. The Germans, under Stanley's command, were to capture it.

The provost marshall counted a measured one hundred to

give the English army time to get away, but the German commander tried to get her to count faster. She then marched her staff back to the prison. We set off cautiously to do battle along the minor back road. We halted at the old cottage-type schoolhouse which also had CLONTONACALLY carved above the low entrance door, with the year 18. . . something – the elements had worn the other two figures away. We listened but could only hear a skylark singing as it hovered above us in the sky. Cattle mooed and a donkey brayed some distance away.

Stanley gave orders to move. He seemed more concerned with our marching step than tactics and demonstrated how to do the goose-step, which he had seen in an old magazine. We tried it, but some of us fell over laughing. A low, flat rick-shifter approached, almost blocking the narrow road and with its haystack brushing the hedge and sticking great clumps to it. The air was perfumed with hay and dried wild flowers. The horse advanced on us, clip-clopping at a leisurely pace. The farmer was nodding and winking occasionally at us. I didn't like the winking bit and sensed danger. Stanley led his army to squeeze past the shifter. I decided to keep to the horse side. Although I was expected to do my part in the coming fighting, I couldn't be taken prisoner as I also had to act out my role as a military policeman and take charge of all prisoners, both English and German, and march them to prison.

Stanley advanced and got behind the shifter. Suddenly they were set upon by a group of Vincent's men – arms were twisted and many of Stanley's army were thrown on to the road and grass verges. Blows were struck in fury. Sissy McCann, a German, surprisingly fought like a tiger but was brought down giggling to the ground by being severely tickled. So, too, Charles suddenly turned into a mad, blind fighting beast, and it took four English to lay him flat. Stanley went berserk when he was thrown to the ground. He refused to be calculated as a prisoner and escaped with half his army to race up the road. I had five prisoners and had to walk them back to the boiler house prison.

Stanley, meanwhile, advanced further up the road, more cautious now. When another hay-shifter came into sight, he had the remnants of his army hide in the hedgerow. It passed, but none of Vincent's men were creeping behind it sheltered by the bulk of the haystack. He got more confident and boldly struck out for the Castle. As Stanley and company came within sight of the stronghold, he gave an order and his army began running and shouting at the top of their voices. Quickly as charging bulls, a group of Vincent's men came out of the hedgerow and cut off their retreat, while further up the road another group appeared as genies out of a bottle to stop their advance. There was a brief struggle, but Stanley and his men were overpowered. I came back to pick up more prisoners. Stanley still refused to become a prisoner, though he was now pinned down on a patch of melting tar in the road.

Vincent surveyed the scene from the top of the Castle, looking through his clumped hands as if they were binoculars. He came down to speak to Stanley and advised him to give in quietly, but Stanley still struggled. He then issued orders. A number of hands grabbed Stanley, a piece of hayrope was produced, and he was bound to a tree and left there shouting at the top of his voice. Vincent then recalled his reconnaissance and observer corps, who climbed up out of ditches and down from high trees.

There was trouble at the prison. The boiler house was full, and the prisoners were revolting because of the coke fumes.

Patsy let them move into the outside well in front of the boiler house entrance. It was reached by about ten descending steps from the playground, and the well at least had some security because of a wall around two sides of it on top of which were iron railings. The prisoners then began climbing the railings and had to be forced back by having their fingers hammered with fists. The worst offenders were Sissy McCann and the once-gentle Charles Temple. Charles had remained the demented beast. Sissy McCann still fought like a tiger, and even tickling had no effect. He overpowed three girl guards sent in by Patsy. He only stopped when Patsy pulled his short trousers down around his ankles. He blushed a deep pink with shame.

Meanwhile Charles had also thrown off his subduers and was almost over the railings. We couldn't pull down his trousers because he had tightened his belt to the last hole. Patsy screamed in a tantrum. Her voice must have been heard for miles. She was inarticulate with fury as she pointed to me and pointed to Charles. I knew what her orders were, or I thought I did. Almost deafened and driven to rage, I took my open hand, put it under Charles' chin and pushed hard. He fell back into the well, hitting his head on the concrete. Blood welled slowly from a cut. He looked unconscious. I went to the fountain, wetted my handkerchief and tended to his wound. I was shaking with fear, and I felt myself turn a deathly pale again. When I looked up, everyone had fled. Charles got to his feet and said he was all right. He walked away feeling his head. He turned with one great tear stuck to an eyelash.

"It was only a game," he said in a disappointed voice. He walked on with the sobs shaking his body.

Vincent came strolling along with his two aides-de-camp.

Once he had won a battle, he didn't take any further interest in events. He was not a behind-the-lines man. Being the oldest boy in the school, he had been given permission to wear long trousers, which raised his status even more. When I fearfully told him about Charles, he said, "It was war. Next time he digs the latrines."

I asked him about Stanley. He thought a moment, gravely shaking his head.

"He faced the firing squad like a coward."

I sort of saluted in his memory and out of apprehension. Vincent and his aides-de-camp casually saluted back, as officers tend to do.

The bell rang for classes to recommence. Miss Flack took us again but for geometry this time. The adrenalin was still flowing through Sidney Carson after the battle. He was talking in class, and Miss Flack said she was warning him once only. Next time he would get the cane. She looked and looked again, but Stanley Lovell wasn't in his place at the desk. She asked if anyone had seen him. There was silence. Patsy began to snigger and was told she would also get the cane. Miss Flack then concentrated on Patsy, asking if she knew anything about Stanley not being at his desk. She said nothing, and Miss Flack left the classroom to report him to Mr Torney. The class went wild when she was gone, throwing paper aeroplanes, ink darts, standing on desks; the boys annoyed the girls by tugging their hair, and the girls taunted the boys by saying, "Hullo, handsome, going my way?"

Vincent and his aides-de-camp sat there taking no part in the hilarity. He was never known to have been punished by any of the teachers for misdemeanours. Nor was he ever considered a teacher's pet. He never picked a personal fight, but if forced to, he ended it very quickly. Miss Flack returned suddenly and caught four, who were told they were to be kept in after school. She said she couldn't understand why a normally well-behaved class had come to act like galoots.

Stanley still hadn't returned, and now the headmaster was beginning to peep through the glass in the door from time to time. He finally came into the classroom and appealed – actually appealed for the first time – for information as to Stanley's whereabouts. There was more silence. He said a search of the local quarry might have to be made for his body, that the police might be called in, that the entire school might have to stay after hours to be made into search parties. Still, no one spoke up. He left the room tutting.

Sidney Carson, a farmer's son, hefty and strong, had still not calmed down. He let out a long, loud fart, whispering loudly, "That came out in a tank."

His face twisted as he tried for another rifter, and though there was no report, those around him stopped breathing and held their noses.

"And that came out in rubber boots," he said, gasping. His red platter face showed its white teeth in a grin like a demented moon.

He was ordered to come out to the front of the class and hold out his hand. He refused to hold out his hand, so Miss Flack whacked him around the bare knees. He raised his foot to kick her, but she caught his foot and threw him to the floor. Just as he was getting up still full of fight, she grabbed the heavy wooden pointer and pinned him to the floor by his throat. He kicked as madly as a fallen donkey. She put on the pressure. He must have gone unconscious, for she slapped his face a couple of times. She dragged him to his feet and was about to knee him, but he had given up and began crying through his bared portcullis teeth, green snatters snailing out of his nose, etc.

"I'll tell my da on you, so I will," he said and opened his mouth wide, but no sound came out for a few seconds. Then he began to bawl. Miss Flack went to the headmaster to report the incident. While she was gone, we imitated Sidney bawling. Sidney stopped but we continued. Miss Flack came back with Mr Torney, followed by Miss Torney, Miss Dobbins and Mrs McNally. They each held a cane except for the headmaster, who held his beloved tae. They stood staring at us without saying anything for a minute until Mr Torney asked, "Who is next?"

Getting no answer he said, "Are any of you asking for a flogging? *Answer me!*"

We answered in unison, "*No, sir!*"

"Good," said Mrs McNally, "or there will be wigs on the green."

Stanley entered, and as he was about to say something, Mr Torney lashed out at him with the tae. He ran the gauntlet of the teachers, receiving various whacks of the cane. Miss Torney, by the time she had sighted her cane nervously, missed, ran after him and missed again. We didn't think it cruel but a great spectacle, something like being at a circus. Some of us even began laughing.

Miss Torney also began to laugh and was ushered from the classroom at a great speed. Stanley sat there staring darkly at all of us.

Later he was called out by the headmaster and got six.

He came back blowing through his hands. He didn't pass a secret note to Vincent to challenge him to a fight after school.

He knew he would be floored with a swift blow to the solar plexus, which was Vincent's favourite punch. I knew I had to be wary, for he was liable to pick a fight with me at the first opportunity.

While leaving the school the next day, I saw Da Carson standing at the gates holding a cutting hook used for harvesting in the awkward corners of fields. He was a bear-like man with heavy bushy eyebrows and had short muscular arms and large hands akin to a bear's front paws. His arse was also as rounded as a bear's. He wore a cap, a dirty grey-striped shirt and a dark suit he once wore on Sundays but which was now speckled with cow dung. Impaled on the dung were a few corn straws. The pupils came out staring curiously at him, and some us hung around to see what might happen next. He waited for the teachers to appear.

To Miss Torney he said, "Ye whoor of an oul maid!"

She almost fell into a ditch with nervousness but continued her dainty fairy steps.

To Miss Flack he said, "Ye need two pups on your lap, ye whoor."

She made towards him but changed her mind and decided to ignore him and military-stepped away.

To Miss Dobbins he said, "Ye Scotch whoor, ye!"

"Scotch? I'm from Ballymena."

"Ye Ballymena Scotch whoor, ye, then," said Da Carson.

Miss Dobbins joined Miss Flack, still protesting at being called "Scotch". They stopped and turned to watch him. They called after Miss Torney. She waved nervously without looking around and continued her journey.

To Mrs McNally: "Ye old whoor."

She wished him a good afternoon and hoped he would sleep it off.

To Mr Torney he said, "Hullo, sir!"

Mr Torney looked at him, raised his soft hat slightly and continued. Da Dobbins then suddenly sprang forward and punched him on the left shoulder saying, "Ye bull's cock, ye. One of your harem's bate my wee Sidney – I'll geld ye!"

He let out a roar and raised the sickle with its shining cutting edge and lunged at him. Mr Torney dropped his attaché case in the road and grabbed his wrist. There was a furious to-and-froing across the road and through a hedge as they grappled.

Finally Mr Torney took the hook away from Da Carson and threw it into a field.

Da Carson raised his bear's paws in the air as if reaching for a flying goose but missed to fall back on his behind. He didn't attempt to get up again until the headmaster was out of sight.

Next morning Mr Torney gave a lecture on primitive man, drawing on the blackboard an ape-type figure with a low brow and bushy eyebrows. We were permitted to laugh. Da Carson's son Sidney also laughed along with us.

I respected Vincent, for he wasn't a bully; also, he acted as if he were about eighteen. But in further wars that he planned – and won, of course – he never give me the rank that I thought I deserved. I wanted to lead the Germans, but it was always Stanley, Stanley, Stanley. He wouldn't even promote me to being Stanley's aide-de-camp. Stanley wouldn't agree, but Vincent could enforce his order. Instead, I was always the military policeman. Looking back now, I suppose he saw something dark in my soul. He even recommended that I join the police force when I was older.

One day our renegade group decided to gather the sour little apples from the crab-apple trees in a barren field near a long-worked-out quarry. We were joined by some of the football team because they had lost their tennis ball. Our group and their group kept their distance and worked on different trees. Vincent and his two aides-de-camp were sitting near the old quarry, planning a battle by placing twigs in a pattern. Vincent held a stick to act as a pointer. This quarry was a dry one because it had no springs to fill it with water. It was maybe about eighty feet deep. Jutting out, about twelve feet down, was a smooth rock ledge just about big enough to hold an adult. I looked over the edge of the quarry and looked down at the ledge long enough for some of my group also to come over and wonder what I was curious about. Some of the football team even came over to peer down. I stood watching until Vincent sent over one of his aides-de-camp to find out what we were peering at.

It was then that I jumped to barely hit the ledge and almost fell forward into the quarry. The landing jolted my whole skeleton, causing my hip joints to almost come out of their sockets. I also hit the back of my head on the rocky face as I flung myself backwards to stop from toppling into the void. Faces were staring down at me twisted with horror. Even Vincent was staring down. I climbed the rough rock face by the protuberances, frozen with fear at the thought of slipping. I climbed on to the surface and sat a while on the wire grass growing from the crevices between the rocks. They all stood there gaping at me and seemed unable to move. I got up shaken to the marrow and walked slowly back to the school, followed at some distance by my renegade group and the remnants of the football group, followed by Vincent and his two aides-de-camp. Nobody said anything. They didn't even whisper.

Suicide was sometimes discussed by parents who usually called it "scugleshoe" to disguise an unpleasant word, but it was always in reference to someone else – like the policeman in Belfast who had recently shot himself because of debt. I knew then my plan had misfired. I had tried what I thought was an act of courage to impress them and to especially impress Vincent that I was worthy of leadership. But I had failed. They all thought the worst.

The news soon got around the small school. It even got to the teachers. I would like to think that no one had told them and that they had merely happened to overhear someone talking about it. Mr Torney, looking very grave, went into all the classrooms appealing for the name of the foolish boy, but he didn't get a name though he threatened to keep us all in after school. Somehow that result took me out of my self-humiliation.

My mother met me at the bus stop, and I had to go into Belfast to do some shopping at Stewart's on the Ormeau Road. When I got back, my sisters told me that Stanley had punched both of them in the stomach on their way home. There were certain rules to be kept about fighting at school, and it certainly didn't involve hitting girls. Once out of the school, it was anarchy. Next morning I sent a secret note to Stanley – passed along in the class by the pupil telegraph – challenging him to a fight after school.

We were in the plots digging, and I was digging extra hard in order to tone up my muscles. Stanley was doing the same. Mr Torney had given up the idea of cultivating a small orchard. The death of the apple sapling must have been the end of the horticultural world for him. We went up to the classroom for dictation. We wrote as usual at speed. A note dropped on to my exercise book. I had no time to open it, but on finishing the class I did. It was from Stanley, and it said he was in a hurry because his mother was ill but that he would fight me on the way home while we ran. I nodded to him.

I raced him down Manse Hill while we both traded punches. We punched past McCormack's Corner, up the Saintfield Road to Carr's petrol-filling station at the fork in the road, and continued up the Ballynahinch Road. I wasn't satisfied that I was hurting him enough, so I raced past him and back-kicked, catching him on the knee. Arse-in-Parsley passed waddling, saying for me to give it into him. An army staff car stopped, and an English voice shouted through the window, "I'd have you in the army if I had anything to do with it, m'lads."

Before the Drumbo Road, he tried to give me a final hefty punch and missed. I followed him up the path of his house flinging punches and rained more upon him as he rang the doorbell. The door opened and an ill-looking woman on a walking stick and in her nightgown appeared. I gave him a final punch, and he toppled forward into the hallway, knocking his mother down.

A few hours later, she hobbled to my house to complain. My mother got out the sally rod and thrashed me. My father gave me another one when he came home from work.

A few days later, during the middle of the night, I was awakened by a droning in the sky. Planes. German planes. Searchlights lit up the sky from an army emplacement somewhere across the fields in front of our house. A searchlight shone on our house, lighting up the rooms until it found its bearings. The planes overhead went from a bass droning to a light droning alternately.

My parents took us all down to the kitchen because it had the heaviest walls. Plane after plane passed over, some directly over our house. After a few minutes we heard seven explosions in the distance, as if from the leading plane as it unloaded its bombs over Belfast. After that, as all the planes began dropping their bombs, all the explosions became as one dreadful never-ending sound. A few planes returned over the countryside, droning lightly now.

We heard heavy lorries outside and saw an ack-ack gun being put into position about fifty yards from us at the top of Killynure Road. It began firing at the planes, shaking our house. A flare parachuted down from a plane and lit up the country for a while like daylight. My father was afraid that a German fighter would then come down to knock out the ack-ack, miss and hit our house. I suggested Vincent's idea of dispersing into the ditches but got a slap around the ears. Father also feared that shrapnel from the ack-ack shells might penetrate our roof. In the distance, a huge red glow lit up the sky from Belfast.

Next morning there was great excitement at school, and we even talked in class and weren't told off. When no further raids seemed likely, order was restored with both tae and cane.

I got four for not carrying my gas mask to school and a further two when I boldly said it would suffocate me anyway. A green extension was added, with insulation tape by an air-raid warden, to the gas mask against smoke gas. I was sure I would suffocate quicker now. But I didn't pursue the matter.

Every night at dark, the sound of feet was heard as thousands of people from Belfast came out the country roads from Belfast carrying bawling babies and dragging along whimpering toddlers. They knocked on each door on the way and asked to be taken in for the night. We shared whatever food we had but quietly cursed their intrusion when they came night after night.

Finally they stopped coming until the next raid.

Vincent left school and went to work in a stone quarry. He had the job of tipping the bogies of rocks into the stone crusher. I sometimes, while coming home from school, went into the quarry and saw him, covered from head to feet in white dust, pull the levers, and listened to the deafening sound of the stone crusher as it rendered the rocks into small ballast for road repairing. He considered himself a man at fourteen, and I knew he didn't like being seen in the company of a schoolboy. To prove his manhood, he told me what he would like to do – in very explicit terms – with Miss Flack. I had been thinking along these lines myself recently, and I asked him if I could pull one of the levers of the stone crusher. He would have none of it, and I left with him calling after me to tell Miss Flack that Vincent McConnell would like to buck her at her own convenience.

We were reading out loud in turns, something from *David Copperfield*, and I was reading the part where "Barkus is willing" when Miss Flack leaned over my shoulder. Her scented plaits fell one at a time on both my shoulders. I could feel the heat from her body penetrate my thin jersey. Her fresh-apple breath rippled through my hair. My face went red and my ears burned.

She said, "I still can't hear you and I'm almost of top of you. Speak up, for goodness' sake!"

After that I spoke even more softly, but she never laid a plait on me again.

One day she didn't appear at school. The next day she also

didn't appear, and the day after that. Soon six weeks had passed and she still didn't appear. No announcement was made by Mr Torney. None of the other teachers said anything either. Mr Torney searched the classroom and took away her personal effects. Then a rumour started that she was a British agent and had been dropped into France, captured by the Germans, tortured and murdered. Mr Torney and the other teachers made no statement to correct this rumour. They didn't even mention her name . . . ever again. Patsy asked Miss Torney where she was and got nothing but silence. I cried that night in bed while my two sisters in the adjoining beds laughed, but not knowing what I was crying about.

Miss Dobbins put up a poster on the wall with a boy on it, a pail of water, a scrubbing brush and large bar of rough soap. The caption read: "Don't Be Afraid of Soap and Water."

She said somebody stank in her classroom and immediately dragged out Skin O'Neill, who had had his head shaved against lice and wore a cheap spit-through jersey. She smelt him as carefully as a dog and then backed away spitting. She told him to go to the cloakroom and wash, as the dentist was coming and she was sure the poor man would faint.

The dentist came and set up his apparatus in the cookery room, which was now being used as a classroom owing to the sudden influx of more air-raid refugees from Belfast. While we sat there watching Miss Dobbins writing on the blackboard, the dentist, helped by a severe-looking nurse dressed all in white, peddled his drilling machine or pulled teeth. The room smelt of methylated spirits as the nurse sterilised the instruments by boiling them on a small stove. Terrible groans would sometimes emanate from the boys and squeals from the girls as a tooth was pulled and loud crying as a tooth was drilled, without anesthetic, while the dentist stepped on the foot-pedal saying, "Shush, shush, shush, shush! It's not as bad as all that."

Stanley didn't even whimper, and neither did I, because I had to follow him into the dentist's chair.

One morning chalked on the entrance door was "BAT IS A BRAT."

Mr Torney had all the boys turn out their pockets in his search for purple chalk. He examined the linings carefully and examined all fingers and found nothing. He didn't bother with the girls.

The army put on a display of weapons in a field next to the school and labelled them. There was a Bren gun, machine-guns with belts, rifles, the empty cases of hand grenades, a Bren gun carrier with caterpillar tracks, light anti-aircraft weapons and bayonets with the points broken off and the cutting edges dulled for our benefit. Everyone had a great time lying on the ground shooting at one another.

Stanley said to one of the soldiers, "That's nothing, look at this."

He took from his pocket a small wooden coffin on which was written "Hitler's Last Stand". He pushed a button and the lid sprung open to reveal Hitler with his penis sticking up.

Fighting with Stanley was so regular that it is impossible to remember every fight. There was never any truce, and now with Vincent gone there were no more collective games of war. I was still not allowed to play football with the rest, nor did I ever have any hope of doing so. I played rounders with the renegades right up to when I was allowed to wear long trousers. Patsy no longer pulled down her white knickers and peed in the fields without inhibitions. Her buds of breast were growing. Charles kept winning the prizes for drawing. I no longer had to pull discarded French letters from my sisters, on the way home from school, when they tried to blow them up thinking they were balloons. They had finally discovered the birds and the bees.

The war was over, and Mr Torney was asking questions like, "What new type of aircraft has been invented?"

Getting no answer, he said, "I'll give you a clue, you uninterested, hopeless pile of humanity: it has no propellers."

Getting no answer again, he said, almost in a rage, "Jet propulsion!"

It was 1946. I was fourteen, and I was leaving school. Those who were leaving – about eight of us – were lined up in front of the headmaster and lectured about the benefits of further education. You weren't handed any certificates or diplomas. There was nothing. There wasn't even a scholarship to be competed for. You were simply lined up, and if he thought you had been outstanding in a subject, you were picked out and recommended for future education. Three of us were picked: Patsy for her English composition, Charles for his drawings and me for my arithmetic. I could see he was fond of Charles, the gentle boy who had never given him any problems, because he talked about six sentences to him. He didn't know where Charles could go in order to progress with his drawings. He did mention a drawing office but withdrew that sentence immediately as having no relevance for Charles' artistic talent. Generally, Mr Torney advised us to tell our parents that we had been picked for further education. He didn't usually write a follow-up letter to them informing them of his decision. Mr Torney said we could send a request to him for a reference, at some later date. He wouldn't write any just now as he didn't know where we might end up. Then he said – and he looked straight at me – "Don't, for one moment, think you can turn me into a liar." There were no handshakes or "good luck" goodbyes. We picked up our schoolbags and left the school for ever.

I didn't tell my parents that I had been recommended for further education. I wanted to be free.

Some time later posters appeared on the hoardings of Belfast: "JOIN THE PALESTINE POLICE. £5 ALL FOUND."

Vincent joined but was back within a year, seriously wounded in a knife attack when he tried to separate two Arabs in a fight.

He recovered and went back to work in the stone quarry as a dynamiter. One charge he set went off prematurely and sent a huge rock through the windscreen of a lorry, killing the driver – one of his former aides-de-camp. Vincent was also struck by a rock but escaped with a broken arm. The quarry owner gave him the money for a return ticket, and he went by bus to the Royal Victoria Hospital in Belfast with his limp arm dangling by his side. His brilliant career as a general was over a long time ago.

Sidney Carson emigrated to Australia. Da Carson bought him land in the Queensland outback. A few months later he died after being bitten by a black snake.

Charles Temple forgot art and went to work in a bakery. I came across him once in a Belfast street when we were both eighteen. He showed me his blackened fingernails and said he had caught them in a dough-roller in the bakery. I wanted to say I was sorry about throwing him into the boiler house well. But somehow I couldn't; I didn't want to go back to those days, during those days.

Patsy became pregnant by her boyfriend at the age of sixteen. Her boyfriend disappeared to England when he heard the news. Luckily her parents didn't throw her out of the house. She went to work in her father's office while her mother looked after the baby.

The cedars nodded slowly in the wind. The crows cawed, but then they always do that.

I climbed back over the rusting gates and jumped on to the road and began walking towards the Castle which Stanley could never capture. I couldn't see the old schoolhouse which said "CLONTONACALLY" and 18. . . something. The whole building had disappeared, or maybe I was too busy looking at a new concrete structure beginning to show through the trees. It seemed to be about four storeys high. . . I don't know, I didn't go near it. But it was definitely a school. A massive one for this part of the country. I saw an old builder's sign nailed to a tree. It said: "Clontonakelly School". The name had been Anglicised, politicalised.

I turned to walk down Manse Hill – no, it wasn't Manse Hill any more. It was called something else. I can't remember. I didn't come here to remember that.

THE YARD

McKay woke his son Jim roughly. It was six in the morning. He shook him until the bed rocked. The boy of fourteen, annoyed at this treatment, dressed carelessly. His room led directly into the next room where his four younger sisters slept. He had shared that room with them up to three months ago, and they had played naughty games together. One night his parents became suspicious and put him in their room while they turned down the convertible settee in the parlour as a bed.

He went downstairs where his mother Mildred was preparing a special work-first-time breakfast. His spam sandwiches were already made up and wrapped in brown paper. His tea can – made from a syrup tin with a wire handle – was on the table. So were two little packets, one containing tea and the other sugar. There was also a small medicine bottle of milk.

He washed in a bucket of warm water and sat down at the table. Nothing was said as McKay and his son ate the special breakfast of porridge, followed by ham and eggs and toast. Mildred sat there drinking tea only. McKay, a stickler for timekeeping, constantly watched the tin alarm clock as it gave off metallic ticks. Even its minute hand could be heard creaking in the silence of the kitchen. It was deep winter and snowing outside. McKay was worried that the bus could be stuck in a snow-filled ditch. Lindsay the driver was allowed to take his bus home at night so as he could make an early start in the morning. But he lived down the narrow Killynure Road near by, and that road just about took the bus's breadth.

Mildred began to complain that it was washing day. With Jim now starting work, she would have to carry the water from the well herself, heat it up on the range in buckets, pour it into the zinc bath, scrub the clothes on the washboard with a bar of yellow soap, pour the dirty soapy water out into the back garden, fetch more water, heat it up, rinse the clothes, cut the buttons off the shirts, put them through the rollers of the wooden mangle, couldn't use the clothes line because of the frosty weather – the clothes would be so stiff they could be marched in – put as many as she could on the clothes horse in front of the range, put the rest on the clothes line in the kitchen, and when they were near dry take out the flat iron, heat it on the range, begin ironing, sew back the buttons on the shirts, cardigans and dresses, fold them up, put them away, starch the collars of the shirts, scrub the floors with soap and bleach, make the beds, scrub the potatoes, clean the vegetables. . . She could do with Jim at home. He could tend to the hens and goat, get the seeds ready for planting in the spring. . .

McKay rose from the table quickly and put his sandwiches, or "piece" as it was called, into his jacket pocket along with his tea, milk and sugar. Jim, about to put on an overcoat, was told by his father that only clerks wore overcoats to work. Mildred put a scarf around his neck and tied it. McKay tore the scarf from Jim's neck and threw it on the floor.

Nothing still was being said as they stepped out on to the garden path into the cold air and shut the door. Mildred looked at her son from the window as they went up the road. They were not a kissing family, but an occasional "Goodbye" or "So long" meant the giver was in good form. Mildred, in her nightdress, went into the cold, down the iced-up garden path and called out to Jim, "So long."

McKay knew it wasn't meant for him and waved his hand to say, "Get inside and don't make an exhibition of yourself."

They walked up to Andersons' house where the bus stop was and waited. Jim was excited by the thought of starting work in the city. A blackbird alarmed inside a snow-covered hedgerow. He also felt regret as he heard his goat bleating in the shed of their garden near by. The Rhode Island Red chickens were clucking impatiently in the hen house, and he wondered if his mother would remember to let them all out.

He had started this smallholding at the age of eleven. McCready, an old soldier who had been wounded at Gallipoli, had helped to start him off by lending him a broody hen to sit on a dozen eggs until they hatched. He also gave Jim a kid goat in payment for gathering dandelion leaves for his rabbits and cleaning out their hutches – which he had been doing from the age of eight. He had also taught him how to kill a rabbit swiftly. It was held up by its hind legs and given a quick chop behind the head with the edge of the hand. He also showed him the best way of skinning it. Chickens had their necks wrung. But it had to be done swiftly with not too much force or the head would come off. The first time Jim tried it, the head came off.

The kid goat followed him like a dog, and he took it on walks down country lanes where it could sample the lush vegetation. When it grew older, the old soldier had said, it would need sired or it wouldn't give milk. Mildred would have none of this. She

forbade her son to take it to the billy goat. He killed a chicken
for the table once, and his father, a city man, couldn't understand how he could do this. They sat around the table eating it
while the father watched the boy to see if he would burst into
tears. He didn't. The boy also kept a black rabbit as a pet which
he played with in the front garden. In its temporary freedom
from its hutch, it would leap into the air with joy. One day the
boy took the rabbit to the old soldier as he couldn't bear to kill
it himself. They sat round the table eating it, and the father
watched the boy, but again he didn't cry. The father was upset.
He thought for a moment that the black rabbit symbolised him.
Jim wanted to be a farmer eventually, but the father insisted that
learning a trade was the best option. There was too much killing
on farms, too much coupling of animals. Mildred understood
the killings but didn't want anything to do with the couplings.

Jim thought of the vegetable garden with its potatoes, carrots
and lettuces, and stared down at the snow on the ground.
McKay told him to straighten himself up and look his best if he
were to be seen with him. He should have combed his hair properly as McKay didn't want people to think he was walking
around with a tramp.

Further up the road from Andersons' house was the Andersons' quarry. Beside the house in a large yard were two steam
tractors and a steamroller used for road-making. Jim followed
them for miles when they were out on the road, fascinated by
the heavy flywheel whirling round and the mighty steam-boiler
that shook the road. Anderson's young daughter Ella used to give
him the *Beano* and *Dandy* every week. She asked him to go for
a walk one day but Jim was too embarrassed. He went red in the
face. When he called at her house for the *Beano* and *Dandy* the

next day, she slammed the door in his face. The day after that he called again and managed to ask her to go for a walk. She slammed the door in his face. Now she was peeping out of the upstairs window at him as he waited at the bus stop. McKay told him not to stare at people's bedrooms. But he did, and she pulled down the blind.

"Didn't I tell you not to stare up there?" said McKay. "They're business people, and you'll soon be only a shipyard worker."

The single-decker bus slid out of Killynure Road with difficulty. At times it swung lengthwise and almost hit the hedge, but Lindsay, a man of sixty, was an expert driver and was able to control it. He was thought of locally as a saint. He had a much younger wife called Lily, who drank and whored down the road at the Ivanhoe. She always wore short white wellington boots. On a wet day her arse would be wet where she had lain down with somebody in a field. She even did it in the snow. Children on their way to school would pick up the condoms, thinking they were balloons, and blow them up. Jim had to knock one from his oldest sister's mouth once. She complained to their father. Jim stuttered and tried to explain to him what it was. McKay's reaction was to call him "a bad bastard in the makin'".

Jim even knew what a Good Thing was – it was poor Lindsay's wife. Lindsay tolerated her, never shouted at her or beat her, but prayed for her redemption. Some of the local men courted her while at the same time saying Lindsay was not meant for this earth.

One day McKay asked his son did he know how babies were made. Jim pretended he didn't know. McKay scoffed. When Jim began to explain the mechanics, his father hit him in the face.

A lone passenger got out of the bus to help put some hessian bags under the back wheels of the bus. He was a man who worked for the Humane Society. Every day he stood at Queen's Bridge in Belfast with a huge shire-horse waiting for loaded drays. The shire was hitched to the dray with two long chains some distance in front of the other horse to help it pull the load over the steep incline of the bridge.

McKay went forward to help at the same time, telling the eager Jim to get into the bus and keep out of the way. Finally the bus made it into the main road. Jim and his father sat silently together. The Humane Society man was up front, talking to Lindsay through the open glass panel.

The bus stopped outside the ex-American army camp where the people from Gibraltar lived. The women were mostly Spanish, and many of them were beauties. They had been evacuated from the Rock when war broke out and were still waiting to return home. A Gib painter and a plumber boarded, heading for the shipyard. They sometimes gave knife-throwing exhibitions during the dinner hour.

At Cedar Valley, just past the police barracks, the bus stopped to pick up the conductor. He was a sour-looking individual who had recently been demobbed from the Irish Guards. He had fought in the Second World War, which had only ended two years ago. The cap peak of his uniform had been altered to come over his eyes in order to force him to stand up straight as if he were still in the Guards. His harsh barking voice demanded, "Fares please, I don't have all day!"

Lindsay smiled in the driver's mirror at the passengers and once swerved the bus suddenly to try and knock the guardsman off his balance.

Passengers continued to get on at every stop. They greeted everyone on the bus until, at the nearest stop to the Belfast boundary, the ones getting on there ceased to be known by the earlier passengers. But there were still slight nods of the head.

Entering South Belfast the bus wouldn't stop now except to let off a few passengers. Trams were waiting with signs mostly saying Queen's Island – an island which the shipyard occupied in its entirety. It was unlikely that the trams would pick up anyone here in this area of trees, detached houses and plush lawns. They would have to move further along Ormeau Road to the "Holy Land", with its Jerusalem Street, Damascus Street and Palestine Street.

Lindsay bade farewell to the passengers at the Peter's Hill Depot. The guardsman checked his ticket dispenser and counted the money.

The trams in an endless line, bumper to bumper, came down the Shankill Road. They were trams of every period. Some, from the beginning of the century, had the front and rear ends of the upper deck open to the weather, though with the roof still protruding. These areas had wooden slatted seats. Other trams were streamlined delights from the 1930s, with leather-covered seats and chrome fittings. One or two, from the last century, had no roof at all. The trolley, connecting the tram to the overhead electrified wire, came out of a barrel-like structure in the centre of the top deck. McKay choose an open-ended one. They climbed the spiral staircase, entered the rear open compartment, slid the door open, walked through the covered section and entered the forward open end. He believed in keeping hardy.

The freezing wind from Belfast Lough blew almost gale force and skirled like bagpipes; the snow danced under the gas lamps before drifting into the open end of the tram and getting into McKay's hair. He never wore a hat or cap, believing that anything tight around the head made a person go bald. Jim followed his father's fashion, though Mildred thought he should cover his head. Most of the shipyard men did. Those from Belfast wore the flat cap favoured by racehorse trainers. The rural men wore great padded caps.

The trams progressed down Royal Avenue, into the centre of the city, and at Castle Junction turned left into High Street and towards the Albert Memorial Clock, then over Queen's Bridge. The Humane Society man hopped off a tram with a barmbrack for the great shire-horse. This fine yellowy bread with currants and varnished-like brown top was a favourite with man and beast.

A carter with an empty dray hogged the tramlines for a less bumpy ride over the greasy square setts. The iron-hooped wheels seemed to have been made to fit into the tracks. Tram drivers stepped continuously on the floor pedal which gave off a cracked bell sound until the carter, with threatening uplifted whip, took the dray back to the side of the road. Bicycles of all kinds – racers, upright heavy ones known as "farm gates", one or two with small smoking engines attached – amounting in all to hundreds, weaved in and out of the traffic of trams, motor-cycles, motor-cycles with side-cars, lorries, vans, double-decker buses, single-decker buses and the odd 1930s car. A thousand or so men walked on the pavements on either side of the bridge.

By now men and boys stood on the outside bumpers of the trams. They filled the conductor's space and the driver's space. When a conductor opened the window and put his hand out for the fares of the passengers on the bumpers, they jumped off. On occasion, a youth might pull the rope to the trolley and send it swinging off the overhead wire. Without power the tram would stop, the conductor would get out cursing and try and juggle the trolley back on to the swinging wire while the endless line of trams gave off their cracked-bell sound in frustration. Amidst all this, a heavy brute of a policeman stood in the centre of Queen's Bridge on point duty. He was known as "the Skipper", for he wore a fisherman's hat in bad weather. He conducted his mighty orchestra with good-natured shouts at cyclists who had no rear lights or roars at a carter who might be thrashing his horse. His half-white-sleeved arms whirled and sucked in the traffic at one end of the bridge and blew it out at the other end.

On the other side of the bridge, empty trams returned to the city centre with illuminated indicators saying Shankill Road, Falls Road, Ormeau Road, Crumlin Road, Ballygomartin Road, Castle Junction or Depot. Thirty-six thousand men and about forty women curtain and soft-cover cushion makers were being delivered to the forests of steel.

At ten to eight, as the traffic approached the dreary filling-bays of the coal quays, the harsh tones of a giant electric klaxon sounded over the shipyard and across the city, sending the sea-gulls screeching and the pigeons flapping. It was known as His Master's Voice. It was saying there were ten minutes left to get to the time huts and pick up the boards (small pieces of wood, three inches by two, with two ears and with a number stamped on top). Bicycles suddenly spurted, motor-cycles roared, but the trams could just go at the same pace, hoping for a gap to get up speed.

A tram conductor was calling out (God knows why, everyone already knew), "Engine Works, Albert Basin, Main Office, Victoria Yard, Thompson Dry Dock. . . Deep Water Wharf ahead." McKay pointed out the main office and told his son to get off there. Did he have his birth certificate all right; did he have the

five pounds for his indentured apprenticeship all right? "Do
your shoelace up, comb your hair or they'll think you're a
tramp." He said he would meet his son at the main gate about
twenty-five to six. When the boy asked where the main gate was,
he was given a look as if he were stupid and told the main gate
was beside the main office.

He went down the spiral staircase and squeezed through the
throng of men and stepped on to the pavement. A huge brass
plate being Brassoed by an old woman said: "HARLAND AND
WOLFF, SHIPBUILDERS. CHAIRMAN SIR FREDERICK REBBECK."

A mass of steel gantries towered hundreds of feet above the
offices. A giant floating crane raised its giant hook above the
workshops. Jim asked the old woman, now polishing the door
handles, where he should go, and she pointed to two heavy oak
doors about sixteen feet high. He grasped the heavy, shining
brass door handle in two hands and twisted it. The door opened,
and he was in a high domed passageway that had a speckled
marble floor with the words "HARLAND AND WOLFF" cut into it
in black marble. Another old woman, mopping the floor, tutted
at him as he walked across it. He asked for Mr McDonald, and
the old lady wondered what a boy like him could want with such
an elevated person. He explained, and she said, "He comes in at
nine. He'll see you for now, seeing you're startin' for the first
time, but I doubt if you'll ever see him again."

Then taking on the role of the elevated person, she said
sharply, "Sit there in the corner and don't fidget. Them chairs
weren't meant for your make."

She kept grumbling as she mopped the floors, casting an eye
towards him now and then. When he moved slightly, she said,
"Ah ah!" and waved a lemon-coloured finger at him.

The traffic outside was lightening. There were longer gaps between the trams now. He heard their trolleys swish by and watched, through a high-up window, the balls of blue electricity as the trolley head jumped the overhead wire.

The klaxon sounded again, and it was 8 a.m. A motor-cycle raced by, roaring at a furious rate. From the city he heard the steam whistles of the spinning mills. The first old woman joined the second old woman, and they both looked at him. When he was about to stand up, the second old lady said again, "Ah ah!"

And the first old lady said, "Your finger marks are all over the doorknob. I had to do it again with a lick of Brasso. A right how-do-you-do, and Mr McDonald nearly on his way here already."

The boy sat still, and the old women became statues. Finally they scuttled into a large cleaning cupboard when they heard the main doors opening.

The office staff were arriving in overcoats, gloves, hats and scarves. Some carried small attaché cases. Dainty-looking girls clip-clopped in on high heels. Perfumes wafted around the grand corridor. One man entered with a placard on which was printed "THE WAGES OF SIN IS DEATH".

Apparently he preached to the toiling masses during his lunch break. He put the placard in the cleaning cupboard with the old women.

More office staff arrived, more perfume, more clip-clopping.

Jim looked at these grand people and wondered fearfully how the elevated one would treat him.

At half past nine, the thin bent figure of an elderly man entered, wearing a black homburg hat and a black Crombie coat. With screwed-up eyes, he raised his hat to Jim. Then discovering his mistake said, "Youth sometimes translates as femininity in old age."

He disappeared through an ornate door into which was carved an early steamship with a steadying sail. The cleaning cupboard opened, and the two old women emerged in the middle of a cloud of cigarette smoke. They tried to waft the smoke back inside the cupboard before leaving.

A secretary emerged from the ornate door, asked him his name and took him into McDonald's office. McDonald was sitting behind a desk, the top of which was covered in a fine green leather edged with gold. He didn't bid the boy sit down but pushed a bell. McKenna, his second-in-command, entered and took the boy's birth certificate and five-pound note. McDonald threw some indentured apprenticeship papers on the table. He signed two of them, then waved them away. McKenna, a fat man aged about forty in a sky-blue suit, took the boy to his office, but he also didn't ask him to sit down, though he sat down himself. His desk was covered in blue leather, but it was of a rougher quality. He then signed both papers and indicated for the boy to also sign. They were stamped, and a red round seal was stuck beside both of McDonald's signatures which McKenna countersigned.

Then McKenna said, "You have been accepted as an indentured apprentice in the woodworking trade by the shipbuilders Harland and Wolff. One half of these indentures you get now; the other half you get when you have completed your five-year apprenticeship. You will – or your parents will – get this five pounds back. Other than sickness, any lost time will have to be made up. That can delay you coming out of your apprenticeship. It is up to you now. You cannot start your apprenticeship until you reach the age of sixteen. In the meantime, we have a position for you as an office boy in one of our time offices. Wait outside please where someone will collect you."

A young secretary clip-clopped in. He put an arm round her waist and said, "You are nice and thin, Dorothy. How do you keep your figure?"

Embarrassed, she made a move to get away from him.

"That's right," he said, "keep away from me and you'll keep your figure."

He looked at the boy hard, as much as to say, "What are you looking at?"

The secretary led him to the corridor and, without a word, waved an arm jangling with bangles to the seat he had been sitting on.

About an hour later a boy of about fifteen entered and asked, "Are you James McKay?"

Jim pointed to himself and asked, "Me? Are you askin' me?"

"Nah, the wee fella behind you," answered the fifteen-year-old. "I'll call you Jim. We don't call people James here in the Yard unless they *are* somebody. My name's Dick, and don't call me Richard until I'm head of the Yard."

He laughed in a voice that went from high to low notes.

"Come on, you're in the Thompson Works."

They went outside, through the main gates and into the main shipyard road. There was just the odd tram passing now. A heavy traction engine was pulling a gigantic ship's engine part on a low trailer that seemed to have twenty solid rubber tyres. It was still snowing, and Dick said it was better to get the shipyard bus though they could walk to Thompson Works in about fifteen minutes. While they waited, shouts were heard coming from the direction of the Albert Basin.

Dick took to his heels immediately in that direction and only stopped for a moment to beckon Jim to follow. Floating on the water was a small floating crane. A diver was having his copper headpiece screwed on. One of the crane crew was turning the handle of the air pump slowly and carefully. Two men helped the diver into the water at the end of ropes. His long red-rubber air pipes followed him. The water bubbled. The diver held in his hand what looked like a measuring rule about four feet long. A harbour policeman came along and tried to usher the boys away, but Dick dodged him so many times that the policeman gave up.

After five minutes the rule floated to the surface before the water started bubbling again. The diver was dragged up from the depths by the ropes. He held a dead man in his arms. The crane crew grabbed the body and laid it on the jetty. The young man was about twenty. He had a gash on his forehead. His face was obscured by foam. As they laid him on his back, a dribble of water came out of his mouth. He had slipped and hit his head on the icy steel deck of the floating crane. The policeman felt his pulse and wiped the foam away from his face with the end of the dead man's jacket, for identification purposes. One of the crew got a tarpaulin and covered the body. The snow fell thick, and soon the canvas disappeared under it. No one said anything. A lorry passed loaded with sheet metal.

They waited outside the main gate until the bus came. It was still camouflaged from the war and had its windows covered inside with plywood. A single bulb from a bicycle lamp burned. In the gloom, Jim glimpsed a man holding a naked circular saw blade for cutting logs. Its teeth gleamed as if it had just been sharpened. The other men held pieces of pipes, tools, a large section of trunking for a ship's air conditioning; a muscular blacksmith held a weirdly shaped piece of iron, blue from the fire. They bantered one another, laughed, cursed, smoked pipes and cigarettes, spat, sang pieces of songs, whistled, jeered and hammered on the sides of the bus as if going on an outing.

Jim and Dick got off the bus at the Thompson Works. Across the road near a dry dock was a partially finished ship on the slipway. About fifty flashes of intense blue light flashed on and off as the welders worked.

"Commere and see this," said Dick.

They walked to the bridge that crossed the dry dock bridge to the slipway. Caulkers made the steel seams watertight with their hand-held caulking machines. The sound of steel being battered was deafening. The caulker was already deaf in his youth. A riveters' fire glowed and crackled with coke brought pneumatically to a white heat. The heater boy threw a glowing rivet from his coke fire. It was caught deftly by the catcher boy – a man in his fifties – with a pair of large tongs. He fitted it in a hole of the steel plate. A riveter held hard against it with his pneumatic riveting machine. His mate, on a staging hanging over the water, flattened the rivet and fixed the two steel plates together. They continued down the never-ending rows of holes; the glowing rivets flew; the metallic chatter never paused. An ill-looking white-faced man in paint-spattered canvas trousers and jacket followed the riveters, dabbing the finished steel plates with red lead. Now and then the red-leader stopped to splutter, spat something out and dispersed it over the deck with his foot.

Dick took him to the small brick time office that was just inside the gates to the Thompson Works and left, saying he would pick him up at dinnertime. The timekeeper was known as Gunner. He got that name because the chief cashier said that when collecting cash from the shipyard bank he was to keep his hand in his pocket to look like he had a gun. An armed gang had once held him up a few years ago and taken a bag of money. The chief cashier said he couldn't have a gun because the robbers might come back and take that as well. Jack was his real name, but so many people laughed behind his back and called him Gunner that he decided to go along with it. Now, when they called him Gunner, it was he who laughed instead.

"I'm Gunner," he said to the boy. "You'll do your two years here. Your job is to collect my boards from every time office in the Yard. Men are sent away from here to work on different ships. They throw their boards into the nearest time office. The board numbers here begin with nine – this is Thompson Works. Beginning with eight is the time office at Musgrave Channel jetty, and so on. Don't try learning too much on your first day. Now go to the sheet-metal shop and ask them for the keys to the gantries."

The boy entered the shop and saw the long lines of benches on which were set every conceivable geometrical design in galvanised sheet metal. Welders, holding wood masks with blue glass apertures in front of their faces, carefully welded the pieces together. The deadly galvanised white smoke curled about their faces. Further up the shop, two men caused a din by hammering some sheet metal into shape with large wooden mallets. Another two were cutting sheets of metal at a high and dangerous-looking guillotine. It was cutting through the metal like paper. One man was digging a metal splinter out of his thumb with the sharp end of a compass. He asked this man for the keys to the gantry. He smiled grimly, sucked his thumb and pointed to a man wearing a brown dust coat and a bowler hat.

The foreman took him into his office which was built like a glasshouse so as he could look all over the vast shop. He sat him down and said, "This must be your first day in the Yard."

The boy nodded and was already guessing he was being made a fool of by Gunner.

"Now look, son, they're playing you for a fool. There is no such thing as keys to the gantries. Sometimes the new boys are sent over here for a bucket of gas or two pounds of electricity."

The foreman stood up to watch somebody in the shop sneaking a read at a newspaper. The boy stood up. The foreman switched the lights in the office on and off to show that he was watching.

The boy said suddenly, "I don't like it here. I want to go home."

"You'll get used to it; now go back to your time office."

"I don't want to," replied the boy.

"What age are you?"

"Fourteen."

"Fourteen, a big boy like you. You've been pampered. I started work at twelve. Spool boy in Jennymount Spinning Mill. I had to crawl under the machinery– and it going like the hammers of hell – to get the spools that fell off. The bobbins were whirlin' above my head like scalded cats."

The boy edged out of the door as the foreman talked on, but now mostly to himself as he looked down at the intricate plans for air-conditioning a new ship.

Jim went back to the office and stood looking at Gunner silently. He wasn't quite sure what to do next.

"You went to the sheet-metal shop as I told you?"

The boy sat down and still said nothing.

Gunner demanded the keys of the gantries in a mock rage, and the boy, angry, arose and squared up to him as if he were ready to fight.

Gunner laughed, patted him on the back and ordered him to fill the tea cans at the boilers outside the blacksmiths' shop. It was near lunchtime, and he wanted his tea before the doors of every shop flew open and the mad crowds rushed to the taps in order to make the best of their forty-minute lunch break. Jim put the tea and sugar in his syrup tin, put the tea and sugar in Gunner's enamelled can with the cup lid and went to the boilers.

An old man was feeding the roaring fire under the large boilers with broken old doors that had come from a ship under renovation. The heat was so fierce that it almost glued Jim's eyelashes together. The wood smoke, mixed with the blistering, melting paint, got into his lungs and made him cough. The scalding water, which made the lids of the boilers dance and steam, was coming out of the taps under pressure. The old man told him to be careful. He said he was seventy-two and asked Jim if he thought he was too old to keep working. Jim, not knowing what seventy-two meant, was silent. He asked Jim what trade he was going to, and when he said a woodworker the old man said good.

"You can be a ship's carpenter and sail a ship out of this fuckin' country." He immediately apologised for swearing at a young boy but said he would probably hear worse in the years to come.

A labourer sweeping up near by was listening to the conversation and said to Jim that woodworking was a stupid trade. Why couldn't he do his time at something modern like an electrician? The boilerman listened, and when the labourer swept up further away, told Jim not to heed him. The labourer was envious, having missed his chance in life.

The boilerman then began to tell Jim about his life at sea and about all the countries he had visited. He had been a deckhand and he had loved the life. They wouldn't let him stay on after sixty-five. He had a wife in the Gold Coast. Her skin was smooth and soft like black satin. He had another wife in Shanghai. Her skin was pure gold. He also had a wife in Belfast. She had a tongue that could cut cold steel. One day he would go back to Shanghai. He thought he might have a child there now. And maybe another one in the Gold Coast. There was nothing like native women. He had been offered a job in Darjeeling as an overseer – whipping the women teapickers when they slacked – but he might end up burning the whip and marrying one of them, so he didn't go. He was saying something about their skin being the colour of strong tea without milk when Gunner bawled from the door for Jim to hurry up.

As he was filling the cans with more steam than the dancing water, the boilerman told him the tale about how Gunner got his name. He also said that Gunner was a fruit merchant and he had better not turn his back on him or bend over when he was around. The boy didn't know what a fruit merchant was. He couldn't understand why you had to be careful of a man who sold fruit. Why couldn't he turn his back on him or bend over when Gunner was around?

Gunner was drying out his Capstan cigarettes (Extra Strong) on the radiator to make them stronger. Also on the radiator was a meat pie in greaseproof paper. Gunner was a small thin man, almost a hunchback. He had a Clark Gable moustache and wore a sports jacket with leather patches on the elbows. He drank his tea, ate his meat pie and smoked his Capstan alternately, and complained about having a bad stomach. A pint of stout with a glass of whiskey thrown into it was his favourite drink. He kept racing pigeons and was going to ask somebody he knew in the plumbers' shop to make a device that could fire a .22 bullet at the falcons that were attacking his pigeons. It had to be small enough to hide in his hand as the predators were too clever for his .22 rifle. The plumber man was a genius – almost German, he was so clever at thinking up different devices. He had ten bob for him if he managed it. He then asked the boy what the boilerman was saying to him. The boy said he was talking about his days at sea. Gunner laughed out loud and said he had got no further than Whitehaven on one of Kelly's coal boats.

"I suppose he told you about his native women."

The boy barely nodded, not wishing to make enemies so soon in his career.

"He's a fruit merchant," said Gunner. "I wouldn't turn my back on him – though I'm old meat – nor tip my toes when he's about."

The boy was puzzling over so many people selling fruit around here when Dick knocked on the door.

"I've got to show him the Musgrave Channel time office, Gunner."

Dick winked and Gunner winked back. The boy was puzzled and apprehensive.

They walked through the Thompson Works and out through the gates at the other end to the Musgrave Channel Road. Running beside it was Musgrave Channel – a stretch of water that separated it from the aircraft factory of Short Brothers. It was a sight that Jim could never imagine.

Tied up at the jetty in a long row were a number of ships. One was an aircraft carrier almost entirely covered in red lead. The red-leaders stood on narrow staging boards suspended on ropes about a hundred feet above the grey channel water. They scraped with wire brushes and hammered the rust with triangular-headed hammers. Fifty feet above them were more rows of boards on which these canvas-suited men stood dabbing on the red lead from paint pails. Their canvas suits were covered in red lead, as were their faces and caps. Each face had a deathly pallor. The snow whirled around them, spiralled, raced along the carrier from stem to stern, turned and raced back again in two-hundred-feet sheets. Now and then a red-leader would stop to beat his blue bare hands against his canvas suit. Some of the suits had splashes of blues, greens, blacks and yellow from other ships they had worked on, but mostly it was red.

Further along the jetty was a huge passenger ship of the Peninsular and Oriental line. It gleamed white with new paint as painters who did the on-board painting swarmed over it in white overalls, giving her her final coat. The ship's klaxon blasted a few times in a test. It had extra steel hawsers – as thick as a man's arm – attached to the bollards on the jetty, for it was undergoing basin trials. The screws whirled and created hills of water as they churned, driving the ship away from the jetty, tightening the steel hawsers until they were rods of steel. The anti-rat collars on the hawsers turned slowly. Dick advised Jim not to go too near the water's edge because should a hawser break a body could be cut in two. A narrow wooden gangway led up to the lower deck with a watchman at the bottom sitting in a small hut in front of which a coke brazier glowed. The gangway, resting on two iron wheels, danced with the movement of the enraged ship.

There was heavy traffic on the gangway as men carried up wall mirrors, cushions, rolls of carpet, wash-hand basins and every other article that would keep a small city going. Others carried toolboxes down to the jetty, having finished their particular jobs. Ship's officers with suitcases were going on board. The arms of the derricks worked methodically, lifting food supplies from the jetty in steel nets.

On another smaller gangway leading through a cargo door, near the bow of the ship, Lascar seamen in skirts, with colourful cloths tied round their heads and leather mocassins with long curly toes on their feet, came off the gangway in a long line, carrying a variety of large vegetable cans with wire handles. They headed for a small brick building which had been converted into a lavatory. Dick said they didn't sit on a bowl but hunkered down and shat into a hole. After that they washed their arses with the water in the cans. He opened his jacket to reveal a knife stuck in an inner pocket. That was for the Lascars. They were fruit merchants. One had grabbed his hand once and stroked it. The next one who did that would have his plums stoned. He advised Jim to make himself a knife. There was plenty of steel lying about on the jetty. All you had to do was bind one end with electrician's insulation tape and take it to the buffers on the jetty and grind the other end into a cutting and plunging edge. At the entrance to the Lascar gangway stood an even more colourful figure with rows of beads around his neck. Dick said he was the Head Sarang. As he said this, the Head Sarang boxed the ears of a Lascar who was in the line coming off.

Dick shouted over at him, "Go on, Gunga Din, bung it in; ye're a better man than me."

The Head Sarang flashed a row of perfect white teeth as he

smiled and beckoned him over. Dick put up his fists, and the Head Sarang laughed so much he had to hold on to the handrail of the gangway.

A group of well-groomed men in suits, also carrying suitcases, went up the main gangway. Dick said they were ship's waiters from Goa. Their faces were not as dark as the Lascars.

Dick said they were civilised. You wouldn't catch them carrying tins of water to wash their arses with.

Jim wanted to have a look on board, but Dick said the watchman was too alert at the moment. Dick had a peep inside the small hut, but the watchman told him to get out of his light as quickly as possible or he would get his toe up his hole. Dick decided Friday afternoon was better as the old watchman would get his wages early. Then he usually had a few bottles of stout and fell asleep.

Out in the aircraft factory side of the channel were four giant four-engined flying boats moored to buoys. They bobbed listlessly, and even as inanimate objects they looked lost and sad. They were up for sale and their future was unknown. Seagulls settled on them could just be made out in the whirling snow.

A captured German ship from the war lay at anchor in the middle of the channel. It was a small, grey-painted merchant ship converted to carry troops. Dick said they would get a raft and go out to her tomorrow. He would take the helm and be captain. He gave a mock Nazi salute towards the vessel and shouted, "*Achtung! Achtung!* Permission to come aboard, *mein Führer?*"

There was a smell of fishy rancid fat in the air as they walked to the next vessel. Her stern was square, and a great doorway led into it. She was so high out of water that one gangway only reached halfway up her starboard side. There, a steel platform had been bolted to her to take a second gangway to the cutting deck. Dick said she was a whaler – a jinx ship. Six men had been killed on her in three months. One man slipped while standing on a staging in the engine room. He grabbed at a pipe to save himself, but the pipe was scalding hot and he fell a hundred feet. When they got to him, his two arms were outstretched with a bolt through each hand. . . and he hanging from a bulkhead. A crown of binding wire penetrated his skull.

"Crucified like our Lord."

The ship was more full of machinery that any other ship as she was also a factory ship. Dick said the smell of whale blubber was everywhere – in the cabins, on the blankets of the bunks, in the galley, everywhere. You couldn't run from it. Even the captain's quarters stank like an old empty tin of sardines. They would sneak on to it next week sometime. The engine room was great. They would race one another to see who got to the propeller-shaft tunnel first by climbing down the pipes.

Further along the mile-long jetty was the huge *Reina del Pacifico*. She had been a troopship and was now being converted back to a passenger ship. Doors and pastel-green wooden bulkheads lay heaped on the jetty, along with a small mountain of tangled pipes, pieces of machinery and old furniture. There was a watchman's hut at the bottom of the gangway, but the old man was fishing with a line further along the jetty. Jim wanted to go aboard and see his father, who was a joiner engaged with the army of other men in ripping the guts out of the ship. Dick said there wasn't time as he had to show him the time hut.

Dick knocked on the door, as it was always locked from the inside. There was a pigeon-hole from which the men drew their boards in the mornings and threw them back in at knocking-off time, watched by a timekeeper in case a man threw in two boards while his mate sloped off five minutes early. They entered the hut, and Jim was introduced to the timekeeper known as Half-Pint, due to his slow drinking in the pub at night while everyone else bought two rounds of drinks to his one. He was a miserable, thin and humourless-looking figure who constantly pushed his piles back up. There were also four boys in the hut.

Dick didn't introduce them. They were also office boys from various parts of the Yard. Jim didn't have enough experience to wonder why they were gathered there.

Suddenly Jim felt an arm around his throat and he was pulled to the floor. One boy pulled his trousers down. He struggled like a wild beast but was overpowered while Half-Pint turned his back and tutted. One boy took a shoe brush and covered Jim's balls in black polish. They held him down while his charlie was also covered. Then they let him go as one and dashed through the door cackling in adolescent voices.

"Now you're in," said Dick as Jim pulled up his trousers, red in the face with embarrassment and furious at the same time.

As Dick was about to go through the door, Jim punched him. Behind the punch were the muscles he had grown while wheeling heavy wooden wheelbarrows of dung from a nearby farm to tend to his garden. Behind the punch were the muscles grown from carrying rocks to make a dry-stone wall. Dick fell through the door and slipped to the frozen snow-covered plank boarding of the jetty. He got up still stunned, just in time for another heavy punch. Dick got up again, feeling his jaw, opening and shutting it to make sure it still worked. He touched his nose carefully and held up three sticky red fingers. Looking at Jim – more in disappointment than anger – he slowly walked away.

Half-Pint stood there a moment, looking at Jim, almost mesmerised. After a moment, he said in a sad voice, "You've just
knocked the shite out of the junior boxing champion of
Northern Ireland."

He took Jim's hand lethargically and raised his arm to promote him winner while pushing his piles back up with the other.

About the "initiation ceremony", he said it was nothing. He'd
seen worse things when he worked as a wages clerk in the mills.
The women painted your balls there with anti-corrosive paint.
But what happened to the young girls was worse. One was
grabbed on her first day, had her knickers pulled down, her legs
opened. An oul doll – who chewed tobacco – spat baccy saliva
right into her minge. The girl's screams was something terrible,
but the winding master pretended he didn't see anything. When
the very same fella was only a loom hand he was a terrible man
for putting his hands up the women's skirts. One day they
grabbed him and put him on the flat of his back on the floor and
pulled down his trousers. One girl had a bottle and forced his
charlie into it while another pulled up her skirt and pulled down
her knickers to let him see oul mossy face. His "lad" saluted, and
the pain of it stuck in the bottle as it expanded had him screeching. Half-Pint nodded gravely and pushed up his piles again.

Jim went back to the Thompson Works, went to the lavatory
and spent a long time washing off the polish. His underpants
were saturated in the polish, and he tried his best to wet them
and rub off the polish, but he had no soap. When he got back
to the office, Gunner sniffed the air and asked him if he had
been made a member of the club yet. Jim didn't answer. Gunner
sniffed the air again and went back to the wages ledger.

*

Jim met his father at the main gates, and they rushed for an over-crowded tram in the long line of overcrowded trams. They stood on the bumpers hanging on to the window wipers. McKay then started to climb up the back of the tram to reach the upper deck. Jim, shaking, began the climb after him. McKay told him it was too dangerous and to stay where he was, but Jim climbed just the same, and his father called him headstrong.

Those who had given up trying to get a tram began the march to the city. Though it was still snowing, the pavements were running with water with the grinding feet.

At Ormeau Avenue, while they waited for the Ballynahinch bus, McKay asked him if he had signed his apprenticeship papers all right, had he given in the five-pound note all right, had he shown them the birth certificate all right? The boy said he didn't want to go back to the Yard any more. When asked why, he didn't answer. McKay told him he couldn't leave because he was now bound to the Yard for seven years. He couldn't leave because that would require McKay's signature, and he was never going to sign away Jim's one chance of a skilled trade. Out of the sixteen shillings a week he would get as wages, four shillings and sixpence would be for his weekly bus ticket; then there were tram fares, his clothes, his overalls when he started his appren-ticeship, his food, his woodworking tools for his apprenticeship – which he would start buying at the weekend because a full kit would eventually cost a hundred pounds.

"I'll be keeping you," said McKay; "then there are your sisters – Mary I'll have to start sending to secretarial school from next year on. That's two years' study. I'll have to start working over-time from next month. It'll be seven days a week to pay the fees. Lilian would be the year after – no, maybe not her. She's dense in a lot of ways. Maybe the stitching room for her. Harriet will get the secretarial course in her place. I've made my mind up about that. Definitely. She has brains like me. Doris, we have time to think about her future. Maybe a shop assistant for her. Not unless she improves at school. Throwing stones, breaking the glass in oul McCready's glasshouse like a tomboy!"

When the bus came and they boarded he continued, "When you're twenty-one, and out of your apprenticeship, and you still want to stay at home, you'll hand in half your wages to the house. But in the meantime, while you're an office boy, we can't afford to give you any pocket money. You'll get some when you start your apprenticeship because you should be earning one pound and four shillings by then. This Saturday I'll have to buy you a suit. You're working now, and I can't have you looking like a tramp. We'll go to Spackman's in High Street."

He began to recite a little ditty:

"When I was a lad I went with my dad to Spackman's.

Now I'm a dad and I go with my lad to Spackman's."

"That's what it says in the window; that's where my father took me for my first suit. I'll pick you out a shirt and tie as well. I still have some overtime money left over."

He then said, "There's a young Gib girl at the back of the bus looking at you all the time. Aren't you going to look back at her? She wants to click."

Jim mumbled something about seeing her all the time on this bus. McKay then wiped the steam from the window and looked through the distorted glass at the snow piled high and browning with the passing traffic.

Jim had been to the Gibraltarian camp a few months ago to see a film. It was all in Spanish and about a girl and a fella and a stern chaperone who comes between them. The fella kills himself with a stiletto and the girl jumps over a cliff. There was no action. It was all talk.

McKay asked him if he had polished his boots before leaving the Yard because there was a hell of a smell of polish.

Jim said nothing and went on to remember the film in the Nissen hut. He knew the girl at the back of the bus was called Dolores because that how her parents addressed her as she sat between them. They constantly admonished her for looking round. Sitting behind her, something made him tug gently on her long black hair. She kept looking around, smiling. Then the parents looked round at him suspiciously. Then all the Gibs began looking at him and wondering what he was doing there. He could have told them that he just walked in to have a look around because he had been here before when the US Army occupied this camp.

He had been here for a children's party at Christmas. They served soup which had jam and cake floating in it. It was American, therefore it tasted good. There were a lot of sweets which they called candy. Each child was given a present, extravagantly wrapped in gold and silver paper, pink bows for the girls, blue bows for the boys. Yes, he had been in this very hut before. A lot of jazz was played through loudspeakers then. The Yanks taught the children to jive. Then they settled down to watch a film called *Orchestra Wives*. The Yanks whistled and stamped their feet every time a woman in the film appeared with hardly any clothes on. All the children laughed and cheered.

"Now she's getting off," said McKay. "At least you could wave. Look, she's still dallying around. She's in no hurry to get home. I wish I was your age again. Look, is that her mother meeting her at the bus stop? Her mother's not bad looking either. There's still that smell of boot polish."

They got off at Andersons' and walked down from the bus stop. The half-moon shone on the snow and cast off the usual pitch darkness over the countryside.

"Did you notice," said McKay, "the hare caught in the head-lamps of the bus when it was crossing the road? Well," he said, continuing without waiting for an answer, "I think it went under the bus. Keep an eye out for it."

A few yards further on, Jim noticed an animal struggling to hop. He ran after it and picked it up by the hind legs. McKay told him to leave it alone. They would bring it home and nurse it until it got better and then let it go. McKay was running and sliding all over the road. Jim chopped it behind the head. It gave one last quiver. McKay pulled the hare from him, in horror, laid it on the road and pushed it to try and make it hop, but its head just flopped.

"Now look what you've done," said McKay. "What did you do that for? What harm was it doing you?" He threw it into the hedge, but Jim recovered it.

McKay followed hesitantly, saying, "I don't know what I'm bringing up. It didn't come from my side of the family."

Jim called to the goat and got no answer. In a panic he rushed to the door and asked Mildred was it all right. She said to eat his dinner first and then she'd explain. He handed her the hare, and McKay grabbed it and tried to throw it through the back door. She recovered it and held on to it until he gave up.

They sat around the table drinking the heavy vegetable soup, followed by meat and potatoes and slices of bread with syrup on it, while the sisters jeered at Jim for being a shipyard man like his father. Mildred joined in and began to scorn the shipyard men as that "yellow-face crowd pourin' out of the gates like diarrhoea out of a cow". McKay looked at her for a long time but said nothing. Jim asked about the goat again, and the sisters began whispering among themselves and laughing out loud before whispering again.

Jim was about to go out to the shed to look at the goat when Mildred said she had given it back to McCready. When she had taken it out the shed to graze that morning, it had butted her; then it ran dragging her after it on the end of the chain. The chain had wrapped around her leg and injured her. She showed her leg, which was black and blue on the shin bone. She also said the chickens would have to go as they were flying over the hedge and into the road. One of them almost got killed by a motorcycle. They would have their legs tied on Saturday morning and be sold to Carse the poulterer. She had made that arrangement already with him. Jim cried. The sisters jeered and the parents shouted at him to have sense – he wasn't going to be a farmer in this life.

Jim skinned the hare while McKay and Mildred went into the parlour to listen to the wireless. While they sat there, no one was allowed to enter.

McKay came out after a time and asked to examine Jim's boots. It was almost a daily ritual going back to when they were toddlers. He wanted to assess the wear and tear. He said he had a right to because he was the one who repaired them on a Sunday. Jim reluctantly took off his boots and was told he was still kicking stones with them. He could see new scuff marks. He was to polish them tonight for tomorrow and not look like a tramp.

The sisters had their shoes examined. He complained that Doris was breaking the backs down because she wasn't loosening the laces enough. Lilian had dried her shoes out too quickly in front of the fire instead of allowing them to dry naturally. Now there were white tide marks on them. Slushy snow soaked them worse than rain. How many times had he to say it? He wouldn't warn them all again but would bring out the strap. Even Jim was still not too big to get a good bleaching.

Mildred stood there silently, not intervening because she didn't want a row in case it went on for a week, after which they wouldn't talk to each other for another week.

She didn't inquire of Jim about his day. He was his father's boy now.

McKay searched in the pocket of his jacket. He had had an extra-long pocket sewed inside for taking things he found while gutting the *Reina del Pacifico*. There was a handful of foreign coins from half a dozen nations. Rupees seemed to be in abundance. There were a couple of army manuals on stripping, cleaning and firing a heavy machine-gun and another one on the .303 rifle, on wartime economy paper, two books – *The Story of San Michele* by Axel Munthe and *The Iron Heel* by Jack London – a miniature telescope, a fountain pen, a silver pocket watch that needed repairs, two new khaki handkerchiefs, a sergeant's stripes still in cellophane wrapping and a miniature of whiskey. He had to be careful passing the Bulkies – these harbour policemen had a keen eye. Mildred shouted at him for risking his job, but McKay said everything would just be thrown away. Jim was asked by his father to pick any two items he wanted, save for the whiskey, of course, which would be put into the medicine cupboard along with the iodine, quinine, Milk of Magnesia, Iron

Jelloids and Dr Brown's remedy for colic. Jim picked the two books.

At eight o'clock the girls were told to get to bed. They asked why Jim wasn't being sent up as well. McKay said he had an extra hour because he was working now.

At nine McKay nodded at him. He went upstairs, and as he was going through his sisters' room they jeered him because of his privileges.

Jim got into bed and began reading *The Iron Heel*. Fifteen minutes later, McKay sneaked up the stairs, saw the light shining under the door, entered and turned it off. His sisters in the other room kept whispering and laughing until Mildred banged on the ceiling with the handle of the brush.

That night Jim had a dream about the goat. It was crying out for him, but he couldn't find it.

He listened to the alarm clock tick and picked it up and held it to within a few inches of his bleary eyes. It was almost 6 a.m. He got out of bed before his father came up to shake him. It was cold in the room without heating. It was never meant to have heating. The glass of the window was distorted halfway up with a thin coat of ice. It was still snowing. He hoped the goat was warm.

Jim was now finding his way around the shipyard collecting the boards from the different time offices, bringing the large wage ledgers, with their plywood covers, to the main offices each Friday for checking by the accountancy staff. While there, he had to help, with about six other office boys, in cancelling hundreds of sheets of National Insurance stamps with a spring-loaded stamper. In charge of this group was an large elderly heavy man with a bald head called Curly, behind his back. The large office he did this work in was occupied by dozens of men sitting at desks checking the progress sheets sent in by the time offices. Some bore the greasy imprint of the black trades: caulkers, riveters, platers and welders who were on piecework or bonuses for achieving production goals. The office staff in their suits, sports jackets and flannels would groan. Some held handkerchiefs to their noses to show their superiority to the islandmen. They didn't work in "the Yard". They worked in an office which was unfortunately in a shipyard.

Jim wandered up to Deep Water Wharf one lunchtime. There were the usual Lascar seamen, sitting in a row, feet over the edge of the jetty, fishing in the shadow of an aircraft carrier that was being completed for the Royal Navy. A giant floating crane was hoisting an engine-room propeller shaft on to its flight deck, and the men on the carrier, steadying its dead weight of hundreds of tons for its final descent, were complaining about it being their dinner hour. Below the pitch and toss school had started.

Gathered in a circle were about two hundred men watching keenly as a man with two pennies on a time board tossed the coins into the air. All heads were raised at the ascending coins, all heads lowered when the coins descended and fell on to the rough planks of the jetty. Somebody would shout:

"Heads!" or "Harps!"

There was then a scramble of the winners to pick up their pound notes or half-crowns. A couple of hundred feet up in the gantries lookouts scanned the roads for any sign of the Bulkies.

Running the pitch and toss school were the two Broderick brothers, supposedly the toughest men in the shipyard. They were rumoured to be ferocious street fighters. Such fighters, being proud of their prowess, don't use weapons. Only the boot and the fist, the knee, the head butt, the grabbing of the male breast – said to be the most sensitive place after the balls – slamming of the bridge of the nose, two fingers poked in the eyes, the grabbing of hair – if any. A man might fall and lie there expecting mercy, but he was quickly pulled up off the ground by the lapels and punched again. Even when unconscious, he still received a final kick.

Jim watched the game progress, the heads rising and falling, the scuffle for the pay-out, the wasted, pale figures who walked away having blown their wages with nothing left to bring home to their wives, the triumphant walking away with about three weeks' wages of others, the desperate who tried to snatch the winnings from the ground and who were tripped up and kicked by a dozen boots, and the one who argued and became hysterical at losing but in not offering any violence was allowed to walk away through the parting crowd.

The Broderick brothers were normally affable. They didn't swagger around like toughs but were quiet and sober at all times and had their share of jokes to tell. Neither of them was a giant of a man. They looked average; that is, they were of average height and weight, but they did have hard, trim bodies. There was no need to fear them on the ordinary level of work relationships. They didn't try to dominate their workmates when working at their trades as plumber and joiner. They could take a punch in a jokey sort of boxing match when fooling around and not retaliate or complain out of anger.

A man might want to get a reputation as a womaniser by spreading stories about himself concerning the number of trysts he was supposed to have had. In due course, one or two women might test him, and if he was up to their expectations, they would spread the word. If he wasn't up to their expectations, they would still spread the word, and he'd be worse off than before. Similarly with violence, a man might lie about being charged in the past by the police with grievous bodily harm in order to keep other men cautious of him. The only difference with building a sexual reputation was that he would rarely be tested. Thus he would become an enigma.

The Broderick brothers did top up their reputations by telling of past battles during their army careers abroad. No one ever witnessed their fights on home ground, though they heard their threats and saw their ability to eyeball someone until he stood down. They abhorred swearing. But if sworn at in a joke, they would simply laugh and appeal to the person to find a better word or words. Yet neither were they religious. They never tried to extend their activities outside the shipyard. The pitch and toss school was their only vested interest. They were continuing a shipyard tradition.

At sixteen, in 1948, Jim left the time offices to serve his apprenticeship in the joiners' shop – a huge hangar where Stirling bombers had been built during the war. About a thousand joiners and their apprentices, wood machinists and their apprentices, two woodcarvers and their apprentices, painters and their apprentices, storemen, labourers and sweeper-uppers filled the hangar, as well as chargehands, foremen, a head foreman and a manager.

It was collar and tie, clean shirt and a white carpenter's apron for the joiners and the apprentices. They did not call themselves carpenters – as they usually do in England – but joiners, who did a variety of work from cabinet making to the making of panelled doors and door frames for the interiors of ships, to heavy teak doors and teak frames for the exteriors, kitchen furniture in beechwood, veneering in bird's-eye maple, spiralling mahogany handrails, complicated twisting stairways and a thousand other things that had to be crafted for passenger liners, cargo ships, frozen-meat ships running from Argentina, whalers and naval ships. The many timbers they worked in were yellow pine, mahogany, Spanish mahogany – usually known as bastard mahogany as the grain had to be planed from both directions – spruce, greenheart, maple, pitch pine, oak, birch, beech, teak etc. One old joiner could tell his timber by tasting the end-grain with his tongue. But it was a dying art, and a dozen timbers had already disappeared.

The joiners' shop was divided into units of twenty benches presided over by a bowler-hatted, brown-dust-coated chargehand. He had an all-glass office which overlooked his section. At the benches worked either two joiners or a joiner and an apprentice.

The chargehand patrolled continually between the benches. There was one forty-minute lunch break with no tea breaks, mornings or afternoons, though a few did manage to have naked makeshift heating elements hidden up inside the bench which they connected to the leads for the electrical sanders. The elements were dipped into the tin can to heat the water. Steam was sometimes seen coming from under the bench, but the chargehand chose to ignore this if the joiner had just been demobbed from the recent world war or had served in the first one.

Also up inside the bench was usually a shelf on which was hidden the "homer" – a jewellery box in progress, some wooden toys, a birchwood breadboard or other small household things. These were worked on when the chargehand went for his break, mornings and afternoons. Warnings were give if a foreman appeared to be coming in the direction of that particular unit. The joiners' shop was open-plan and so large that to stand at one end and look towards the other end was to see only blurred unrecognisable faces. When a figure came into focus wearing a bowler hat and suit, the warning was given by throwing a small block of wood. When the manager came around, he also wore a bowler hat, but with a more expensive suit.

Various small urinals were placed around the shop, but if anything more was involved, then the personnel had to leave the shop and go to two fifty-foot-high sliding steel doors and exit through the wicket gate to the yard and the lavatories. At the entrance to the lavatories was an all-glass office with an in-and-out turnstile. The clerk took your time board, noted its number, wrote it in his ledger, put down the time you entered and, on leaving, the time you left. Seven minutes was allowed for each visit, morning and afternoon. If you ran over this time, the clerk ticked you off. If you ran over the time seriously, like say by fifteen minutes, then you were reported to your chargehand, interviewed by the foreman, passed to the head foreman and threatened with dismissal by the manager. If an apprentice, you went through the same procedure but were threatened with being "sent home" for a month without pay. Arriving home with that news usually meant all hell broke loose. At the side of this lavatory block was a door for the chargehands, the key of which was collected from the lavatory clerk. They had whatever time they wanted, for they didn't have boards; nor did they have to sign in or out at the time offices. The foreman and the head foreman shared another small building and were allowed to carry their own keys. The manager had his own personal lavatory and an attendant who opened the door for him.

There were two large lavatory blocks at the back of the joiners' shop. One had a clerk called George, a thin, sad-looking little man, who read the horse- and dog-racing papers most of the day. He was liberal in overlooking the time spent in his lavatory. Though if you overdid it, you were given a long steady stare as you picked up your board. About five hundred yards along was the second lavatory run by "Fat Fred", a severe disciplinarian. He didn't have much custom, and his lavatory was only visited when George's was full to overflowing. Fat Fred had many of the more timid put through the foreman gauntlet. The aggressive usually threatened to wait for him after work and knock his head from his shoulders should they be reported. This worked even for some of the apprentices, usually the more hefty ones.

George's was not really a lavatory but a meeting place. It had seen, over the years, betting men, religious zealots, philosophers of various schools of thought, would-be novelist and poets, those learning French, Spanish, German, Icelandic, communist plotters, thieves, hard men, moneylenders, musicians, amateur entertainers such as comedians, pioneer karaoke singers, looka-likes of a few Hollywood film stars, young boxers on the way up, older boxers on the way down, a couple of professional ex-world boxing champions, amateur wrestlers, a professional wrestler who had once fought the great Mike Demetrius, weightlifters, two ex-professional footballers with knee trouble, a Jewish deaf-mute joiner who taught the police ju-jitsu in his spare time, ex-servicemen of the First World War, ex-service-men of the Second World War, those who had been prisoners of the Turks, the Germans, the Japanese, lickspittles – better known as bumboys in the local parlance – vendors of cigarettes bought from Goan saloon waiters of passenger ships in for repair, a Finn, a native American who had been stationed in Northern Ireland with the US forces and returned after the war, a white American similarly, Scots, Welsh, English, an apprentice joiner whose mother was an Indian born in India, rural men divided into the various counties. . . and those who had no distinguishing features. But most had to be somebody. A few would become famous, a few notorious.

Behind the lavatories was a vast area where massive logs of hardwoods and softwoods lay seasoning. Beyond that in the sea channels were chained logs floated for extra-special seasoning.

This area, known simply as "the Logs", was also where apprentices went when challenged to a fight.

Not far from the Logs were the huge sheds where the logs were cut up by massive, frightening circular saws and bandsaws, and the shop where the saw doctors sharpened the massive saw blades until they flashed an aggressive smile.

Into all this came Jim, without a formal welcome of handshake or nod. He was taken to share a bench with a boy of about seventy-five. Old Jacob had a full head of hair that was still a startling black. He was working on a pair of very intricate mahogany handrails for a stairway in first class accommodation on the *Reina del Pacifico*. The old man had restarted work during the war when the call went out for more skilled workers. The wartime workforce rose to 70,000. He had worked on the wooden dummy aircraft carrier that had been built as a decoy. Somehow he had been deliberately overlooked when the war ended because of his great skill as a woodworker. He once worked on the *Titanic*. He didn't say so himself, but an old painter remembered him working on board that ship.

Jacob grunted at Jim and went on cleaning the joints of the handrails. The handrails, clamped and padded in the vice, rose in the air like some demented pythons that had visited a taxidermist. His toolbox was of a size that only two men could lift. He had a vast collection of wooden hand-moulding planes of the nineteeth century, a great number of wood chisels, mallets, drills, hammers of every size, spokeshaves, saws, six sizes of granny's tooth, braces, bits, gouges of all sizes, woodcarving tools. On his bench gleamed the razor-sharp cutting edges of chisels and a heavy piece of dowel which he used to rap the knuckles of any apprentice who dared to touch any of them. He scanned Jim briefly and went on carefully working while Jim stood watching him and wondering when he would be invited to work on the handrails. But Jim was living in a fool's paradise. Such work was as sacred as if it were to be an offering to the gods. Old Jacob called harshly for glue, and when Jim didn't immediately react – as no one had explained anything to him so far – he said, "Glue. . . there, boy, glue. . . glue. . . are ye deaf? Glue, glue!"

An apprentice at a nearby bench swiftly went to the electric boiler – bolted to a concrete pillar – and quickly stirred one of the iron pots, broke the skin and handed it to Jim. The glue had a sickening smell of boiled bones. Jim put the pot on the bench. Jacob looked into it and shook his head and opened his mouth in a dry soundless snarl that showed three yellow teeth and about five black teeth. The glue was not of the right consistency and needed a little more water. The helpful apprentice poured in some water and put it back in the boiler to heat.

Jacob understood that the glue needed time to cook again, but he had no patience with mere boys. He told Jim to sweep up the shavings and sawdust around the bench, and on no account to knock the brush head into the handrails.

Thus there was a week of glue boiling and sweeping, cleaning the bench off and watching as the old boy slowly and carefully worked the mahogany with his nineteeth century tools.

The chargehand was called Andy, but everyone above his rank was addressed as "Mr". He had been a horse-handler pulling artillery during the First World War and bore the purple imprint of a horse's hoof on his face. His nose lay sideways. His smashed cheekbones had healed wildly. His mouth was now diagonal. He spoke mostly through his nose as his mouth had limited movement. Eating his sandwich meant breaking off pieces with his fingers and pushing them into his mouth, rolling them around with his tongue until, saliva soaked, they dribbled down his throat.

He had spent the last thirty years in pain, but for all his sufferings he remained tolerant of humanity. To have survived the terrible battle at Mons was a miracle he never forgot. He realised that the boy was going to get nowhere with old Jacob, so he put him with one of the Broderick brothers called Ned.

Knowing that Ned ran the pitch and toss school with his brother lent an air of excitement to the transfer. Ned set him to work immediately on the carcass of a chest of drawers, to clean the dovetails that had come from the machinist.

In the centre of the shop was an area where all the woodworking machinery was: circular saws, bandsaws, the pneumatic dovetail machine, the wood-turning bench, the router machine, the mortice machine with its chain teeth and the tenon machine with its horizontal whirling blades. The wood-machinists, in leather aprons and covered in wood-chippings and sawdust, worked carefully, as loss of concentration even for a second could mean a lost finger or even a lost hand in the whirling blades.

Ned said the first thing an apprentice did was to make a tool-box from yellow pine. He went to the wood pile at the end of the unit and carefully picked out a suitable length, then took Jim to the sawyer, give him the measurements and asked him to put it through the circular saw. The sawyer was a powerfully built man of average height. He had wrestled the great Mike Demetrius in London and won. In a return fight in Athens he had lost. He had three fingers missing on one hand and two missing on the other hand through working the saw. His crab-like left hand guided the timber through the saw while his right hand pushed. Jim was apprehensive that the man might lose another finger on his account. The yellow pine was then taken to the pneumatic dovetail machine, where the operator stopped working on drawers to put it in the hissing machine. It was taken back to the bench, glued and assembled, quarter-inch ply-wood being used to give it sides. It was then sawed almost in half length-wise to form a lid, hinged and brought to the paint section in a corner of the shop.

The chargehand painter had lost a leg in France during the First World War and now had a heavy metal one issued by a military hospital in 1918. He got a painter to paint the box black and then went limping across the shop, the metal leg seemingly to lead the way.

Old Jacob's son died at the age of fifty. He turned up as usual for work. First Andy tried to make him go home again and, getting no response, called on the manager. The manager, with his head foreman, talked to Jacob and assured him that while he was gone no one else would take over his work on the mahogany handrails. Jacob tried to negotiate maybe taking half a day off and returning at lunchtime, but he was persuaded to take off the whole day to make the funeral arrangements. On the day of the funeral he turned up for work again, and the management again had to persuade him to take the day off.

While he was gone, Andy noticed something about the handrails that disturbed him. There was something wrong, though they looked like the perfect example of fine craftsmanship. The joints were so good they were hard to see – it was as if the timbers had grown into one another. He examined the plans on Jacob's bench thoroughly, measuring and remeasuring the handrails with his three-foot rule, looked at the plans again, went to his office and looked at the master plans for the first-class saloon, noted the staircase and its sweep as it turned left and then right into the saloon. Then he saw the mistake – a left turn was right and the right turn was left. And the same with the other one. It was the most terrible blunder. He couldn't have them adjusted because the joints would be gaping, and if the joints were recut, the handrails would be at least three to four inches short. Also, the handrails were due to be delivered to the French-polishing shop in a few days' time, and a few days after that they had to be transferred to the ship for fitting. The foreman wouldn't be able to deal with the problem and would have to see the head foreman who would, in turn, have to see the manager of the joiners' shop for a final decision. The horse-shoe imprint on his face turned a more vivid purple as his face turned white. He also began to sweat. He would be ticked off for not supervising the old boy enough. But old Jacob was beyond supervision. To even stand and watch the old fellow working for five minutes would be a humiliation for him.

The manager said old Jacob would have to be dismissed. He would like to retire him, but the rules were that he had to sack him because the ship's manager would want to know why the handrails hadn't been delivered on time, and he would have to explain the full circumstances. There was also the matter of the marine architect reporting the handrails as missing to the ship's owners. They could all be in trouble then if they tried to cover up for the old boy. Andy was given the job of sacking old Jacob.

Jacob arrived for work. He was standing outside the time office at seven to draw his board instead of his usual time of ten to eight. The timekeepers hadn't even arrived yet. When he did draw his board, he entered the empty shop with its hanging lights glaring a bluey-yellow. The overhead trunking was vibrating as it pumped out the tepid air that was supposed to heat the shop in winter. A few pigeons flapped in the steel girders of the roof, sending down glittering streams of wood dust as they passed the lights. Jacob waved his arms to frighten them away from his area in case of any of their droppings landing on his handrails. The lime could burn into the mahogany very quickly and produce black spots. He sat there a while watching two mice chase each other under a bench. The dark silhouettes of trams passed the wired windows. He edged himself off the low stool as his knees were beginning to play up again and turned to the bench. Someone had moved the plans! An apprentice? Maybe another craftsman? Or even Andy! He screwed up his eyes and saw the pencil marks. He looked at the handrail and saw that the pencil marks followed the curves and sweeps of the handrails.

Someone had altered the plans to suit his interpretation of how the handrails should be constructed. Or maybe someone was showing up his mistakes! He looked around the shop slowly and in the distance saw the figures coming through the turnstiles of the time offices. He quickly put on his glasses and looked at the plans. The pencil lines had been initialled by the manager. He put away his glasses very quickly as the first men arrived at their benches. The ten to eight klaxon blew. The newly arrived sat down on the stools they used for sawing timber on and began greeting one another, reading morning papers or complaining about how cold it was in the shop.

The eight o'clock klaxon blew, and the shop was now full except for the few unfortunates who had the pigeon-holes of the time offices closed in their faces and the turnstiles locked. It was a day's pay lost. The woodworking machines began one by one. The high-pitched scream of the planer began like some dive-bomber and drowned out the circular saws, the routers, the spindles, the bandsaws, the tenon machines and the morticing machines. Mallets beat on timber, handsaws sang in a chorus. Andy put on his bowler hat and brown dust coat and peered through the glass to make sure that everyone was on his feet in his section. He also looked towards Jacob's bench and knew that all his experiences on the Somme weren't going to help him with this one. He had known Jacob ever since he had been demobilised from that war and had been visited by him at the military hospital on his return to Northern Ireland from that slaughter. He looked again. Jacob was sitting down on his stool. He had taken out his pipe and was rubbing a plug of Warhorse tobacco in the two hollows of his hands. Now he was lighting up in great clouds of smoke, sucking on the pipe at even intervals while tapping down on the lighted tobacco with a well-scarred thumb. Smoking was not allowed in the shop. Doing it meant instant dismissal. Andy thought a moment while watching Jacob. The joiners and their apprentices watched him from behind the carcasses of furniture or opened a door in the frame they had just hinged or peeped at him through the rails of birch plate racks, still working but slower now. Once or twice they glanced towards the glass office to watch Andy's reaction. The strong tobacco wafted over the benches, and one or two young apprentices coughed. Someone with an axe he was using on a baulk of teak raised it, whooped and did a sort of war dance. The native American raised his axe and whooped back. They all knew the old man was up to something but didn't know quite what it was. Andy knew and decided to act.

He approached Jacob's bench in a slow march, put his hand on the shoulder of his old friend and said, "No smoking is allowed in this shop. You should know the rules by now. The penalty is instant dismissal. Sorry, but I have to let you go. Pick your tools up within a week."

Jacob rose without a word, tapped the ash out of his pipe, put on his jacket and walked slowly away. Soon, all that could be seen of him was his clouding figure receding into the vastness of the joiners' shop.

Jacob got home and began washing the dye out of his hair.

He also put his glasses on.

Ned told Jim many stories about his war experiences in Crete. About the ill-planned drop by German parachutists. How they had used every weapon, including anti-aircraft batteries, to kill them before they even reached the ground. How he was wounded in the foot in Greece and was picked up by German stretcher bearers. One of the "Germans" spoke English in a Southern Irish accent. He asked the "German" how he got the accent. The "German" said he was from Mullingar and had joined the German army in the Channel Islands. He had been a fisherman on a trawler out of Cork, but it had gone aground on Jersey. Ned told him that only for being on the stretcher he would get up and give him a kick in the balls. The "German" dropped his end of the stretcher and said, "You fight for the English. I fight for the Germans. Maybe we're both eejits. Now fuckin' walk!"

The normally calm Ned went into a tantrum and said one day he would go to Mullingar and – if the fucker was still alive – kick him to the deck.

One evening when Jim was going back home in the bus, he noticed the Gibraltarian girl was not sitting in her usual seat. Passing the Nissen huts he noticed a lot of activity. There were lorries, vans and buses being loaded with suitcases and trunks, men, women and children. They were on their back to the Rock. He cursed himself for being so timid. For a long time she had caught this same bus and was usually alone. That had been his only chance, for when she got off at the camp she was usually chaperoned by a member of her family. He was caught in the agony of being in love at a distance. He even found out her surname by slipping into the camp one Sunday morning and reading a noticeboard where her name and photograph were pinned for some beauty queen event, even her hut number. But there were all sorts of problems on his mind – he still didn't have the money even to take them to a cinema.

Then he thought he could have asked her out for a walk. He

cursed his lack of confidence in the end. Blamed his father and his mother for still beating him, and he now an apprentice.

Finally a few months later he wrote to her in care of the General Post Office of Gibraltar and told her of his shyness and reminded her that he once tugged her hair at the camp film show while she was sitting with her parents. He got a reply four weeks later which turned out to be a rejection for the stamp was put upsidedown on the envelope. She said his letter had been opened by her mother and that she had got into trouble and to please not to write again for he would never get an answer. They were the same age at sixteen, but she seemed to be a woman while he still felt like a boy. He blamed himself again and blamed his parents. He cursed himself again and he cursed them.

At work he made mistakes and didn't care. Ned took responsibility for the mistakes, but Andy wouldn't allow him to and isolated Jim at a bench by himself and gave him no work of any kind to do for a month. He stood there at the bench thinking of the girl and growing more angry all the time. He went to the lavatories and stayed as long as he could, arguing with his friend, a religious zealot, about the existence of God. His friend didn't reject him even when he said the most diabolical things about God and all religions. On going back to his bench Andy looked at his watch and threatened to report him to the foreman. After that, whenever he left his bench, Andy quite deliberately looked at his watch to time him. Jim could then only stay seven minutes while everyone else was allowed twice that. He didn't have the time to go round all the groups at George's and listen into the discussions on politics and women, nor join in laughing at the latest jokes about the Englishman, the Irishman and the Scotsman, nor listen to the hard men discuss last Saturday's fight outside Caproni's Ballroom down in Bangor. How the hell some of these apprentices got the money for drinking was beyond him. They mustn't give any wages into the house, whereas he had to give everything in and only got back his bus fare for the week, plus about four shillings pocket money. He wanted to run away again.

He went to the Royal Navy Recruitment office in Donegall Street one Saturday morning to join, but they said they couldn't take indentured apprentices without the written consent of their fathers. He went to the offices of a shipping company and got a form for a job as a saloon boy. He filled it in, forged his father's signature, posted it off and was called in for an interview a week later. He had a medical, was accepted and went home to await a sailing date. He never got that letter, nor the next one asking him to reply urgently. His father had intercepted the letters. He found them behind the bookcase months later. He was to join the *Reina del Pacifico* sailing out of Belfast for Buenos Aires in her new peacetime role as a passenger liner. They had sailed, both girl and ship. His father laughed, his mother laughed, his sisters jeered. They sang mockingly:

"I joined the navy to see the world
But what did I see?
I saw the sea
I saw the Pacific and the Atlantic. . ."

In the black pitch night he went into the garden and looked up in the sky that was brilliant with a million stars. He couldn't find one that would guide him anywhere.

Old Jacob died three weeks into retirement. He never did collect his vast collection of tools. His widow sent word for them to be put up for auction. That was the tradition. An old woodworker by the name of Denis passed the word around the joiners' shop. The tools were displayed over several benches and on the wooden-block floor of the shop. At lunchtime he climbed arthritically on to a bench and opened the auction. His apprentice handed up each tool, and he described each one – how much was left of the iron of a wooden try plane or jack plane, the wonderful steel of the chisels. Mostly the apprentices bid, as they were expected to build up their tool kits over the five years of their apprenticeship. They got them for knock-down prices as a joiner wouldn't bid against an apprentice.

Finally all that was left were the nineteenth century hardwood tools of moulding planes, routing planes, hardwood cramps of every dimension and other tools that only the older generation had any knowledge of. Jacob's huge toolbox went unsold, and his rejected tools were put into it. His widow gratefully received the money but didn't want the box or its remaining tools. The box lay in the joiners' shop for months, and when the widow died it was quietly taken to the heating furnace, broken up and, with its tools, cast into the greedy flames.

After two years in the joiners' shop, Jim was transferred to work on the ships for two years. His last year of apprenticeship would be spent back in the joiners' shop. He was sent to a new oil tanker that had just come off the slips. It was just raw steel and had its bulkheads newly red-leaded. There was not yet a scrap of timber put in by the joiners. The caulkers and riveters vibrated the steel with their pneumatic tools while hooded arc-welders, wearing asbestos armlets and rawhide jackets, sent out huge flashes of intense blue light as they looked through the smoked glass of their face protectors. He was warned not to look at the intense light as it could cause a "flash" in the eye equivalent to having sand there. He was also warned not to piss in the corners of the ship as some welders had bolted a live cable there to prevent that. "Make your water over the side of the ship."

The temporary lights in their protecting cages, strung on the cables, ran through the ship and cast a pinkish light as they reflected on the red-leaded steel bulkheads. Outside was the sound of shipwrights' adzes as they chopped at teak planking to be laid on the steel exterior decks. Behind them, as they laid the formed planks, a shipwright hammered oakum into the joints with a copper-headed hammer, while behind him another poured boiling pitch on to the oakum. When it dried, the surplus pitch was removed with scrapers, and, finally, the deck would be run over with a roaring planing machine.

Down on the jetty the pitch-boiler rattled and sent up great clouds of smoke from its wood fire and acrid smoke from the boiling pitch. A man broke up, with a sledgehammer, great cakes of hard pitch and fed it to the boiler, while another turned the tap and filled an iron bucket with the flowing blackness and hoisted it aboard with pulley and tackle. There were two men engaged in filling the iron buckets. The right-hand man had developed a right arm with a bulging bicep and powerful forearm muscles, while the left-hand man had this on his left side. Also, the leg on that side was powerfully developed. When they walked they seemed to have to repeatedly change direction in order not to go round in circles.

Now the platers were putting into place an inch-thick steel plate aft on top of the donkey-boiler room. The jetty crane was hoisting it on board on steel cables, and it was being lowered carefully. A gang of platers' helpers attached ropes to it and were hauling it into position as the craneman peered down at them from a hundred feet up. The helpers began to sing what was supposedly the song of the slaves who once hauled the barges along towpaths of the Volga: "Oh Oh Oh!. . . Oh Oh Oh!. . . Oh Oh. . . Oh Oh Oh Oh. . . Oh Oh! . . . Oh Oh! . ."

One plater who had been in the Royal Navy shouted to another, "Know what this plate's for? I'll give you two guesses."

Getting no reply he said, "Foundation for an anti-aircraft gun. There might be another war."

The sheet-metal workers were busy installing the air-conditioning trunking on the iron lugs of the deck head. Behind them came the asbestos workers putting netting-wire around the trunking. That finished, they mixed the rough porridge-like flakes of asbestos with water in steel basins and began plastering it on to the wire-netting, at first with their hands and then with wooden trowels. That particular area they worked in looked as if it had had a snowstorm. Flakes of white asbestos danced in the pinkish glow of the temporary lights like a blizzard under street lamps. The faces of the asbestos workers looked as if they had been hit by a bag of flour; it was in their hair, on their eyelashes and stuck to the hairs of their forearms. There was much coughing and spitting.

The joiner marker-out, after sighting his plumb bob, marked the steel deck and deckhead by punching an indented dot into the steel with a hammer and centrepoint. Along came the welder and welded the lugs to the markings, followed by a red-leader who dabbed them. The sheets of one-inch marine plywood were craned aboard; the labourers carried them from the well deck to below decks; the joiners and their apprentices drilled the sheets top and bottom and bolted them to the lugs; door frames came and were fixed; French-polished doors were hinged. The cabins of the crew's quarters were being formed, each with a porthole. All of this took many months.

Discipline aboard ship was not as strict as in the shops. No one was tied to a fixed position. Tea cans could be boiled, but unofficially, on the riveters' fire for a morning and afternoon tea break. The fire was so fierce that the can had to be held at arm's length on the end of a piece of steel rod. The pneumatic-driven coke fire threw up minute pieces of coke that sometimes went into the can and turned the tea grey. Jim learnt to prevent that by floating a sliver of wood on the water. How this worked to repel the coke no one could explain, but it worked. Others plugged in the usual naked electrical element and dipped it in the can for a few minutes, but the coke-fire tea tasted best of all.

Once, when he was on deck one lunch hour, he and a number of apprentices looked over the side of the ship and saw a huge school of Portuguese man-of-wars. The apprentices seized rivets and bombarded them, cutting many of them to pieces. They used up all the riveters' rivets and looked around the decks and began throwing planks of teak at the jellyfish. Then the planks ran out, and they began using the coke for the riveters' fires, but these lightweight missiles had no effect. They went below decks and gathered up all the joiners' bolts they could find and went up again to continue the bombardment. The sea now had an armada of teak planks floating around the ship. The starting klaxon blew, and they ran back to their jobs, fearful of the riveters and the shipwrights. Jim threw one last defiant block at a seagull. An old joiner coming up the gangway spotted him. Jim put on an aggressive front as the elderly man approached him.

"That seagull could be an old joiner back from the dead," he said softly and give a slight smile.

Jim felt ashamed and almost cried out, "I wish you was my father!"

He didn't throw anything else ever again at the seagulls, nor even at the man-of-wars. The other apprentices continued throwing the expensive resources of the earth into the sea. One had devised a trick of putting a lighted cigarette butt into a piece of bread. The seagulls usually dived for thrown bread and caught it in their beaks. One got the lighted-cigarette sandwich and flew off swallowing it. Fifty yards further on it dived straight into the water and was carried away by the tide, its wings flailing in agony. Jim shouted at the plumber's apprentice, who invited him down to the jetty for a fight. Jim got a bloody nose. He wondered how the old joiner would have handled the situation.

Still, it was a more liberal atmosphere on board ship. Though there were still the chargehands, they didn't wear bowler hats but caps and dungarees. His chargehand had a marker-out and keyman, who supposedly had the easier jobs, but who were called bumboys behind their backs either through envy or from their being suspected of giving information about the others to the chargehand. Smoking was not allowed, as in the shops, but most did smoke, holding the cigarette hidden in the palm of the hand as in the manner of the "old soldier". The head foreman of each trade, accompanied by his foreman, usually came on board once a week to inspect. They wore bowler hats and suits but were a more understanding version of the shop variety. If they caught someone smoking who was of their particular trade, they told the chargehand, who then told the smoker to be more careful in future and, as a way of penalising him, took him off door frames and put him to the heavier work of erecting the plywood bulk-heads.

The man to watch out for was the ship's manager. He wore a bowler hat and well-cut suit with highly polished shoes. He was known as a "hat". The only one with a bowler hat who was designated as a "hat". But he was never quick enough, for he was always spotted in the distance meandering along Musgrave Channel Road with his head draughtsman, who usually carried about a dozen rolled-up plans under his arm. The temporary lightman would go to the electrical breakers and turned off the entire lights of the ship twice in rapid succession as a warning that a "hat" was soon to be on board. Everyone was then on their best behaviour until he left.

Just before twelve thirty, the workers gathered on the well deck near the gangway, with their cans, to await the klaxon that summoned lunchtime, or the dinner hour as most knew it as. The ship's manager stood at the head of the gangway like a border collie to keep them at bay. This was his daily routine. The workers had to keep at least a fifty-yard gap between them and him. Anyone wandering over this invisble line was asked if he thought he was better than everyone else.

One day an asbestos worker by the name of Joey the Jap – who had been a prisoner of the Japanese – came forward in a terrible fit, crossed that invisible line, headed for the gangway, and said to the manager, "The Japs didn't stop me gettin' water and neither will you!" He then headed down the gangway to the boilers on the jetty.

The "hat" said nothing, seemed to swallow his humiliation, but took out his notebook and wrote something down. . . as three hundred workers watched him. Later that day, while he was on the jetty inspecting a lump of machinery for the ship's engine room, a heavy plank of teak was thrown over the tanker's side. It landed at his feet, denting the heavy timber jetty. He never looked up but went on inspecting the machinery.

About a week later, a joiner by the name of Clifford the Head Case stepped over the invisible line and was asked the usual question by the "hat". Trying to copy Joey the Jap, he mumbled something about Belgians not stopping him. . . he stopped suddenly unable to finish the sentence, tore at his wild mane of hair and swore at the manager. The manager – deciding to make a bigger fool out of him in front of an audience – took off his jacket and challenged him to a fight down on the jetty. Clifford, in declining the fight, nodded his head violently up and down like a horse. The drips that usually hung from both nostrils spread across his face. Three hundred men roared with laughter. The "hat" also laughed – maybe for the first time in his life. Clifford then retreated back over the invisible line, shadow boxing. The next day another baulk of timber landed at the manager's feet.

Clifford had once been in Purdysburn. When taunted, especially by the apprentices and some of the black trades, he would tell them he had a certificate saying he was sane. He then asked his tormentors if they had a certificate.

The work continued: the red-leaders taking their turn in coming out of the vast oil tanks for air every half-hour; the asbestos snowstorms; the mighty cranes swung and lowered, hoisted, swung; the blue-white flashes from the welders; the rat-a-tat of the riveters; the teeth-vibrating din of the caulkers; the almost rural sound of the shipwright's adze on teak; the buzz of the circular saws below decks; the singing, the bantering, the happy smiles on Friday payday; the loudspeaker voice of the born-again preacher patrolling the Musgrave Channel Road at lunchtime; the grim faces coming back from the pitch and toss school at Deep Water Wharf.

One morning Jim read in the paper that the body of a man had been found in the waters off Twin Islands just north of Queen's Island. It was Gunner, the time clerk. He was dressed in a heavy khaki greatcoat. No suicide note was found. Everyone knew him. There was gloom over the shipyard that morning. No one could figure out why he had done it except to say he had a bad stomach. Somebody said that suicides by water always dressed in warm clothing against the freezing waters.

Next day Jim decided to toughen up, so he went, at lunchtime, to join a group of all-weather swimmers at Deep Water Wharf. It was winter and sleeting. He took off his clothes to his underpants and dived into the freezing waters to join the other swimmers. The cold was numbing for a while, but he swam vigorously and then began to enjoy it.

Jim came out of the water and put his clothes on over his wet body as the other swimmers did. Walking back to the tanker, his body glowed with warmth.

One day a few weeks later, when the swimmers were having their usual lunchhour dip, there was a shout from the flight deck of the aircraft carrier and frantic arm movements for the swimmers to keep clear. Up on the deck stood a man in his underpants limbering up: jumping-on-the-spot, whirling his arms around his head and doing knee-bends. He did this for maybe five minutes. A crowd gathered to watch, and a number of them began to chant to egg him on but were quickly silenced by the rest of the men. Tension began to build up in the now-silent crowd – some took off their caps to beat the dust out of them.

One man took off his cap and began wringing imaginary water out of it. The diver moved closer until his feet half-curled over the edge of the deck. Down below was a hundred foot drop to the grey waters on which floated quickly dissolving sleet. All that could be heard was a voice from the nearby pitch and toss school shouting, "Heads!" or "Harps!"

The diver put his hands above his head, palm to palm, bent his knees slightly and pushed himself off into the void. He flew through the air in a perfect arc to hit the wharf waters with scarcely a splash.

He was down in the depths, with the eels, for what seemed a long time. When he surfaced there was no applause. They didn't even laugh when he stepped ashore bollick naked, having lost his underpants in the depths. The pitch and toss school were still not diverted but continued as usual. The crowd drifted away still silent, and a few shook their heads as if they couldn't credit what they had seen. Jim had respect for the diver – for risking his life, taking a chance and winning.

There followed then a serious accident in the engine room of the tanker. A fitter was crushed when the propeller shaft slipped from its blocks while he was working under it. A crane couldn't be used as the accident happened right inside a tunnel where there was barely standing-up room. Jacks had to be fetched from the whaler further up Musgrave Channel Road. The first aid man was summoned from his post in the Thompson Works, but there was nothing he could do but hold the man's trembling hand. He wasn't allowed the use of morphine as he was only a medical auxiliary. The shipyard ambulance had to be sent to the Royal Victoria Hospital at the top of the Donegall Road–Falls Road junction to fetch a doctor.

The jacks from the whaler weren't heavy enough to take the weight of the huge brass propeller shaft. They shattered. There was scarcely any room in the tunnel to get a team in to try and lever the propeller shaft up – it only needed a few inches. In the end, the shaft was cut in half by acetylene burners to make it lighter. The doctor arrived back in the ambulance to administer the morphine, but the man was now unconscious. He was carried from the tunnel on a stretcher to the engine room proper where the crane had lowered a huge steel bucket. The stretcher was laid across the top of the bucket, and two of his workmates got into the bucket to hold the stretcher. The crane lifted the bucket to a great height to clear the funnel and wireless mast of the ship and lowered it to the jetty. The ambulance moved off at speed with its bells ringing, but it didn't go far before slowing down to a normal pace. The man had died.

At knocking-off time, the workers raced for their bicycles in the bicycle racks. The watchman unlocked the long cable that was usually put through the frames to keep them secure. They cycled off, mingling with two old Ford V8's, motor-cycles, motor-cycles with sidecars, converted bicycles with small engines attached to the front wheel and the Riley car of the ship's manager. Feet tramped by the thousands as they made their way to the trams. The cranes stopped quivering, and all was quiet except for the sound of seagulls and the crackling of the watchman's coke brazier.

Left in the bicycle rack was one lone bicycle belonging to the dead fitter.

The weeks rolled on, and there were two more deaths. A huge packing case loaded with engine parts fell from a crane and crushed a labourer to a rat flattened boneless by a car. Then a red-leader died the same day in the tanks from a heart attack.

The ship's furniture was brought from the joiners' shop, scribed to the deck and bulkheads and fixed to keep it from moving.

The black trades left the tanker, their work done. The finishing trades then came aboard: the painters with their paint pots, brushes, large filling knives, scrapers and stools; more joiners with their stools; electricians; a carpet layer for the senior officers' quarters and the captain's cabin; four Italians to lay the terrazzo floor for the captain's bathroom. The red-leaders were now standing on rigging over the side of the ship painting it cream, while the painters on board painted the exterior white. Below decks two painting squads were applying a thick filler to the raw wood of the plywood bulkheads with their wide knives. A red-leader was up the wireless mast in a bosun's chair painting while two more, also in bosun's chairs, painted the funnel black with a broad blue band around it.

Stools were an essential thing to have for cutting timber on or standing on to reach the deckhead. Sometimes one disappeared, and a joiner or a painter would scour the ship looking for it. The man in question would be enraged as he went on deck, went below deck, into the tanks, up again, along the alleyways, even down into the engine room. This was the stool he had made ten years ago. This was the stool he sat on at lunchtime and ate his "piece" and drank his tea on. This was the stool which he carried to the store's hold where a group played rummy during lunchtime or to the captain's quarters where they played chess or checkers. Then he might spot it being used by a young painter or electrician. He had to hide his rage, for there could be a stand-up fight on the jetty. Usually something humorous was thought up like, "Two men will meet before two mountains can. Oul han', that's my stool."

He usually got his stool back and walked away talking to the stool. "You run away next time and I'll call the polis."

Now the tanker was gleaming. The ship was also producing its own electrical power now from its dynamos. The deep-throated siren was tried out a number of times. The tanker's steam derricks were even beginning to lift their own supplies on board. Tons of pig-iron was brought for ballast and shifted around in the bowels of the ship until it achieved the right stability. The ship was tied with extra hawsers and basin trials begun. The propellers thrashed the water to white and everything seemed all right. The lifeboats were brought aboard and hung in their derricks and lowered to the water for testing.

Three tugs appeared one morning and pulled and nudged the ship into the middle of the Musgrave Channel. She was then towed by way of Twin Islands to the Thompson Dry Dock. The tugs had extra-large propellers. Their powerful engines roared, and black smoke belched as they pulled the tanker at the end of ropes thicker than a man's arm.

One tug nudged the ship gently to the entrance of the dry dock and then left to rejoin its companions. The ship floated in very slowly, aided by a squad of dock labourers pulling it on ropes. The huge gate swung closed and the water pumped out. Heavy baulks of timber were jammed in on either side to keep the ship on an even keel as she sank with the lowering of the water to her bed.

While Jim was wandering around the dry dock, he noticed a man with a shotgun. He fired both barrels at a flock of pigeons and brought most of them down dead. The ones still fluttering injured on the stone quay he grabbed and wrung their necks and threw them into the already full wheelbarrow. He then wheeled the barrow to the furnace of the dry dock pumping station and burned them.

The tanker had its bottom scraped of barnacles and painted by the red-leaders. The plimsoll line markings were done by a signwriter, who also painted on the ship's name and its port of registration. The tugs returned and took her back to her berth.

The finishing trades were being thinned out as the ship neared completion. One day when Jim returned from lunch, he discovered his toolbox had been broken open and a number of tools stolen. He told the chargehand, who said he could do nothing about it but advised him to be patient. Jim asked why, but the chargehand said nothing. He had to borrow tools from some of the joiners in his squad. A day later he returned from lunch and found a pawn ticket on his toolbox. The ticket listed his stolen tools. When he got two pounds together, he recovered them.

All trades were off the tanker now except for the few who would accompany her on her voyage to the measured mile off the coast of Scotland for shakedown trials. The crew came on board.

The ship was run at maximum speed, and two joiners still on board went round looking for dropped doors which they had to take off and plane. Electricians looked for electrical malfunctions, and fitters for problems in the engine room. The ship then returned to her berth, and the last of the workers went ashore.

At last the ship was ready to sail for the Persian Gulf. The crew stood on deck, the officers in uniforms; the master, splendid in his gold braid, stood on the bridge. The ship's carpenter wore a white boiler suit. The ship's lights blazed as she was towed towards Belfast Lough. Her creators on the jetty gave her a last farewell wave and wished her luck.

Jim went on to work on a refrigerated-cargo ship, insulating the holds with cork. Then to a Castle line ship which was being refurbished for the South African run. Notices aboard warned the crew in Afrikaans and English about consorting with Bantu or Cape Coloured women.

His last year in the shop was uneventful. He watched the charge-hand go around some Fridays with a list in his hand. The join-ers blanched as he got near, fearing they were on the list for redundancy. The ex-footballers, the hard men, the would-be novelist, the unpublished poet, the Native American, the white American, the big hearty Finn, the deaf-mute Jew, Ned Broder-ick who had fought the Germans, those who had fought the Germans in an earlier war – all blanched as the man with the horseshoe imprint on his face advanced. As he glanced at them, they tried to tell by his face if they were on the list. Andy could have no facial expression due to his injuries. Jim momentarily despised them all and went on with his work.

A few months later he went to the main office and picked up the five-pound deposit and the other half of his indentures. It was maybe the greatest moment in his life so far. He was a fully fledged woodworker now. He was free to leave his job, free to leave the emotional claustrophobia of his family. He went home and gave the five pounds back to his parents. Even with handing half his wages into the house, he now had more money than he ever had before. His father had been made redundant, but said he would be back in work in a few month's time as two ships would be launched by then. He would have a rest in the meantime.

Jim worked on in the joiners' shop. Andy made the rounds with his list from time to time. One Friday he suddenly blanched with the rest. He was shocked at his reaction. Andy passed by him. He still had a job, but Friday mornings were becoming excruciating. He was still living at home after all his resolutions about freedom and independence. His father criticised him if he returned home with the smell of alcohol on his breath. His mother didn't seem to like his girlfriend. She didn't like any of his girlfriends. His girlfriend hinted about marriage, having children. He felt like Carson's dog now.

One bright sunny Saturday morning he went to the Carson farm to buy potatoes. The dog was usually chained to its kennel night and day. It rushed at him and the leash broke. It did its usual act of barking furiously and hopping on its hind legs around the boundary of its designated area. He didn't even need to step back. It was unaware that it was free.

He didn't quite know what freedom meant any more. He looked back to the age of sixteen and tried to remember what he meant by freedom then, but all he could remember was the longing to be free. All those former ambitions to join the Royal Navy or the Merchant Marine and even the army on one occasion – while working with Ned Broderick – didn't attract him any more.

One evening while reading the newspaper, he turned to the brief "Jobs Vacant" column. A well-known dance hall in the city "required the services of a Ballroom Supervisor". He immediately wrote off for an interview. He got a reply a few days later, giving

him a time and date. Next morning he gave his notice in to Andy.
Andy said that anyone leaving the Yard on their own accord was
sure to get on in life. This immediately bolstered his confidence.
He didn't have a job any more, only the promise of an interview.
He said goodbye to his workmates and didn't answer any of their
questions when they asked him what he might be doing in the
future. They said he would be back within a few months. A few
were even convinced that he had got the sack.

ELSIE

He had said in his letter of application that he was quite capable of dealing with unruly elements, that he could do all the latest dances – the quickstep, the foxtrot, the waltz, the tango to a lesser degree but he was practising – that he had taken part in dancing competitions and won two bronze medals and a silver, that he had been a pupil of Betty Staff, danced at John Dossor's, White's, the Plaza, had been to Caproni's in Bangor, dance halls in Lisburn and Armagh. The advert in the newspaper had invited young men, preferably not over the age of twenty-five, to apply for the vacant post of ballroom supervisor.

It gave the address as Chichester Street in central Belfast. He got back a letter giving him a day and a time for an interview. It was pointed out to him that they had had many applications for this post and that it would be advisable to appear about one and a half hours earlier than the time given for the interview. Each applicant would hear his name called out within the environs of the ballroom. He looked the word "environs" up in the dictionary. His interview was for 4 September 1953, at three o'clock.

He got there in his dark suit, his polished shoes and with his hair brilliantined. There was already a long queue outside the Plaza. It stretched halfway down the street. He walked casually past the queue to take in the opposition. Some of them were already in their forties, so he eliminated them. A number though young had flattened noses. He eliminated them as failed boxers – good ones had few marks on them. Some were too small, a few were too tall and gangly, and some were much too young.

There were a number of well-dressed ones like him, but they didn't wear their clothes properly. They would have to be eliminated.

He kept on walking, pretending he wasn't going to be part of that queue. When he did go to the back of the queue, he left a large gap and looked into the window of a car salesroom selling brand-new Volkswagen beetles for £431. He could almost smell the new rubber of the tyres through the window. The paintwork was crisp, and the interior upholstery was as smooth and clean as a washed newborn. He kept looking as a man in cavalry twill trousers and Donegal tweed jacket inspected one. The man was pulling white five-pound notes out of his pocket as casually as if they were scraps of paper. He even dropped one and didn't bother picking it up for about ten seconds. One of these five-pound notes was a week's wages for some people. The wage for the job he was applying for was £6 10s. 10d. He had been getting almost £7 as a motor mechanic, but it was a dirty job. He had soaked his hands in the bath for hours and cleaned his fingernails until they were almost red with blood. He had an idea the manager would glance at his hands.

The gap was filling up with those who had seen the queue and, without an authorised letter of interview, were joining it on spec.

He decided to stroll along the queue again to examine finger-nails. Some of them had nicotine-stained fingers. He eliminated them as he didn't smoke. Others had dirt under their fingernails. Too bad.

A bald-headed, flat-nosed man in his early thirties, in a dinner jacket, came out of the ballroom and called out some names. A few of them followed him in. At the same time, a number of young men came out. Some looked glum, some pretended they were happy, and one or two said out loud to the queue, "Don't waste your time, the job's gone."

Some of the queue jeered at this but a few did leave. It began to rain, and he sheltered in the doorway of the car salesroom. One or two had taken out combs and were running them carefully through their hair so as not to disturb the Brylcreem that had set their hair to a quiff. He elimated all Brylcreemed heads. They weren't aware of the subtlety of brilliantine.

It was about a quarter to three, and most of the queue had gone, leaving just four. He didn't include himself in that group.

He decided to close the gap and moved up behind them. They were wishing one another good luck. He smiled to himself: "Do they mean that?" One had been a carter. His firm had sold the horses and bought lorries. He couldn't drive and now had no job. One was unemployed. He had always been unemployed except for snow-clearing in winter. One was a joiner but wanted a change from woodwork. And the fourth was a lorry driver who wanted the extra money the job of ballroom supervisor would give. They looked at him, but he didn't tell them anything about himself. They sort of eased away from him and began talking in a group.

The bald-headed man came out again and read out all their names. They entered the foyer of the ballroom, and he told them to sit down. A young man came out of the manager's office with his head down and went into the street cursing to himself.

The four went in one by one and each came out with either

his thumb raised in victory or hands in pockets with a couldn't-care-less air.

The bald-headed man called for, "Mr Martin. Gerald Thomas Martin," then whispered, "You've made it. He liked your letter."

Gerry entered the high-ceilinged office with its photographs of dance competitions framed on the walls and various silver cups in a glass cabinet. The floor was thickly carpeted. Behind a huge desk sat a man with brown-tinted, permed hair. On the desk was a triangular piece of polished wood with a brass plate announcing him as Mr Berkley Black, manager. He held, in his small, white, fleshy hand, a gold-plated cigarette holder. He stood up to shake hands. He was a man of about six feet with the same podginess as his hands. His suit was tailormade, and he smiled as if smiling painfully through his tears. He sat again like someone with back trouble who had to wear a corset. He looked at Gerry for about ten seconds and then looked down at his application letter on the desk.

"Though we must keep order in this ballroom, Mr Martin, I do not approve of fisticuffs," he said in an English accent. "We talk them out, and if that doesn't work we have the police take them out by the back door. But most important of all, we bar them. They must never be allowed back. This will hurt. We are the biggest ballroom in Belfast, if not the biggest north and south of this country. We have the biggest and most well-known bands in the United Kingdom. We are the most glamorous in a city of what comprises of small dance halls."

He said "dance halls" again with venom.

"Our top capacity is about two thousand on a Saturday night. Mr McClaron is under-manager and will oversee you and Mr

Evans. Mr Evans and you, in turn, will oversee the female staff
on the door and the cloakroom staff. Do you have a dress suit?"

Gerry was not prepared for this question. He said yes.

"Good. That is your winter wear. During the summer
months, you wear a white tuxedo with a red bow tie and cuff
links with a spot of red on them. We have a tuxedo which might
fit you."

The manager stood up with his usual pained smile and shook
Gerry's hand. He lifted the phone and asked for Mr McClaron.
The bald-headed man entered the office. Gerry followed
McClaron, who showed him over the huge dance floor with its
polished-hardwood floor and tutted when he spotted a black
spot of chewing gum. He called out for Mavis, the cleaner, but
Mavis didn't answer, so he called out for Nelson, the lavatory
attendant. An elderly man came shuffling forward with a hand
to his ear to act as hearing trumpet. McClaron pointed to the
chewing gum.

"What's this! And don't blame Mavis."

The old man stood there, his arms swaying like dead
branches.

"Get it off this floor!"

The old man shuffled away whimpering like a child.

Gerry looked at the tables covered with linen cloths, the table
lamps on them, visited the lights box – was introduced to the
electrician and his assistant, was shown behind the revolving
band platform.

"We have Nat Alton and His Band here from across the water
on a year's contract. Each band changes on the hour. You be here
two minutes early and take a hold of this handle. Mr Alton alter-
nates with Billy Duggan and His Boys – our local band. As soon

as either band begins to play," he began singing in a surprisingly good voice, " 'When the music goes round and round . . . round and round. . . round and round. . . oh oh oh eh eh eh ha ha ha . . .', the other musicians should be already in their positions back here on this revolving platform. Get the nod from the band leader first and then turn the handle slowly to cast them into the spotlights. The band that was on will then be back here."

He repeated the instructions a number of times and emphasised that this was the big time. Gerry was shown the table marked "Reserved" for the ballroom supervisors by the side of the band stage, shown the locker room and introduced to a Mr Evans, who was in his mid-twenties. He spoke with an English upper-class accent but said he was really Welsh. Gerry was told there were two sessions a day: one from one o'clock to three and an evening session from seven to eleven, except for Saturdays which started an hour earlier at six and ran to midnight. They sold no alcohol, and no alcohol was allowed on the premises. If it were seen in anyone's possession, it was to be confiscated. No one was allowed in who looked and behaved drunk. People were allowed to leave for a short break, but strictly speaking they could be recharged admission. No passes were given, but it was up to whoever was on the door to remember the faces who asked to leave and remember them when they came back. And above all, jiving was not allowed. Strictly ballroom dancing here.

Mr Evans took Gerry to a quiet corner and, looking around first in case somebody was within earshot, asked, "Have you ever heard of Indian hemp?"

Before Gerry could answer, he said, "It's mostly Indian seamen who bring it into Belfast. It's a drug. A leg-opener. If you want to protect our women, sniff the air a few times for funny cigarettes. Also, we don't let Indian merchant marine crewmen in here – not people with nightshirts and tea towels wrapped around their heads. You might see them sometimes at Barry's Amusements in Blitz Square with their odd-looking leather moccasins with the curly toes. We've sold the Indians an aircraft carrier. The crew's over here to collect it from the Yard. It wouldn't surprise me if they tried to get in here. Only let in the officers. If they're not in uniform, you'll recognise them because they wear suits like us.

"And that reminds me – nobody gets in without a tie on. As well as that, the tie must be sober. I had to turn somebody away the other night because he had a tie that lit up, then flashed on and off. You could just about see a naked woman on it. This is not a circus. This is a ballroom."

Gerry was to start work on Saturday, to be here at five for six. A letter confirming this should arrive in two days' time.

Gerry left the Plaza feeling triumphant. It was still raining, but his spirits were high. The rain even seemed perfumed and added to his joy at getting the job. No more greasy garages for him. The only problem was he needed a dress suit.

He walked up Chichester Street to near the City Hall and crossed the road into Donegall Place, down to Castle Junction and turned right into High Street. Loud music was coming from Barry's Amusements in Blitz Square. Blitz Square was an unofficial name for the wasteland caused by German bombers in 1941. Later it became known as Red Square when the communists began holding meetings there. There was the smell of electricity in the air as the bumper cars careered around with their trolleys sparking on the overhead wire netting. The drivers were mostly schoolboys in school uniforms with skullcaps and black

and yellow scarves wrapped carelessly around their throats. They
pronounced their "ings" and finished their sentences even when
shouting hysterically as they collided.

He crossed over to the other side of High Street and passed
across the mouth of the narrow Pottinger's Entry. A strong smell
of Guinness was coming from the pubs there. A thin-faced youth
with blood on his face suddenly came running out, followed by an
enraged portly middle-aged man holding a bottle of stout. Being
unable to catch the youth, he threw the bottle at him but missed.
It shattered in the middle of High Street. A carter drew his horse
up so quickly to avoid the glass that it almost sat down. A trolleybus, seeming like a small house, swerved violently to avoid the
dray. The carter, in hessian-bag apron and highly polished leather
leggings, jumped to the greasy square setts with sparbled boots
and raised his long whip towards the driver of the trolleybus who
was leaning out of the cab swearing. A crowd gathered to watch
the fun as the pocket-sized driver jumped out of the cab and put
his fists up. The whip lashed around his face and the crowd booed.
The little man got under the carter's guard and pummelled him in
the stomach. The crowd cheered. This had no effect on the burly
carter. It was his turn now – he grabbed the trolleybus driver by
the scruff of the neck, like a terrier with a rat, lifted him off his
feet, carried him to the dray, grabbed the horse's nosebag and
stuck his head in it. The crowd booed. A passing Crossley tender
with its police, sitting back-to-back and holding .303 rifles
between their knees, skidded to a halt.

The trolleybus driver was now spluttering corn as he tried to
explain to the platoon sergeant. The carter removed the broken
bottle from the road and took no further interest in the pro-
ceedings. The sergeant called out for witnesses, but the crowd

didn't respond and began slowly to drift away. The impassive police still sat on the tender staring ahead at nothing in particular. Finally the trolleybus driver was ordered back into his cab. He drove off picking corn out of his hair. The carter encouraged the horse forward with a great "Getup'er that!"

The police tender slowly followed the dray as far down as the Albert Memorial Clock before losing interest and diving for Musgrave Street Police Barracks.

Gerry got to Spackman's just in time before it shut, asked the price of a dress suit and was quoted £20. He didn't have £20. He had his back wages of £7 from the garage, but he had already given half of that to his mother for his keep. It was no use asking them for a loan. He wouldn't get it. They didn't believe in lending money to either him or his younger sister. It could make them apron-string children.

He went to the County Down Railway Station in Midland Street and took the Bangor train. The train was already filling up with shipyard workers. Some of them still wore their greasy overalls and paint-spattered caps from work. He edged away from one individual who smelt of yellow ochre while moving his legs from someone in the opposite seat smelling of heavy engine oil. He glanced at the man and saw that his dungarees and jacket were black and shining with many dried-up layers of oil. His mate beside him was running his hands through his hair to get rid of the white pieces of shredded asbestos. Then he swept it off his lapels saying, "Some people should travel second class like the rest of the clerks." He took out a Gallaher's Blue and lit it, though it was a no-smoking carriage.

A man with red-rimmed eyes protested, which brought the comment, "This is a workmen's carriage."

After that they all lit up while red-rims held a handkerchief to his mouth.

Gerry got off at Holywood, glad to be done with oil, grease and dirty fingernails. He walked up from the station to the small estate of newly built houses with neatly tended gardens and trees in the streets. As soon as he got indoors, he heard the key in the lock, and his father Derek came in wearing a clean pair of dungarees with collar and tie. He carried a ripsaw which he was going to sharpen that night for the next morning.

"Are you too good for me now?" he asked his son.

Gerry looked at him, puzzled for a moment.

"You must have seen me get off the train, yet you hurried ahead of me. In case somebody thought we were related?"

Gerry said nothing as he knew his father was in bad form and was looking for an argument which might turn into a shouting match.

Irene, his mother, came out of the kitchen with two steaming plates of stew and banged the plates down on the table as a warning. She also said nothing and went back into the kitchen.

Derek went upstairs to wash his hands. Maisie entered in office clothes and immediately shouted to her mother in the kitchen not to get her anything to eat. Irene came out and asked why. Maisie didn't answer but went upstairs and came down immediately, complaining that her father was having a bath when Friday was his bath time. Irene told her daughter that she seemed to have a bath every time she came back from work. It was bad for the skin to go as far as that every day. Maisie laughed towards Gerry, to bring him into the argument. Gerry said it was a good idea. Derek, who wasn't having a bath, came down, heard Gerry's comment and said, "You'll be wearin' high-heel shoes next."

Gerry mumbled something about ignoramuses, and his father said, "If you get that job, you'll get all the fighting you want. But be careful they don't kick you when you're down."

Gerry looked at his father and saw his mouth was hard with bitterness. They never had got along very well, but things seemed to have become worse recently. Irene looked at her husband with loathing, then softened and asked him if he was tired tonight.

Maisie said nothing but felt there was something about males she didn't understand. Or maybe, at nineteen, she had stayed too long in this household. They ate in silence, and Gerry could hardly swallow the food. His father's stinging words still went round in his head. He felt like crying, but those days were over with. Any other man who had said that to him would get an immediate punch on the nose.

His mother said, "One day I'll be carried out of this house and the rows will stop."

Maisie went upstairs, and Gerry followed her and asked if she had £20 to loan. He had to buy a dress suit and he would pay her back in instalments. She asked him if he wasn't taking on too dangerous a job as a chucker-out in a dance hall. Gerry corrected her towards ballroom and ballroom supervisor.

Maisie laughed and said, "You're a brave one! Good. Throw off the overalls and never put them back on again. Nobody appreciates you when you work with your hands."

She promised to take the £20 out of her post office account the next day. She went into the bathroom and ran the bath.

Downstairs the living-room door was open, though he was sure he had closed it before following Maisie. His parents were whispering when he entered the living room. He knew by their faces that they had eavesdropped on his conversation with Maisie.

They began talking out loud about how the back garden needed the hedge cut. . . how the grass needed mowed. Derek said they were all lucky to live in a house like this. The repayments were steep, but luckily he still had his job with McLaughlin and Harvey, and the company had a full order book building new houses. Irene mentioned her part-time job cleaning the minister's house. Derek mentioned the financial contributions his son and daughter were making. One day Maisie would get married, but that seemed to be a long way off as she had been going with that fella only for a few months. Gerry, she said, looked as if he was about to sow his wild oats in taking a job in the dance hall. Derek interrupted her by pretending he didn't know if Gerry had got the job or not. Gerry said it was a ballroom, not a dance hall. Derek said he should stick to his trade. Maybe one day he could set up a garage of his own. It was easier to set up a garage than a dance hall. Gerry said ballroom again, but with emphasis, and then said it wasn't polite to listen in to other people's conversation. Irene said she and Derek weren't other people.

Derek said, "You're borrowin' money from your sister. That's almost a month's wages. How will you be able to pay it back?"

Gerry said it had nothing to do with him. Irene said it did. Derek said he had, with great financial sacrifice, sent Maisie to a secretarial school for two years. He had put up with the poor wages Gerry got during his apprenticeship as a motor mechanic. If he ever left here for good, it was expected of him to send money or he wouldn't be welcomed back home, even for visits. Irene said that was a terrible thing to say to his son, although she did think it was a tradition. Derek said he did it as a young man – sent money home. He said he didn't always know whether his family loved him or hated him when he was sending money. When he stopped sending money home, he soon found out they hated him. He discovered their true natures. But even if they hated him and he had been aware of it, he would have still sent them money. That was the tradition, and as far as he knew it was still a tradition. Anyway, Gerry, in borrowing money from his hard-working sister, was heartless. It was the beginning of dance-hall life to borrow like that. Gerry didn't say ballroom again. He was imagining a brick wall.

Derek had two more mugs of tea and went into the back garden and came back with his sawhorse. He took the ripsaw and sighted it with one eye and straightened it before putting it between the two pieces of wood with just the teeth showing. He tapped the holders lightly with a hammer and took out the triangular saw file, put on his glasses, held the sawhorse down with one foot and was about to file when Irene said, "Where do you think you're livin' now?"

"It's rainin' outside," he said, and bent over the sawhorse again.

"Go into the garden shed; you're not filin' here. Do you hear me: I said to go out the back to the shed. Are we livin' in that house in the country?"

His mouth hardened with bitterness again, and he left with the sawhorse, dropping the saw-set as he went, cursing to himself as he bent to pick it up.

Maisie entered the living room wearing a towelling bath robe and with a towel wrapped around her head. She took off the towel and bent near the open fire, letting her hair dangle over her face towards the red coals. Irene told her to be careful as she could smell singed hair already. Maisie said she had heard there was such a thing as a portable hair dryer now, but they were far too expensive. Irene looked at Gerry as much as to say, "And she's lending you £20."

Derek came in sucking his hand and said, "With all the arguments in the house, I'm being brought bad luck. I've just gone and cut my finger to the bone on the teeth of the saw. Look at it!"

Gerry said he was going upstairs to have a bath but he would forgo the high heels.

"You had one this mornin'," said Irene. "The skin'll be peelin' off you in no time – like the Americans who have two showers a day, so it's said."

When he had gone, Derek said Gerry was starting to get "a wire about himself", that after the dance hall he would need all the baths Holywood could provide. Maisie said ballroom, and her parents gave her a startled look before Derek said, "You'll both catch it in the big wide wide world when youse leave this house."

"'Youse'?" said Maisie and laughed.

They both looked at her again, but this time it was with the look of a chastised dog. Derek warmed his finger at the fire to congeal the blood, and Irene said, "That's what they used to do a hundred years ago. Away and wash it and put an Elastoplast on it."

He went to the kitchen and she shouted, "The washbasin!"

Before he went to the small washroom downstairs, he asked Maisie if she thought he needed a haircut, but she said for him to go and wash the pomade out of his hair first as she couldn't tell – it looked like a greased rat was sitting there on the top of his head.

He held up his hand to prevent his finger dripping on the floor and asked, "How many times am I supposed to wash my hair. . . Miss?"

"Every two weeks," said Irene, "or you'll take the natural oils out of it."

"Once a week. . . at least," said Maisie firmly. "Once for men and twice for women."

Derek washed his finger and came out saying, "Is he goin' to be up all night in that bath?"

Gerry tried on the dress suit in Spackman's, and the assistant said, "Like a glove! You dress to the right I see. Try on this pair of trousers."

Derek changed behind the curtain and came out to acclaim by all four assistants. They fussed over him, tugging and pulling the jacket at the back, pulling the trousers down slightly over the shoes.

"Now look in the mirror," said one little old man; "what do you see? Oh youth – who needs anything more!"

"Except a shirt, pair of black socks, and a bow tie," said a cynical voice from behind the counter.

Gerry peeped at himself in the mirror with embarrassment until he was gently prodded by the little old man to a straightened-up position.

"Forgive yourself, like yourself. Life is short." He reached for a large mirror. "Perfect at the back. No need of bespoke."

The same slightly cynical voice said, this time from the store-room, "Call back next week."

The little old man suddenly barked something in German and went to the storeroom. He came back and said to Gerry, "Is this what I get for taking a failed medical student back under my wing – to bite the feed that hands you?"

He spluttered and gasped for air, trying to get the quotation right while a voice from the storeroom laughed.

Gerry handed over the money. It was put into a pneumatic tube, there was a rush of air and away it whizzed to some back office. Another rush of air and he got his receipt. The little old man showed him to the door, shook his hand and wished him luck for his grand occasion.

Gerry was in the locker room at the Plaza. It was ten to six on a Saturday evening. He felt self-conscious in the dress suit with the shining satin lapels and the black stripe down the seam of the outer leg. Evans was talking about his two years doing National Service in Malaya. He said he was a second-lieutenant. He showed Gerry a photograph of a massacre there. Chinese men, women and children were dead, piled up on top of one another on the ground.

"Those communist bastards did that," he said.

McClaron, of average height, took a deep breath, stuck out his chest, tucked in his chin and said, "Who keeps a photo of somebody else's massacre? Maybe you helped do it, I'm beginnin' to think." He left smirking.

"Silly bastard!" said Evans.

McClaron re-entered immediately.

"Silly bastard! You don't call someone a bastard in this town unless you're prepared to put your mitts up. And don't show that photo again. There's no politics in this ballroom. I'm in charge of you here, and you'll go to the office and see Mr Black. He'll shoot you down in flames. Silly bastard."

He left with his flattened nose vibrating as he snorted. His hands were in fists, and the longish hair around the rim of his bald pate had risen.

Evans waited a long time before saying silly bastard again, and then said, "Watch him, he's a hard man. That's what you call idiots like that here, I believe. Watch him dive into fights on the floor. He takes them all on. The silly bastard. He's been warned not to do it, but he just keeps on doing it. Let them fight. The police get the survivors. That's their job. That arse-head, with his physical endeavours, is turning these premises into a dance hall. Now, Gerry lad, you look like a reasonable sort of chap. Take my advice – don't get hurt. Fighting is for thicks. Swing the lead and you'll get your pay just the same. There are plenty of women coming in here tonight. They are on a platter. Take your pick. Most are common, but there are some beauties."

McClaron came back and looked at Evans suspiciously. Evans began to sing a song in Welsh under his breath.

McClaron said, "I know the words of that. Remember, I know the words of that."

Evans left to patrol the dance floor. McClaron asked Gerry if Evans was talking about him behind his back and said, without waiting for an answer, "He's a lazy cunt. Why in the name of fuck would his kind come to a place like Belfast unless he was hidin' something? Come on, I'll start you on the door. Fuckin' shite! Fuckin' whoor!"

They walked into the carpeted foyer, past the potted plants in great brass pots, to the entrance area. The box office behind the cash grill was busy churning out tickets as people drifted in.

They were mostly young couples in their best clothing. Some of the males had handkerchiefs peeping out of the top pockets of their suit jackets. The girls had on pretty dresses over which they wore dark wool overcoats. Each stocking had a seam down the back. A few had wedge-heeled shoes, while others wore high-heeled court shoes. Some carried vanity cases. All of them had a handbag of some kind.

"Coortin' couples," whispered McClaron; "no trouble. They come early and they leave early before the steam builds up."

Billy Duggan and His Boys, a quartet consisting of drums, double-bass, guitar and clarinet, began playing. Billy was on clarinet and then changed to saxophone, after which he began singing in a passable voice:

"Shrimp boats are comin' there's dancin' tonighhhhhht. Shrimp boats are comin' there's dancin' tonighhhhhht . . . so will you hurry hurry hurry home. . . hurry hurry hurry home. . . Shrimp boats are comin' there's dancin' tonighhhhhh-hhht. . ."

Four young girls arrived giggling. McClaron asked one what age she was. She said she was sixteen and her friends gave their ages as sixteen, sixteen, seventeen – no, eighteen. Nearly eighteen. The one claiming to be eighteen wore white ankle socks. Her legs were still blotched and slightly purple from puberty. McClaron thought a moment. The girls stopped giggling and began to look very serious. They looked even younger now.

"Sorry, girls," said McClaron. "My opinion is you're underage."

"And what age are we supposed to be?" asked the girl in the ankle socks.

"Whatever age I think you are."

One of the girls broke down and cried. McClaron told them

there was a past pupils' dance in a hall off Cornmarket. The Plaza, he said, was a serious place. There would be a lot of wicked people coming in tonight. They drifted off.

"Young skins," said McClaron. "Watch them, they'll be back when we get more crowded. They'll change their tactics and come in one by one, attachin' themselves to any half-drunk boy, and they'll throw him over when they get inside. That's how fights start."

He waved through two young men dressed in what looked like standard-issue suits as they were about to pay at the cash grill. They were thickset and over six feet tall. One was about to salute, then suddenly remembered too late but ended up giving a half-salute.

"Military police," said McClaron, "from Palace Barracks, near where you live. Off duty and useful to have in a fight.

"Don't let the boul Berkley Black see you do that. Better still, don't let me see you do it. I'll decide. This is my game."

A girl attendant dressed in tight nylon pants and a Crimean War-style dress jacket rushed to her post near the cash grill while adjusting her pillbox hat.

"Late again, Betty," said McClaron, "third time this week, and worst of all on a Saturday."

Betty ignored him and began greeting the incoming crowd with good evenings. McClaron took Gerry aside out of earshot of Betty.

"Can't do much with her. That's Black's piece of stuff. Can't understand it. You should see his wife! She would send you pantin'. Or maybe she can't stand the oul cunt."

People drifted in more and more now until a queue began to form down Chichester Street. A drunken young man was in the queue at the cash grill. He nodded to the cashier who refused him a ticket, saying, "Go home and sleep it off."

He began arguing and said in a slurred voice, "Why's everybody tellin' me to go home and sleep it off." His voice rose. "It's the last thing I want to do on a Saturday night."

McClaron took him by the lapels and pushed him backwards through the glass doors into the street and into the arms of a huge doorman dressed in a greatcoat and peaked cap. The doorman gave the drunk a close, low, almost unseen punch that had the young drunk rolling in the gutter. An old woman passing in the street, wearing a black shawl over her head and shoulders to the waist, said, "Ach, that's a terrible thing to do to a young fella."

A white-faced, deprived-looking youth with her said to the doorman, "Go on, ye dyin'-lookin' cunt!"

The doorman picked up the young drunk, dusted him down and handed him over to two passing policemen. The doorman then stood to attention and gave the policemen a mighty military salute.

Black, who had somehow got wind of the incident, came into the foyer dressed in bespoke evening wear with a frilly white shirt. He took Gerry and McClaron aside.

"What happened?"

"He was causin' trouble," said McClaron and looked at Gerry for support. Gerry didn't reciprocate. Black knocked on the glass door with one of his many ring fingers. The huge doorman entered, taking off his cap. Black asked again what had happened. The doorman said he had been attacked by the young drunk and had just pushed him away. Black silently waved him outside again him and stood watching the doorman.

"Why does his head shake like that – Parkinson's? Haven't you noticed it before, Mr McClaron?"

McClaron lied and said he hadn't. He also wasn't going to tell Black that he had seen the doorman fight off a gang of five when he, McClaron, had refused them admittance one Saturday night because he didn't like the look of them. They had sharpened bicycle chains that wound round their necks under the collars of their jackets, reaching down inside the lapels. A piece of thread was attached to either end of the chains to run across the top button of the jacket to keep it in place and concealed. Despite the flailing sharpened chains, the doorman had flattened two and seen three run off. A useful man to have on your side.

Just at that moment, Black spotted another young drunk near the cash grill. He was dressed in a uniform of the Royal Air Force. Black nodded to Gerry and then watched. Gerry, now scared by the recent incident and almost intimidated by the throng pouring in, approached the RAF man and said, "I'm sorry, we can't let you in just yet. Have a couple of walks round the City Hall and then see how you feel."

The RAF man shook his hand and walked out. Black gave a painful smile to McClaron and went back to his office. While this was going on, the young girl in the ankle socks was persuading a gauche-looking young man to buy her a ticket; then after a pause, a second girl linked herself suddenly to a rugged farmer's boy. His face reddened with embarrassment as she whispered something in his ear. The third and fourth girls decided to hold up a slightly drunk-looking young man. McClaron, disgusted at Gerry's passive behaviour toward the RAF man, decided to do nothing but watch Gerry handle the next drunk. The slightly drunk young man mumbled something about the girls being his sisters. Gerry decided to let them all in.

Betty went up close to Gerry and said, "This place is full of jailbait tonight. If any of them get up the chute they'll be in court accusin' and wearin' their school uniforms. And you'll be responsible."

McClaron came over and said to Betty, "Don't get too big for your boots. You're talkin' to a ballroom supervisor. I'll have you shot down in flames."

He then beckoned to Gerry and whispered, "She's right – I doubt if they even have hair on it yet. Just pray their mothers don't come here lookin' for them. Black'll riddle you."

Billy Duggan and His Boys were playing, and Billy was singing, "And the music goes round and round, round and round. . . oh oh oh ha ha ha ee ee eh. . ."

His band faded out to give way to a bigger sound of many saxophones – alto, tenor and bass, flugelhorns, clarinets, trombones, drums, clashing cymbals, a piano going manic, and with a great thumping bass. . . and above it all a female singer sang, "And when the saints. . . and when the saints. . . and when the saints go marching in. . ."

The crowd at the cash grill pressed forward impatiently, and the floor of the ballroom resounded to a thousand pairs of feet. Evans and McClaron came to the foyer, and Evans said he was relieving Gerry on the orders of Mr Black. Gerry followed McClaron as he pushed through the standing crowd to the edge of the dance floor. A huge mirrored ball revolved slowly above the scene. Spotlights of all colours flashed and swept over the crowd. A white spotlight picked out the singer, Deborah Gold. Another, smaller spotlight shone off the figure of Nat Alton, showing up his tall lanky figure and his sunlamp tan. A man in his fifties with greying hair, he wore grey flannels and a multi-coloured shirt and waved a baton at his blue-suited, bow-tied musicians. But mostly he faced the dance floor and winked at any attractive girls he saw. Johnny the pianist played furiously while talking to a girl at the side of the bandstand.

The big band played on, running one tune into another non-stop.

Deborah was now singing, "She wore red feathers and a hoolie hoolie skirt. She wore red feathers and a hoolie hoolie skirt. She lives off fresh coconuts and fishhhhh from the seeee. . . ah ah ah. . ."

McClaron spotted a couple of jivers in the middle of the dancers and said it was only spite to try and jive to that tune.

Suddenly from the light box, a mighty spotlight of about fifty kilowatts shone on the two jivers, especially on the girl's bare back. They tried to get away from the heat, but the spotlight followed them. The boy began to rub the sweat off his face. The girl's back began to turn red. The electrician melted them down until they decided to do a foxtrot. McClaron put a thumb up to the light box.

McClaron and Gerry patrolled the fringes of the dance floor, asking people to take their feet off chairs, turning round on occasion to face cocky young men who jeered at them behind their backs. They soon shut up, fearing a bar on them or maybe a smack on the mouth from McClaron. A well-dressed woman of about thirty was checking in her handbag at the depository at the back of the dance floor. McClaron said, "That's Mrs McKidrick. Her husband owns Golden Cabs. She only shags sailors in uniforms. Though Evans claims he had her once inside one of the emergency exits."

They walked on a bit.

"Do you see them two fat Jews in the grey suits leanin' against the wall. They're brothers and own the half of Belfast. I've never seen them dancin' yet. And I've been here since the American Red Cross handed the Plaza back in 1946. They're so mean they'll only take one girl out of here and share her between them. One night they left with a lad of about eighteen. I think they could well be bicycles."

Further along, in a corner, a scuffle broke out. McClaron told Gerry to get Evans. Evans yawned and followed Gerry slowly.

In the corner, two large men held an equally large man by the arms and were bouncing him off the wall and shouting to their victim, "Say you're sorry. Say it!"

"It's your turn," said McClaron to Gerry.

Gerry approached and asked the two men politely to stop battering that man against the wall. One of the men, still battering, and without turning round, said, "Shove off, Mac!"

"Then say you're sorry," said Gerry to the victim. "I don't want to have to scrape you off the wall."

The victim, now dazed and bent at the knees, said sorry.

"Louder!" said the first man.

"*Louder!*" shouted the second man.

"Louder," said Gerry.

The victim roared, "*Sorry.*"

They let him go and he fell on to his hands and knees. While this was going on, Evans was sitting at a table talking to a young woman in a low-cut dress. The two men approached Gerry. He wasn't trembling or afraid. He had contained the situation, and he guessed that was all Black required of him.

They shook his hand and said, "Business, that's all, Mac. Just business. No hard feelin's?"

One of them then said, "Where's that baldy fucker. I'll break every bone in his face!"

But McClaron was nowhere to be seen. Gerry wondered if he was being a coward. He thought, "There are only three of us to control a crowd of about two thousand on a Friday and Saturday night. David had only one Goliath to face. I can only live by the science of the possible." Evans was now stealing a kiss from the girl and rubbing his hand up and down her bare back.

Gerry went to the locker room to change his shirt. The air-conditioning was not coping with the two thousand hot bodies, the heat of the spotlights and the fifty kilowatt picking out yet another two jivers. He was just in time to see McClaron put a knuckle-duster back in his locker.

McClaren sort of sneered about his intervention at the battering wall and asked him, "Do you know who you were tanglin' with?"

Gerry said, "I can't say that I care. It's all settled now."

"Fuckin' Silver McKee and his mate. You must have heard of him. Comes from the Markets. Cattle drover and car-tyre thief. It takes ten peelers to arrest him. He has this arrangement with Stormy Wetherall. He comes here one Saturday, Silver the next Saturday. If they ever meet then that would be a fight. The best street fighters I've ever seen. Stormy's from the Shankill. They don't fight over anything as stupid as religion or country. They just hate each other. It's only pure hate. That cunt Evans still sittin' on his arse?"

Gerry changed into a fresh shirt and went back to the dance floor. Deborah was singing "Stormy Weather" to Johnny's solo on the piano. Three girls at the side of the bandstand now competed for the piano player's attention. He spoke to each of them in turn without missing a note.

The music went round and round as Gerry turned the handle. Billy Duggan and His Boys came on playing "My Little Black-Eyed Suzy". Billy sang this song. Billy loved this song. The music went round and round, then round again until Nat Alton and His Band played the last waltz. There was a great scramble by the males for the females.

This was the moment of truth for the fellas. Most of the younger ones still lived with their parents, so unless you had a place to bring the girl to, you ended up kissing in a doorway, hoping for a promise of a walk over Cavehill the next day, Sunday, when you might be able to try something. Then again, if you were serious about the girl you kissed her on her doorstep and asked her out to see a film on Monday. But then again, you got to know those who would take a grope in a doorway or, even better, a mutual groping leading to a mutual wanking. But gropers, Gerry soon found out, were just gropers who never went the full hog. When he mentioned the Botanic Gardens beside Queen's University, one refused to go there because it was full of fruit merchants. He mentioned about taking a taxi to Ormeau Park, but she said there were scouts – peeping Toms – lying in wait. The girl he took to Cavehill one Sunday and kissed while she lay on the grass cried great tears when he touched her breasts. He took her to her home in silence. She refused a goodnight kiss, and he knew what she wanted was a steady boyfriend. He wanted a steady girlfriend. He had destroyed that possibility.

He blamed the hedonistic atmosphere of the ballroom. It was a gold mine, and he wanted all of them one minute and a particular one the next.

Evans came in one Monday with two large lovebites on his neck. McClaron said he did that to himself to show off and try to make-believe that he had picked up a hot thing.

One Saturday night Gerry picked up a girl nicknamed Gypsy Rose Lee because she always wore very large circular earrings, had curly hair and wore colourful clothes. They went to Ormeau Park and let the peeping Toms peep. They went to the Botanic Gardens and ignored the fruit merchants with their sacred song sheet music under their arms.

It was dawn and he smelt strongly of her. The glamour of the ballroom was far behind him as the birds started their chorus. He asked her out to see a film on Monday, his day off. She refused, laughing at his naivety. He was glad, as otherwise he would have felt guilty in not wanting her as a girlfriend. He left her home and then thumbed a lift on the Hollywood Road from a milk lorry.

Walking up the road that separated the Palace Barracks from the officers' detached houses, he saw a conscript soldier on the doorstep breaking firewood. The officer's wife was shouting for him to hurry up. Through the wire of the barracks, a soldier in khaki overalls was on his hands and knees picking up matchsticks as a punishment for some offence he had committed, while a sergeant stood two feet from him and moved when he did.

Gerry went into the house and crept up to his room where he found shirts on the bed which his mother had washed and ironed. She had also gone through his wardrobe and washed his pullovers. He still owed Maisie £20. Irene came out of her bedroom and whispered to ask him why he was coming home at this hour. He said nothing, and she said he was probably out with some oul tramp all night. She said there were three letters for him that looked like girls' handwriting. Some more tramps, she asked? He said nothing. As a matter of fact, he wasn't speaking to either parent very much any more. They could never understand his new life even if he wanted to tell them. Although, to be honest, he did speak to his mother on occasions, but only to call her "a fuckin' old whoor!" when she called his girls tramps again. Even if he was going steady he would never bring a girl back here.

Derek wanted to know, "Why did you call your mother that terrible name?"

Gerry didn't answer. Derek kept asking this question every time they were together. Gerry finally answered him.

"Keep to your side of the fence or you'll get what's coming to you!"

Irene screamed with fear, and Derek wanted to throw him out right there and then, but Irene said no.

Maisie asked for her £20 occasionally. One day she said she was getting engaged to her boyfriend. He was an army sergeant in Palace Barracks. Irene almost fainted and said she was lowering herself. Maisie said he was only on National Service, it wasn't his fault.

Derek asked, "A sergeant already and he's only doing two years?"

Maisie said he was a very good soldier and was promoted quickly. When his time was up, he was going back to Scotland where his father had a beef-cattle farm. Derek said beef farmers only reared for the killing.

"Did you think they were pets?" said Maisie.

One day the sergeant called at the house and asked for Maisie. They didn't invite him in. Maisie had to talk to him on the doorstep. The sergeant, before he left, asked Maisie for his father's boots. He would clean them as they had never been cleaned before, army style. Derek, intrigued, came to the door and said hullo and handed over the boots. Irene, in the background but not coming to the door, shouted out a reluctant hullo and disappeared into the kitchen.

Later that night, in his barracks, the sergeant entered the barrack housing the new entrants, bawled one of them out of bed and told him to clean the boots until his face shone in them. He quickly showed him how to smooth the leather of the toecaps with a heated soup spoon. After that he threatened to have him confined to barracks for a month counting every grain of gravel on the barrack roads if he didn't have the boots like mirrors the next morning. The poor lad was up all night, and when dawn broke he was counting gravel just the same.

Derek was delighted with the boots and wanted to invite the sergeant to tea but Irene said, "There will be no soldiers in this house. They are the lowest of the low."

A few weeks later Maisie fell desperately ill. She was diagnosed as having tuberculosis and was removed to Whiteabbey Sanatorium. The sergeant spent all his spare time at the hospital holding her hand. He only left when her parents arrived on visits. Irene blamed the soldier for Maisie's tuberculosis. His father had cattle. That's where it came from. The neighbours weren't to hear about her condition. If there was too much curiosity, they would say she was in the Royal Victoria Hospital with pernicious anaemia.

Gerry still owed her £20. He had often seen the sergeant on the doorstep in the past. One day he met him while he was drilling some new reluctant recruits along the road where the officers lived. He marched along with him, while he barked out orders. He didn't know what to say to this little muscular Scotsman with the craggy face so he asked him, "Do you do shoes as well?"

"Only fathers'," he said, and screamed out an order for a soldier to do twenty press-ups on the road for his dumb insolence.

"One for each pound you owe your sister."

"Well," said Gerry, "it's a good job I don't owe her a hundred, for your man there's sweating already."

Jock, who was called Jock, said, "Sorry talking about the money, but it was your daddy told me. It's a good sign for him to tell me a family secret. I might be your brother-in-law yet." He held out a hand, the palm of which seemed to be made of wood, and Gerry shook it.

That summer he wore his white tuxedo with a red silk bow tie and red screw-in buttons on his shirt. Out of the top pocket of the tuxedo was a red silk handkerchief. On a Saturday afternoon, American sailors came in from a visiting warship. They began to jive with the girls. Some danced with two at once. McClaron told one hefty sailor to stop jiving.

"Sir," said the sailor, "that's all I can do."

Gerry advised McClaron to relax the rules for once as the sailor had probably been cooped up for weeks on board ship. McClaron became annoyed at having his overlordship challenged and ordered Gerry to tell the sailor to stop the jiving. Gerry refused the order and sat down at the reserved table to wait for a girl attendant to bring him tea.

Jiving was not a moral issue. It just took up too much space on the dance floor. That afternoon there were only a few hundred in, and most were female. McClaron complained to Berkley Black. Black came out of his office in hunting gear and carrying a riding crop. He looked towards Gerry and gave his usual painful smile. McClaron was overruled. Near by, Evans leaned against a pillar yawning.

Nat Alton and His Band played listlessly, as was their wont on afternoons. Momentarily the band became alive as they played a jive number: "Chicken on the Hop". Then they played a few Glenn Miller numbers to please the sailors. The sailors sat down with girls on their knees, waving the band away. Glenn Miller was OK for their fathers' generation. McClaron told a girl to get off a sailor's knee. The girl refused, and McClaron tried to pull her off. The sailor whacked him. McClaron slid across the dance floor like a puck in ice hockey. Two massive Shore Patrol sailors, with long wooden truncheons, came forward to arrest the sailor. Black flew out of his office to intervene. He wanted no arrests. He didn't want sailors being dragged out of his ballroom in daylight hours in front of the Saturday shoppers. A compromise was reached with the sailor shaking hands with McClaron and saying "sir" again.

The latest girlfriend of Johnny the pianist sat on the knee of a sailor, glancing now and then at Johnny. He took no notice.

She took her vanity case to the bandstand, opened it and dumped out his underwear and a couple of shirts, which he had given her to wash. He still took no notice. She picked up a pair of underpants and threw them into the works of the open piano. Some of his notes muted as the clothing caught in the hammers. Johnny played on, an amused smile on his unshaven face.

Deborah didn't sing. She sat there looking forlorn. Nat scarcely twirled his baton. The music went round and round.

Billy came on and sang his usual "Little Black-Eyed Suzy" in a hangoverish sort of way. His bass player didn't dance with the bass fiddle, as he did in the evening session, but more or less leaned on it for support. The sailors drifted out bringing some girls in tow. A couple of housewives got their shopping out of left luggage and left.

The music went round and round. Nat had the band in the lowest gear possible. A quickstep became almost a waltz. A waltz had the remaining couples tripping over one another in slow motion. At the close of the session, the saxophones squeaked, the trombones barely vibrated, the maracas sounded like they had two seeds in them, the clarinets squealed like piglets, the piano had the mute keys of a practice piano, the cymbals scraped like rough sandpaper, the drums were light rain on a tin roof, the flugelhorn was a kid's bakelite toy. The spotlights were ten-watt bulbs. The mirrored orb hanging from the ceiling ceased to revolve or reflect. The greyness of Nat's face shone through his suntan-lamp tan. Never had so many walked out on Nat before. The American sailors, having acquired more cosmopolitan tastes on their voyages, had torpedoed him. He longed to be "back in town", meaning London. The dance floor was empty well before the last note. Berkley Black was furious and decided to drop out of the weekend fox-hunt in the Mourne Mountains.

Evans laughed. McClaron was still enraged enough to head-butt his locker. Gerry thought about being a motor mechanic again but remembered the dirty grease under his fingernails. He looked at his hands – they were soft and white.

Nat was across the street trying to start his Lambretta scooter.

He kicked and kicked but it wouldn't start. It was raining. He had on his long, brown leather coat. His patent-leathered foot kicked again. His miniature Yorkshire terrier, usually between his feet on the scooter, whined to be away. Gerry, having changed into his everyday suit, stepped into Chichester Street. He saw Nat still kicking. Knew what was wrong with the scooter but decided he wasn't going to help. He wasn't going to be his mechanic and be downgraded as a result. Maybe a push would help, but he wasn't going to be a rickshaw man either. He had a message from Black for Nat – be in his office *now*! He didn't pass on the message. He watched Nat wheel the scooter towards the City Hall. Gerry could have told him he was going the wrong way for a garage. He didn't. He would tell Black that he couldn't find Mr Alton.

Evans had suggested to him that the Irish were too helpful and friendly for their own good. He said they would always be subservient. He had lived in London and occasionally mixed with the better section of the Welsh diaspora. He could talk with a Welsh accent, but he didn't want to be taken for a peasant. His public school accent made people sit up here. The same thing in London.

Gerry looked at the Volkswagens in the window of the car showroom for a long time. Nat Alton's musicians came out complaining about the rain. Billy Duggan's Boys came out, watched where Nat Alton's mob was going and went in the opposite direction. They liked Lavery's pub a few doors along the street but decided it was Mooney's in Cornmarket for them. Evans came out with a girl and said he would see her on Sunday but in the meantime he was with friends. He tapped Gerry on the shoulder and invited him to go with him to Lavery's. Gerry

didn't drink, but Evans said he could have a coffee and a sandwich. Nat's crowd were going to be in there and when they had
a few they were different people. McClaron came out and asked
Gerry if he had given Black's message to Mr Alton. Gerry said he
couldn't find him. McClaron said the band was liable to be shot
down in flames, riddled to a man. Evans intervened to say, "And
woman."

Evans went on to say that local managers didn't have that
power. That all power came from London headquarters. He
then continued, "Do you mind awfully, Gerry and I are with
friends."

Lavery's public bar had the usual bunch of men, in flat caps,
reading sporting papers and giving each other tips for the dog
races that night. Nat's musicians were sitting in a corner. Deborah was there pressing a bell to order a Number One, which was
a half pint of mild stout.

Evans said to Gerry, "Why don't we move to the Chichester
Room upstairs? What is the point of going native?"

The bantering of the "natives" was almost deafening. Above
Deborah's head a sign read "No Singing."

The bass player was arguing with his girlfriend, who worked
as a waitress in a restaurant in Great Victoria Street. She was slipping him her tips, and he was throwing the coins on to the table
and shouting, "What fucking good is that to me!"

Deborah intervened to say, "Calm down; we'll buy you a
drink."

He rose from the table and went to the lavatory. Deborah said
to leave him alone. He had been a prisoner of the Japanese during the war. He had been a lovely bloke before that. Deborah
said they should split up when buying the rounds. Her husband,

one of the trombonists, who looked like Glenn Miller with his rimless glasses, agreed. The smell of Guinness was overpowering to Gerry. It permeated everything. The bell was rung, and the barman came to take the orders. It was Number Ones all round and a coffee and sandwich for Gerry. The bass player came back and immediately launched into how his car was rusting away "in town".

He looked around for his girlfriend, but she was gone. Deborah told him to drink up, they'd all be back "in town" one day.

The girl with the vanity case came in and sat beside Johnny. She kissed him and said she was sorry. She opened her vanity case to get lipstick. Johnny suddenly reached into the case and pulled out an American navy-issue pair of underpants. He held them up for everyone to see.

"A lot of meat could fit into this."

The girl's face went red with embarrassment, but she managed to laugh and then gave a little sob. Johnny flung the pants across the bar. They landed on the back of an old man who didn't seem to notice. The customers nudged one another as the old boy went to the lavatory with blind, faltering steps and came out again with the pants still sticking to the back of his raincoat. The girl laughed hysterically. Johnny held her hand and smiled.

Drinks came at a steady pace, and Evans was telling a joke in a mock Welsh accent. It was about a native Welsh speaker who had difficulty speaking English. The preacher was giving a parable on a boat that sank when it hit the rocks of evil.

"So, if you have a hole in your bottom you'll sink, too."

The bass player suddenly grabbed Deborah's hand and twisted it. She said, "Ouch, you've broken my fingernail, you silly sod!"

There was a lot of talk about playing in Liverpool, Birmingham and Glasgow. About how Nat used to play at the Savoy, Claridge's and the Park Lane Hotel before the war. He was even heard on the radio for six months. Times were getting bad, said Johnny.

"Getting?" interrupted Deborah.

Johnny said he wouldn't be surprised if they all disappeared one day. Elvis Presley was topping the American scene. He would finish off London soon. He was also filtering through to the provinces. They scoffed at this and began ordering more drinks.

Evans challenged Gerry to drink a glass of lager and lime. He said it wasn't a real drink, more of an old woman's drink.

Gerry said he didn't drink. Deborah told him he was right – don't drink. She then scolded Evans as an evil little swine. Evans took this as a compliment. Gerry reached for the push-button of the bell. Deborah tried to push his hand away. He pushed the bell. The barman came. She apologised and said it was a mistake.

Gerry said he wanted a bottle of lager and lime. The barman brought it.

Deborah asked him his age. When he said twenty-one she said, "And you've never had a drink. Well. . ."

"I'm in rude health, thank you," said Evans.

Deborah continued, "And why haven't you had a drink?"

"Because," said Gerry, "my father didn't drink. He convinced me that alcohol was poison."

"And why did your father not drink?"

"Because *his* father was a drunk. He had seen enough of it."

"Don't drink," she said; "it's in your family. Please don't. . . for little me?"

The others laughed and urged him on. He hated the taste but the effect was beginning. He looked at them and saw them as the most beautiful people on this earth. Deborah was frowning.

He pushed the bell again, but Evans sharply told the barman to go away. Gerry sat there, and this most wonderful feeling of calm came over him. He said he felt grand. He laughed and began to tell jokes for the first time in their company.

Deborah said, "One drink makes you feel like that? Stop it!"

"Oh, come on, for goodness' sake," said the bass saxophonist, "you know we couldn't get through tonight without a few drinks. Look at this afternoon!"

"That was Nat's fault. He's the leader and he was down in the dumps."

"Just for a change," said one of clarinettists.

"It's her, always *her*," said the bass player; "she needs a fucking good shagging. He's married to his dog. We would have eaten it if we had it in the camps. And ate him as well." He didn't laugh at his own joke – though they all laughed – but beat the table frantically with his fists.

"Watch your hands," said Deborah; "you're playing tonight."

Elsie, Nat's mistress, came in. She was beautifully dressed, as if she were about to have tea at the Ritz. Her long dark hair ran down her back. Her hazel eyes seemed to suck Gerry in to her very soul. She sat down looking slightly depressed. Deborah ordered her a gin, and she drank it down in one gulp. Then Elsie rang the bell and ordered everyone a a double-Irish despite their protests. Deborah snatched Gerry's whiskey and poured it into her own. The smell of whiskey was sickening to him anyway.

Elsie remained silent, but they all knew what she was suffering with Nat. He had a scooter – to give the dog fresh air –

though he could afford to buy a car. He hadn't made love to her in months. She was twenty-four, and she had missed months out of her life. She wanted a baby, but Nat was never settled anywhere. He bought her the finest clothes and jewellery and had a detached house rented for them on the upper Antrim Road with a regular charwoman. He had made a fortune touring America before the war and had held on to it and invested wisely. But she was lonely and sat upstairs at the Plaza in Nat's dressing room while he twirled his baton downstairs. Behind his sunlamp tan a ghost of a man lurked. Gerry gazed at her and gazed at her until she gave him a little enigmatic smile. She still sat there silent.

Deborah said to Gerry, "We are merry now. We can carry on."

Betty, beside the cash grill, was good evening-ing everyone coming through the door. Gerry was standing there in a jovial mood after his bottle of lager. He also joined in the good evenings. The large doorman outside, controlling the queue, was also trying to control his head from shaking. It was cold and windy outside. A policeman entered to shelter from the weather. He had his usual .45 revolver in an open-topped holster and his greenheart truncheon in a black leather case attached to his belt. He opened the top catch of his tunic and then offered Gerry a cigarette. Gerry, who didn't smoke, took the cigarette. They both lit up. Betty hissed over to Gerry to remind him he wasn't allowed to smoke while working. In nicking the cigarette he burned his fingers.

"Do you see who's in the queue?" said the policeman. "Stormy Wetherall. Is he allowed in here?"

"As long as he doesn't cause trouble," replied Gerry.

"It looks like he's caused it already," said the peeler; "his arm's in plaster and he's here with four of his pals to protect him. Still, it's nothing to do with me. I'll give you a tip. You're surrounded by a gang. What do you do? Run? No. Get down on your knees and beg them to let you go? No. No. I'll tell you what to do – pick the one who's doing all the talking, grab him by the lapels, pull him forward and at the same time knee him in the balls, finish off with a head-butt. Whoever takes over the talking, deal with him in the same way. There'll be a gap in that gang. Walk through it slowly and Bob's-your-uncle." He fastened his uniform and bade goodnight before he left.

McClaron came and asked if the policeman was looking for him. Gerry explained he was just having a break.

"He's my peeler," said McClaron, working himself into a fit. "I'll decide who he talks to. Now he's gone, and I wanted to tell him Stormy Wetherall was here with a broken arm."

Both bands were in great form. Deborah sang sweetly. Nat, still in a bad mood, was forced by the momentum to smile through his lamp tan. He motioned to Gerry and asked him to go up and see if Elsie was all right. He called her his wife.

Elsie was half drunk. She asked, in the most beautiful English voice, clear and with perfect diction, devoid of class connotations, for Gerry to send up Johnny. He explained that Johnny was playing. She locked the door and said Gerry would do. She began taking off her clothes. When Gerry went to the bolted door, she called him a coward. Gerry obliged her. She said to call back for another session while Nat was doing his session.

He told Nat that Elsie was all right. She was sleeping.

He went back but she was weeping. She told him to go away. She had been drunk and he had taken advantage of her. His heart beat fast with fear.

"And you didn't even use a French letter. Not even one," she added.

He felt relieved by her intimate accusation and felt he would see her again. He went down and told Nat she was all right.

The American sailors began coming in. Some were supporting one another. Berkley Black had given orders that the American navy was to be unhindered – unless one or two became violent.

They made for the lavatories and pissed in the wash-hand basins.

The old attendant told them, "Take your Pennsylvanias out of my nice clean basins."

"Ah, come on, Pop," said one, "that's a custom in the US."

"I've been there," said the old boy, "and you don't put your Penn where's it's not wanted."

"Where were you there, Beelzebub?" asked another.

"Oregon," said the old fellow, "in the pit, sawin' with the two-hander. One on top of the log, one in the pit."

"I bet you were in the bottom of the pit, Pop."

"What makes you think that, sailor?"

"There's sawdust on your shoulder, Pop." He laughed and said, "I was in a bar downtown. . ."

"You're downtown already," said his pal; "you better believe it."

"Anyway, this guy tells me there's sawdust on my shoulder. I look and kinda brush it off. But there's nothing there. The guy laughs, 'I'm telling you your head's cut.' Good one?"

They laughed. The old fella rushed away to mop up a multi-coloured pool of vomit.

The fifty-kilowatt didn't burn that night. McClaron kept an

eye on Stormy Wetherall, from a distance. Evans pranced around as if he didn't work there and invited a young lady to sit with him at the reserved table and asked to be served ice-cold ginger ale in small glasses – it would look like whiskey. Near by, the sailors drank from Coca-Cola bottles half-filled with Southern Comfort. Black kept in his office and prayed for the American navy to cast their anchor in some other waters.

The last notes were played, and the pressure was on to get the crowd decanted on to Chichester Street. The cloakrooms were busy handing out coats and bags. Evans asked Gerry if he would go halves on a bottle of Black Bush whiskey. They would go to the Embassy Club along with Nat's people. Billy Duggan would be there with his musicians, but that was unavoidable.

After the doorman pulled the expanding gates across the entrance to the the Plaza, Berkley Black told him he was on a week's notice and wished him to have a nice Sunday. The doorman gave a full military salute.

At the club entrance, Evans told the doorman there, in his best accent, that they were with Nat Alton's party. A small band played in the darkened, soft-lighted club. It played badly, and a male singer gave a poor rendition of "That Old Black Magic". Nat and his people sat at one side at two long tables. At the other side of the room sat Billy and His Boys. They laughed and sneered over at Nat's party. Gerry and Evans sat at a small separate table in order not to have to share the whiskey. That was Evans' idea. He said Nat and his friends were sitting on their booze and drinking everyone else's. When that was finished, they would have their own and they wouldn't share. Gerry didn't understand whiskey. He poured a great tumbler of it and drank it down like lemonade. Evans asked him to go to the bar and get some UBs for chasers.

While at the bar, he came upon the girl with the vanity case. She was now with a dentist, and he was very drunk and horribly jealous at Gerry talking to his girl. He made a wild swing and Gerry ducked.

A group of young men in zoot suits appeared to be discussing cars – other people's cars. Gerry struggled through the throng of half-drunken doctors, solicitors, journalists, scrapyard merchants, comedians and dancers from the Empire, and a lookalike of Betty Hutton complete in cowboy hat and six-shooters. She was top of the bill.

They had a UB each and hid the rest of the drink before going to Nat's table. He sat there like a squire lecturing his parishioners. It was all talk about music and how Johnny should arrange some new numbers. Elsie was there but she wouldn't look at him. Gerry danced with the sixteen-year-old wife of the sixteen-year-old drummer. She said they were from Brighton and she had known her husband since they were four. When the music stopped, she said to stand about until they played the next number. This happened three times until he took her back to the table against her will. He tried to catch Elsie's eye, but she gave that ugly yawn that women sometimes make to say they aren't interested.

Gerry went back and recovered the cache of drink and poured another full tumbler of whiskey and drank it straight down. Anaesthetised by now, he didn't taste the so-called horrible liquid nor feel its burning in his stomach. Then he was under the table holding on to the bottle of whiskey with a death grip while Billy peeped under the tablecloth trying to persuade him to share it. When he looked again, His Boys were there, peeping under the tablecloth from each leg of the table. They prised the whiskey bottle from him. He crawled out on hands and knees. The band was on the ceiling and the singer was singing "Mammy" upside down. Evans rescued him and sat him at Nat's table. Elsie clung to Nat and hid her head behind his back as he discussed an arrangement of "Blue Moon". The musicians made various mouth-sounds to indicate their instruments.

Nat looked at Gerry a moment and said, "I don't like people who get drunk."

Elsie cringed, and Gerry had enough consciousness left to say nothing for her sake.

Deborah said to Gerry as she eyed Elsie, "You seem to have had a busy day."

Evans got him into a taxi, and they went to his lodgings near the university. The landlady was waiting up for Evans, and he scolded her for that. Her one-legged husband, who used to tread the boards as a music-hall comedian, walked in as unsteady as a duck and began to tell jokes at breakneck speed. He rounded off his patter with a comical song about Lloyd George. Evans applauded and nudged Gerry, who did the same though the walls were beginning to revolve again. It was three a.m., but the landlady insisted on making tea and toast. Then she suggested that Evans share his bed with Gerry as she didn't have a spare room. It was natural enough then to share a bed with another male. It was still the age of innocence and trust. Gerry agreed without a murmur. And though Evans grabbed for his balls while he was drunkenly singing as he lay on the bed in his underwear, he dismissed this as playfulness.

After breakfast that Sunday morning, Evans took him on a tour of the large four-storeyed house and pointed out rooms where various professional people lived. The top floor was occupied in its entirety by a professor of philosophy. He was away in Fermanagh fishing in the loughs. Evans entered his book-filled library and showed Gerry that this "great" man was also reading shilling detective novels. Evans was evidently in awe of this intellectual giant. Gerry asked him if the professor was from here – meaning was he from Northern Ireland.

Evans looked at him as if he were stupid, saying, "He's English, of course!"

"What's his name?" asked Gerry.

"Oh, I don't think his name would mean much to you."

They began walking through the tree-lined streets in the university district, into Stranmillis Road, and from there to Great Victoria Street. The usually busy thoroughfare was almost deserted, with only the occasional car passing. A tramp known to all in the city as "Poor Fella" was foraging through the litter bins at the trolleybus stops. A flapping tattered poster on a wall advertised "BUCK ALEX. LION WRESTLER. TWO PERFORMANCES DAILY." The poster didn't add "EXCEPT SUNDAY". That was too obvious. Buck was known to keep an old lion in the tiny backyard of his tiny house. It had broken-off teeth and filed-down claws. It was fed mostly on loaves of bread and surplus army corn beef; also, it was rumoured, stray dogs. Those who still kept pigs in the tiny backyards local to Buck would occasionally sell him a sickly piglet for the lion to maul and get his natural instincts back.

Gerry started relating these stories to Evans, but all he said was, "Oh, yeah? Oh, yeah?" and murmured, "Silly clod."

When they came to the Great Northern Railway Station, Evans said they should pop in. He would show him a most comic sight, if the idiot was out and about today. The great blackened hall echoed to their footsteps. A few people sat on the benches – rural types with small attaché cases and wearing rough overcoats and battered soft hats with sweatbands. One of their women wore a severe-looking small hat favoured by the "saved". Her thick stockings rippled with the pumping of varicose veins. A porter was scraping off the many layers of old posters on an advert board. He began to laugh and called his mate over. An old faded poster had come to light. It showed, in caricature, a fat, round little man in a rough jacket and heavy shapeless trousers carrying a small attaché case. Sticking out of his back pocket was a tin. The slogan ran, "ANDREWS HEALTH SALTS FOR A GOOD BEHIND".

The great engines touched the buffers, but only one of them had a wisp of steam coming from it. A boy with a dirty face rattled the drawer of an solid iron chocolate-dispensing machine until the porter came to chase him away. Addressing nobody in particular, he said the machine last had chocolate in it twenty years ago.

Evans looked at the huge clock high up in the smoke-greased roof occasionally as its iron hands quivered forward in an undecided fashion. Over the city, church bells rang continuously in a variety of rhythms. Bantam cocks crowed from the backyards of the nearby Sandy Row.

Gerry asked Evans about this comic event he was supposed to see. Evans shushed him and said listen. A steam locomotive was blowing its whistle somewhere near Stockman's Lane. A slow droll male voice came through the loudspeaker:

"The Dublin to Belfast train is now arriving at Platform Six. Those waiting to meet passengers should not impede the ticket barrier. Thank you."

Clouds of steam hit the blackened glass of the roof and drifted out through a broken window. The grease-ingrained floor of the station trembled slightly as the train rumbled slowly towards the buffers. Soot-covered pigeons flapped lazily to the high ledges of the ironwork. Two policemen and a sergeant entered the station to peer at the five passengers coming through the ticket barrier. One of the policemen nudged the other – a passenger was carrying a suitcase as if it were heavy though it was obvious, by the handle not bending under the supposed weight, that it was empty. The man was dressed in what he must have thought to be Californian style. He wore a light sky-blue suit with a silk, hand-painted, lurid tie of purple, pink, blue and green in the pattern of a hummingbird. On his head was a tweed pork-pie hat with a red feather in the hat band. But the most startling thing of all: he looked like the twin brother of Tyrone Power, the Hollywood actor. A spitting image. He stood under the clock, looking at his watch impatiently as if his party, who was to meet him, was late.

"And what would Tyrone Power be doing in a dump like this?" said Evans, and chuckled.

Gerry said he once saw Burl Ives passing the City Hall and it was him. Evans scoffed. People, continued Gerry, said the same thing about Burl Ives until they saw his photograph in the paper. Gerry also said Laurel and Hardy were once at the Grand Opera House for a week. He saw them on stage. Evans scoffed again. Gerry said if he wanted proof, then he should go to the Midland Railway Station at York Road. They stayed in the station hotel and had their hair cut across the street in a barber's used by ship-yardmen. The barber still had a photo of them in the window and underneath it said, "We Cut Laurel and Hardy's Hair. Why Not Let Us Cut Yours?"

There had been crowds from the houses near the docks – oul shawlies and all – patting them on the back and trying to kiss them. Some of the oul dolls were crying. They couldn't believe that they were here – right here in Belfast.

"If what you are saying is true," said Evans, "then they must have been on their way down . . . the poor sods."

Gerry was so excited in telling this story he didn't hear Evans' caustic remark.

Gerry went on, "I was there – Stan Laurel and Oliver Hardy wore black berets!"

"So you think this could be the real Tyrone Power?"

"No. He's a French polisher in the shipyard. I heard about him. But this is the first time I've seen him."

"I wonder why he makes a prat of himself like that?" said Evans.

"He gets the train at Finaghy Halt, only one stop away from here. Every Saturday and Sunday. Three times on Saturday. Once on Sunday."

"Why didn't you tell me you knew all about him?" said Evans angrily. "You've wasted my time standing here."

"I only go to see real people like Laurel and Hardy," replied Gerry.

They had lunch at Fusco's, just at the beginning of the Falls Road. Evans felt uncomfortable being here, but there was nothing else open. Evans kept his voice down, and when he did speak it was in a phoney Welsh accent, which made him sound as if he were talking into a wooden barrel, reflecting its hollowness.

At the next table, a group of young men from Catholic Action were having a heated discussion with a group of young communists about the existence of God. One young girl communist was saying, "If God is so all-powerful and infallible, can *He* make a stone He can't lift?"

There were cries of, "Unfair! Unfair! You're perverting this discussion."

Ma Fusco, a heavy-breasted woman, went to the table and said, "I hope God doesn't run up a bill He can't pay. We're closing now, darlings."

The streets became even more deserted, with only the occasional trolleybus passing. Hymns rang out from a number of churches as they passed. A preacher on a soapbox at Castle Junction directed his wrath of God towards a lone bus inspector sitting in his kiosk.

Halfway down High Street, they stopped at the Sportsman's Club. A small figure of a man appeared out of a doorway and said to Evans, "Sign us in, mister." The man had the shakes and dragged on the butt of a saliva-wet cigarette.

Gerry didn't tell Evans that the man was a former flyweight champion of the world.

Evans used his accent to cajole his way past a well-dressed doorman and smiled to himself. Inside were the usual doctors, dentists and hardware merchants. No scrap merchants or cartyre thieves from the Markets here. All "ings" were being given full expression. No "Norn Iron" instead of Northern Ireland. Gerry doubted if the ex-champ would have got in even when he was the reigning champion.

Frank Forester, of the Frank Forester Dance Studios, was buying two bottles of Black Bushmills whiskey at the bar. The barman was wrapping them carefully in tissue paper while Evans commiserated with Forester about his recent problems, but he seemed in a desperate hurry as he watched the barman. His face was deathly pale against his black, longish hair, which was slicked back in the manner of a Spanish gypsy dancer. Only a few days ago, at the inquest on a young girl who had gassed herself, the judge had told Forester in a suitably grave tone of voice:

"This young girl in a cheap cotton dress came to your dance studio, and you took full advantage of her, of that I am sure, after listening to the witnesses – you, a sophisticated man of the world. Now she is dead. She, being of eligible age but barely so, means that I don't, regretfully, have the power to deal with you. I therefore hope you will, one day, face a higher court than this one."

Evans continued to commiserate with Forester. He said thank you a number of times, but it was obvious that he wasn't going to invite Evans back to share the whiskey. When he was finally able to leave, he fled down the stairs under Evans' glare. Evans was now in a dreadful temper, and he walked out of the club without buying a drink. Gerry followed.

Outside the ex-champ again asked Evans to sign him in. Evans stood as if on the parade ground.

"My good man, the only place I am willing to sign you into is your nearest forced-labour camp. Good afternoon to you."

They walked to Cornmarket. The Imperial cinema was showing the Charles Laughton version of *The Hunchback of Notre Dame*. It was open to the British armed forces only – the Sabbath Day Society ruled. Evans announced himself as Captain Evans and Gerry as Second-Lieutenant Martin at the box office. The girl asked for their warrant cards.

Evans replied in his best accent, "Two tickets for the balcony and don't let me have to fetch my commanding officer from inside your dingy premises. . . my girl."

The girl pressed the ticket machine. Going inside, Evans said, "Subservient. . . as usual. You people never learn."

Nat Alton's contract was finished, and they were going back to "town". Gerry went down to the Heysham boat shed at about seven p.m. to see them off on their night-long journey to London. Or rather he was there to get a last glimpse of Elsie. Nat had never again sent him upstairs to see if she was all right, nor did he ever speak a word to Gerry again, preferring to glance coldly at him. He guessed that Elsie had confessed. It was rumoured that Nat had sent her to London for an abortion, to one of those professional clinics near Swiss Cottage that looked like a residential house. So Evans said, eyeing Gerry and waiting for his surprise or comment. Gerry remained mute. Indeed, she had disappeared for six weeks. Evans eyed him again.

Nat was in tears as his dog had just died that morning. It was also rumoured he had it in a guitar case in order to bury it in his brother's back garden in Edgeware. So Evans said. Evans wasn't there at the boat shed, of course. He exchanged his day off only too willing for Gerry to see them off, saying at the same time, "Give her up. She's a whore. I had her inside the emergency exit a few times."

He then waited for Gerry's reaction, stepping back from him a few yards.

Berkley Black wasn't at the boat shed either. The girl with the vanity case was there to see Johnny off. Johnny was in the wellington boots he usually wore when riding his motor-cycle. But he had sold the bike months ago. He hadn't shaved either. He also wore a stiff rubber raincoat without a shirt under it. It was rumoured he had become addicted to Indian hemp while in

Belfast. Or so Evans said. Gerry shook hands with everyone and asked where Nat was.

"You mean Elsie," said Deborah and kissed him.

"He's already on board," said the bass player, "in first class. With Elsie."

"Don't be so cruel!" said Deborah.

The musicians made their way to the economy-class gangway. The ship blew its siren. A great cloud of steam poured out of the huge whistle. The dock labourers took away the gangways and released the steel hawsers from the bollards. A tug, blowing clouds of black smoke from its funnel, strained to pull the ship from its berth and into the middle of the Belfast Lough.

Gerry walked away with the girl with the vanity case. She still had three of Johnny's shirts, some underpants and socks, unwashed. She said that Gerry and she had lost the most important people in their lives. She suggested a drink somewhere. She had a room of her own. Maybe they could go there afterwards and comfort one another. They had the drink and they went to her room. All he did was talk about Elsie until she threw him out.

Ambrose and His Orchestra arrived at the Plaza with the survivors of the other big bands that were being shot down in flames by the arrival of rock'n'roll. The music went round and round for a time, then, suddenly, Billy Duggan and His Boys were no more. Billy had got tired of singing "My Little Black-Eyed Suzy". He was last seen, in dungarees, looking down an open man-hole in Donegall Place for Belfast Corporation.

Gerry resigned from his job at the Plaza. The place was unbearable for him now. It was empty even on a Saturday night, without Elsie. He went back to his old job as a motor mechanic and got himself a flat in Belfast. He never got that new Volkswagen. Only an old Morris car. He was still so stricken with Elsie that he was almost paralysed. He couldn't be bothered with the task of picking up girls. Instead he put an advert in the personal column of the *Belfast Telegraph* and was answered by a hairdresser from the country town of Auchnacloy. She was a shy little mouse of a girl with slight acne. She was also called Elsie. They married within a month.

Maisie died in Whiteabbey Sanatorium. He still owed her £20. Jock came over from Scotland to put flowers on her grave at Carnmoney.

Gerry didn't see his parents any more.

McClaron was transferred to Glasgow and was knifed to death in a ballroom when trying to break up a fight.

Evans was last seen in a Dublin street. He said he was the manager of the five-star Shelbourne Hotel, in his best accent. It seemed odd then that he just happened to be strolling along Gardiner Street. A street well-known for its bed-and-breakfast houses and its grey bed sheets.

Gerry took Elsie to London for a week's holiday. They stayed in a bed-and-breakfast hotel across the road from Euston Railway Station. They visited Piccadilly Circus with its empty glare of neon advertisements. Walked through Leicester Square. Walked past a theatre performing *The Mousetrap*. Marvelled at the porters of Covent Gardens as they carried high basket towers of fruit and vegetables on their heads... but mostly for the few American tourists. Glimpsed St Paul's Cathedral through the grey gloom of a London sky. Saw Tower Bridge. Crossed London Bridge and wondered why it was so special – it was nothing like the nursery rhyme. And rode the Tube round and around on the Circle Line.

On Friday evening, a day before leaving London, he looked up the *Evening Standard*. They caught a bus to Streatham High Road. The weather was damp and cold. He found the venue. The cream paint was peeling from the front of the building. On either side of it stretched dilapidated-looking shops selling a variety of cheap goods, suspicious-looking meat and wrinkled potatoes. Picked out in twinkling little white lights, a sign read "Nat Alton and His Band". A variety of people were going in, including a bunch of lads with Elvis Presley-style haircuts, heavily greased. There was the usual huge uniformed doorman on the pavement with the ballroom supervisor in the usual dress suit inside looking out through the glass doors.

At the last moment, Gerry changed his mind about going in. Elsie was disappointed, so he tried to make it up by taking her to a fish-and-chip shop. The chips had been reheated several times – crisped to the toughness of matchsticks. The tiny piece of fish was imprisoned in a slab of half-cooked dough. The tea was semi-warm – the tea leaves probably recycled with a pinch of washing soda until they turned white. The bread was spread with the most inferior margarine. Even the vinegar had been watered down. The neon reflected on the hardened grease on the dirty white tiles. The steam from the fryers drifted in clouds, condensation ran down the windows in rivulets. He lingered as long as possible until Elsie complained about getting foundered from the draft coming in from under the gap of the door. The gap was big enough to let a rat in. He felt sick, and they made for the street.

They had a walk along the High Road, looking in the windows of every shop they passed. One hardware shop was advertising oil stoves at £7 – one and sixpence a week on the instalments system. That explained the wafting smell of paraffin coming from the side streets now being shrouded in the gathering smog.

Eleven p.m. came. They walked to a large hut-like structure against the kerb of the road. It had huge iron castor-type wheels as if it were mobile. But the castors were rusty, and it didn't look as if it had moved for many years. Besieging this meat-pie stall were about twenty Dickensian-looking Teddy boys dressed in black with velvet collars on their jackets and bootlace ties down the front of their shirts. Most had duck-arse haircuts. They stood on heavy sponge-rubber soles while passing a bottle of HP sauce around. Their harsh accents echoed down the High Road. Gerry said hullo to as many as possible. They looked at him as if to say, "What's his game?" They congregated uneasily, as if putting their heads together for a rugby scrum. One ventured, "You alwight, cock?" and another, "Bit parky tonite, guv." Then they all laughed at their enforced formality.

Gerry bought two meat pies and two cups of tea. One of the Teds passed them the sauce bottle.

A few hundred people drifted out of the dance hall. Within minutes they had disappeared. The smog was thickening and whirling around the yellow sodium streetlamps. Gerry wondered if Evans would stand here on a cold winter's evening hoping to get a glimpse of the Elsie of his repetitive dreams.

His wife Elsie was now freezing cold. She begged for them to leave. Bits of old newspapers, dampened by the smog, limped down the High Road in the wind. He put a sixpence in a chewing-gum machine, but it was empty and didn't return his money. He banged the machine, and a window opened above the shop and a voice shouted, "Oi!"

Elsie was so docile she didn't even ask, "What are we doing here?"

He was angry with himself for putting Elsie through this, but the musicians hadn't come out yet. Nat and Elsie hadn't come out, especially Elsie. He began to slowly walk away when Elsie – his wife Elsie – said, "Was that the Nat Alton at that dance hall in Belfast?"

He didn't correct her to say "ballroom".

"I only went there once when I was staying with my auntie up in town."

He said, "Up in town, back in town. What town!"

She couldn't understand his sudden anger but went on, just the same, to say, "The music was lovely. Who knows, you might have been dancing there that night. We might have met and then went out courtin'."

They walked on, looking for a bus to Euston. As they passed the meat-pie stall, he decided he loved her. He stopped, hugged her and kissed her for a long time. Right there on Streatham High Road. The Teds cheered. Gerry waved them goodbye. Elsie, overcome by his sudden new-found attention, cried and laughed with joy, then cried again.

He didn't hear the Lambretta ridden by Nat with Elsie on the pillion. He didn't hear a new small dog yap between the feet of Nat as the scooter passed them slowly in the descending smog, muffling the sounds, blotting them out from sight.

LILY O'CONNOR

Can Lily O'Shea Come Out to Play?

A bestseller in Ireland and Australia, a fascinating story of growing up Protestant in Dublin.

This vivid memoir of a childhood in the 1930s and '40s is marked by its narrator's consciousness of her status as an outsider, for Lily is a child of a mixed marriage, baptised a Protestant but living in a Catholic community. The originality of this account of a working-class childhood is its portrait of a spirited girl coming to terms with her difference. At its heart this is a universal story of childhood; of hardship and joy, of violence, poverty, pleasure, humour and, over all, humanity.

ISBN 0 86322 267 6; Paperback

DENNIS COOKE

Persecuting Zeal: A Portrait of Ian Paisley

"Stunningly insightful. . . well researched and attractively presented." *Fortnight*

"The Cooke 'report' on Paisley is reasoned and unemotional. But it is also daring in a place where sectarianism drives men to murder." *Observer*

"A rounded and authentic picture. . . A very valuable book." Eric Gallagher, *Methodist Recorder*

ISBN 0 86322 242 0; Paperback

Two Jack Taylor thrillers from Ken Bruen

The Guards

"Edgy, pitch-black humour. . . With few, if any, antecedents *The Guards* is one of the curiously rare Irish crime novels, and the first set in Bruen's home town of Galway." *Guardian*

"A masterful black novel, full of unforgettable characters and a never dissipating cloud of menace that mirrors the persistent Galway rain, coming down hard on all concerned." *Bizarre*

"Both a tautly written contemporary *noir* with vividly drawn characters and a cracking story, *The Guards* is an acute and compassionate study of rage and loneliness. . . With Jack Taylor, Bruen has created a true original." *Sunday Tribune*

ISBN 0 86322 281 1; Paperback

The Killing of the Tinkers

"Bruen's writing is lean, mean and deliciously sharp." *Time Out*

"Irish writer Ken Bruen is the finest purveyor of intelligent Brit-noir." *The Big Issue*

"A soul-mate of Jim Thompson's, or maybe of James M. Cain's, he has a cast of characters which rates high on the deadbeat scale." *The Irish Times*

"Bruen uses a clipped, telegraphic style – reminiscent of James Elroy's *White Jazz*. . . he infuses his story with a brand of humour that is alternately sly, bizarre, ribald and very dark." *Booklist* (USA)

"If Martin Amis was writing crime novels, this is what he would hope to write." *Books Ireland*

ISBN 0 86322 294 3; Paperback

Marie McGann

The Drawbridge

"Marie McGann is a real find. She writes with the exhilaration and defiance of youth and the wisdom of age. A moving and triumphant novel." *Fay Weldon*

"*The Drawbridge* is an assured debut, offering no pat answers. . . At its heart [it] is about love in its many forms, and the struggle to throw off the shackles of defensiveness and self preservation and at last attain the freedom to love without fear." *Sunday Tribune*

"This is a first novel with the kind of story established writers would die to produce. . . A page-turner, a delight, a revelation. . . I loved this one." *IT*

ISBN 0 86322 271 4; Paperback

Jennifer Chapman

Jeremy's Baby

"A page-turning tale of contemporary mores." *Rosemary Friedman*

"Set against a backdrop of Aga cookery, weekend lunches in the country, arts review programmes on television, it's also a novel about birth and death, love and jealousy, friendship and betrayal. . . But it's in the development of the characters, and in the author's near-scientific fascination with the workings of their minds, that the book's strength lies." *Sunday Tribune*

"Anything Jennifer Chapman writes must be taken seriously." *The Times*

ISBN 0 86322 277 3; Paperback

Two Dublin novels from John Trolan

Slow Punctures

"Compelling. . . his writing, with its mix of brutal social realism, irony and humour, reads like a cross between Roddy Doyle and Irvine Welsh." *Sunday Independent*

"Three hundred manic, readable pages. . . *Slow Punctures* is grim, funny and bawdy in equal measure." *The Irish Times*

"Fast-moving and hilarious in the tradition of Roddy Doyle." *Sunday Business Post*

"Trolan writes in a crisp and consistent style. He handles the delicate subject of young suicide with a sensitive practicality and complete lack of sentiment. His novel is a brittle working-class rites of passage that tells a story about Dublin that probably should have been told a long time ago." *Irish Post*

ISBN 0 86322 252 8; Paperback

Any Other Time

"Trolan's portrayal of a hopeless underclass is both convincing and chilling. . . he has a rare and genuine gift for dialogue, and his characters' voices ring true. A relentlessly grim, but undeniably powerful novel." *Sunday Tribune*

"His second novel, *Any Other Time*. . . is a starker more shocking read, but it is wonderfully written and confirms Trolan's talent. . . Such is the power of Trolan's writing, and so skilful his descriptions and characterisation, that before long I was mesmerised by the seedy world I had landed in. . . Trolan writes from the inside, and it shows." *Books Ireland*

"This is an Irish *Trainspotting* with perhaps a greater degree of realism. . . A tragic story of the wasteful loss of youth and innocence – a baby scrambling over her overdosing mother's breast instinctively to hear her mother's final laboured heartbeats. This is no fairytale and it has no fairytale ending." *Irish Post*

ISBN 0 86322 265 X; Paperback